I0694388

TROUBLE WITH TRAVIS

CALL HIM DADDY SERIES
BOOK 1

CHRISTINA HOVLAND

*My brother-in-law, Kasey, said he'd fix my coffee maker if I
dedicated this book to him.*

I really needed my coffee maker fixed.

CHAPTER 1

RACHEL

"Not like that." Rachel Gibson shook her head even though her client couldn't see her. "Don't be afraid. You can't mess it up. Do it just like I showed you. Once it's aligned, then slip it right in. Boom. Done."

She glanced at the digital clock on the top corner of her laptop.

Crap, crap, crap. She was so late. A-freaking-gain.

She normally didn't take clients in her bedroom, but she'd turned off the camera, so it wasn't a big deal.

"I think I've almost got it," the deep male voice assured in a tone that was not assuring.

Rachel stilled, took a deep breath, and did her absolute best to relax the tension from her shoulders.

Perfection is not measured by degrees. It is created by degrees. She played the mantra over in her head. This particular adage was the extent of the philosophical genes making up Rachel's DNA. Seeing that most of her genetics came from a family who preferred to crack jokes at inappropriate times to deflect from thoughtful conversation, it was a miracle she'd inherited *any* deep thoughts.

That said, *this* philosophical saying was her go-to in the reality of her daily activities as the owner, manager, and only employee of her very own virtual personal assistant company. Also, as a mom to her two boys. Twins.

Anyway, perfection was within her grasp, degree by degree—if she could simply keep her shit together.

Or get her shit together. Either way.

She let out a sigh, watching her client's progress on the screen. This client was in California, so their time zones were close. Rachel was in Denver, and thanks to the beauty of the internet, she could work virtually with clients nearly anywhere. Although the new Australia client was starting to seriously cost her on missed sleep.

"Darn," he said. Once again, he fudged the design. Perfection would not happen for him with this graphic design lesson.

"Just line it up," Rachel encouraged. "Don't overthink."

Most days, her uncanny ability to find solutions to client issues was outweighed only by her inability to deal with her own crap. Sometimes she even considered taking up the joke-cracking schtick that worked so well for her brothers and parents.

"I can't get it. I'm telling you," he replied, frustration lacing his tone.

Man, she did not have time for this. She had to get out the door. They'd need to reschedule for later, which stunk because she didn't have time later.

Hell, she didn't have time *now*.

"Okay, wait, I think I did it." James sounded as relieved as she felt.

Thank goodness. She glanced at his work-in-progress on the screen of her laptop. Oh, thank, thank, thank goodness. Yes, he had it. She released a long breath.

"I can't believe I got it." He laughed, switching the video monitor from the graphic design program on the screen to his webcam. "You're the best, Rachel."

He gave her two thumbs up.

Even though he couldn't see her, Rachel couldn't help it… she smiled. One more happy client. She'd been working with him for the past hour so he could create his own graphics for his start-up company. He'd finally figured out how to copy and paste and now he knew how to move the images around. Perfection by degrees. Her motto in process.

"I'll practice some more and then we can chat in a few days," he said, the pleased tone of his words causing that bloom of pride she adored so much in her job.

"Let me know if you need anything else," Rachel said, raising her voice into the speaker of the MacBook placed precariously on the edge of her dresser. She'd set down the computer so she could simultaneously apply her eye makeup while observing his progression on the screen.

They said their goodbyes, and she closed the laptop. Then she yawned. Last night had been another doozy. Could she get away with crawling into bed to sleep for the next eight hours? No. She could not.

Because the load of shit that needed to be done would not do itself.

That was the answer to that.

Accepting her newest client (the Australia guy) was the perfect supplement to her income. Unfortunately, she'd never been good at pulling all-nighters. Not even when she'd been an undergrad or when her twins were teeny tiny, itsy-bitsy, cutie patootie babies.

One step at a time, one project at a time, one client at a time, she was making all the things happen all the time. After all, the difference between boiling water and hot water was only one degree.

The difference between crossing the finish line in first place or second place was usually a matter of millimeters.

And the difference between "horribly late" and "let's just reschedule" was nearly always separated by Rachel's underestimation of time management.

"Rach?" her best friend Molly called from downstairs. "C'mon, hustle up. We're going to be late."

Yes, they were. But what was she supposed to say when James had needed an extra hour this afternoon? She did what she always did. Solved. The. Freaking. Problem.

"Coming," Rachel hollered, hoping her voice carried out the door and down the staircase.

"Late," Molly called back.

"Two seconds," Rachel called again. Rubbing the remnants of concealer over the dark bags that seemed to have permanent residence under her eyes, she quickly pulled her hair up into a twist, securing it with some corkscrew bobby pins her mother-in-law insisted she try.

Former mother-in-law.

The meemaw to her twin boys.

The momster who usually always got whatever she wanted, even though Rachel couldn't quite figure out how she did it.

A quick pop on the scale on her way out of the bathroom and she'd be on her way. One swift step. She could do this. Gah. She hated this part of the day.

She closed her eyes when the digital display blinked, and she considered whether the three cookies she'd eaten after lunch were going to prove to ruin her afternoon. Deep breath and she opened her eyes, glancing down.

Shit.

Damn, that thing was being a total asshole.

For the record, she'd eat the cookies again just to spite it.

Also, they were really yummy and a gift from a client.

They'd arrived at her doorstep warm—with bonus ice

cream—and what was she supposed to do? They were meant to be eaten warm. So she ate them…warm. That was what one did with divine cookies.

"Rachel, seriously," Molly called, but her tone sounded as though she'd just discovered the remnants of a dozen warm cookies from Heather's Cookie Co. on the dining room table, and she didn't really care if they were that late.

Double crapola.

"Don't eat those," Rachel shouted, grabbing her favorite sling-back black sandals on her way out of her bedroom, her toes sinking only briefly in the carpet because she was on a sprint.

Dammit, Molly was as good as Rachel for spiderlike senses around carbohydrates and sugar. Rachel should've put them away. Of course, her best friend would find the residual cookies.

But Rachel had plans for them—there were four left. Two for each of her boys.

If Molly ate one, then there would be only three and that meant an argument that Rachel did *not* want to referee. So if Molly ate one, then Rachel would have to eat one, but she'd already had plenty, and she didn't really want the scale to be more of an asshole because her best friend ate a cookie.

That made sense, right?

"Seriously, Molly, don't eat that." Rachel took the steps two at a time, skidding around the bottom of the bannister, deftly stepping over errant Legos scattered like land mines, past the corner of the office she'd set up there.

Yes, she *could* cut the third cookie in half for the boys. While that might teach them a lesson in sharing, it brought more challenges and probably the food scale to get an exact weight so things were *precisely* fair.

So it'd just be easier if—

She scooted around the corner into the dining room where the box lay open on the table.

Cookie in hand, Molly's dark curls bobbed against the exposed pale skin of her shoulder as she turned to Rachel. Rachel, who had reached the room three seconds too late.

Molly lifted her looked-to-be-recently-threaded eyebrows as she bit, her hazel eyes sparkling with the perpetual perkiness that had become her brand.

Rachel made a strangled sound.

"Wha?" Molly asked as a few errant crumbles fell from her lips.

Rachel took a breath as her cell buzzed in her pocket.

"Want some?" Molly asked around the mouthful of carb-laden goodness.

Rachel shook her head, glancing at her cell. A client.

She needed to take this.

"Don't pick that up." Molly's eyes turned to slits. "We'll be even later. Not just cookie late, but client late. You know we can't be—"

"It's Cassie." Rachel stared as the number flashed on the screen.

"Cassie?" Molly asked.

"Client." Cassie had a tendency to try to do things herself that she really should let Rachel handle. "It's probably important."

"It's after hours," Molly said, totally correct in that assumption.

Rachel bit at her bottom lip. Molly wasn't wrong...yet...

"*That* is why you shouldn't pick it up." Molly clearly knew better than to reach for the phone, since she and Rachel had been friends forever. But, since they'd been friends forever, Rachel knew Molly's fingertips must itch to grab the cell and bat it out of reach. Crush it under her tennis shoe. That sort of thing.

"It is after five," Molly continued. "*We* have a Little League game to get to. Your kids and my kid are expecting us not to be late. And boundaries are important."

"What if *the call* is important?" Rachel wished she had powers of telepathy so she could reach through the signal and determine if it was something that needed to be dealt with before she picked up and made them both late. Later.

"What's the likelihood that it's not something that can wait until tomorrow?" Molly asked, her tone one of soothing comfort that usually worked for getting her way.

Molly had a knack for getting people—everyone—to bend to her will. Sometimes she used the brute force of her personality and sometimes, like now, she used a gentle touch. Molly was diverse in her manipulation techniques like that.

She'd make an excellent mother-in-law someday.

Rachel warred with herself and the decision at hand. If she answered the call, she'd be late, but her client would be happy. If she didn't answer the call, she'd be only a little late and Molly would be happy.

"My clients hire me because they know I'll always go above and beyond." Her heartbeat increased even as she glanced at her friend. The above and beyond thing was right on her business cards. In bold italics.

"True." Molly continued nibbling the cookie but kept one eye on Rachel and one eye on the phone. She also started toward the door.

"Not answering is *not* going above and beyond," Rachel declared.

"Don't make the boys wait," Molly said quietly, turning to her friend. Her understanding of the battle going on inside Rachel was abundantly apparent.

And that's what did it. The boys.

Her boys.

Rachel wouldn't let her boys wait.

"I'll just catch up with Cassie in the car on the way." Still, Rachel had to force herself not to return the call.

Her phone immediately rang again, as it did regularly throughout the day and often during the night, too. Since she was a virtual personal assistant, she had three large clients. In three very different time zones.

This was her job. Her business. The thing that, aside from her children, brought her the most joy.

Most days.

This time, however, it was her ex calling. The father of her eight-year-old twins and the supposed-to-be one-night stand that turned into *way* more than either of them had bargained for.

Mouthing, *I'm sorry*, she immediately pressed the phone to her ear. "Gavin?"

Molly rolled her eyes, shaking her head, while making gagging noises unbefitting the cookie she still worked on.

"Rach." He did not sound like he was anywhere near the baseball field, or in a car on the way to the baseball field. No, he sounded like he was in an airport.

A slight feeling of vertigo pulled at Rachel, like the gravitational field of the earth seemed to get stronger.

No. He needed to be at the game. The boys were so excited.

She gripped the phone in her hand and closed her eyes.

Gavin's a good guy. Gavin's a good guy. Gavin's a good guy.

"What's up?" she asked, hoping her perky tone betrayed the inner turmoil swirl, willing him to say he was on his way to the game to see their boys even though she knew deep down he wasn't and she'd work her magic and all would be well. The only one who would pay the price was her.

"Dakota has a last-minute installation in Boston," Gavin said, obviously distracted because he was Gavin. Distracted. "We're heading there for the weekend. I'll be back in time to help set up for the boys' party, but we're going to miss tonight."

Yes, gravity. Her legs felt heavier by the second. "Gavin, they want you there."

They need you there.

"If I could be there, I would, you know that."

She did. Sort of.

He sounded genuine. Then again, he always sounded genuine. Genuine was Gavin's thing. If Gavin had a thing.

Dakota and Gavin had been engaged for a while. He worked tons of hours, in an office. Dakota, meanwhile, had carved out a name for herself as an artist who painted, and sculpted, a variety of animals in bathtubs.

Yes, this was a thing.

Dakota worked tons of hours with this gig and was, as Gavin had explained, kind of a big deal. Rachel didn't mind her. She was nice to Rachel's kids, and that's what mattered.

Meanwhile, Rachel also worked tons of hours…from her home office, so custody and the majority of childcare had been delegated to her.

Which was fine because, as she'd insisted and they'd agreed, the boys needed her stability.

"Rachel?" Dakota had apparently confiscated the phone from Gavin.

"Hey, Dakota." Rachel struggled to hold her phone and pull on her shoes simultaneously.

Dakota? Molly mouthed rolling her eyes dramatically with more gagging sounds.

Rachel nodded, ignoring her friend to focus on the conversation. Molly hated Dakota.

"Gavin and I sent the boys a surprise for their birthday. It'll be there tomorrow. I hate to ask, but would you mind—"

"I'll grab a video for you." Rachel hopped to stand, mentally rehearsing what she would say to the kids so they wouldn't feel the entire sting of this disappointment. *Your dad wanted to make it tonight, but he had to go to Boston.*

Don't worry, he has a big surprise for you both.

"You're the best." Dakota's muffled voice sounded as though she'd covered the speaker before she spoke.

"Not a problem." A birthday surprise was an excellent

distraction. A birthday surprise was something for the boys to look forward to. A birthday surprise was the perfect redirection for their disappointment.

This wasn't the first time she'd helped Dakota and Gavin co-parent virtually. It wouldn't be the last, she was certain of that. Gavin was not a hands-on kind of father. Then again, he hadn't really signed up to be a dad, so she did her best not to make it miserable for him.

"Bye, Rach." Gavin's voice sounded like an echo, since Dakota still had the phone.

"Bye," Rachel said, thumbing the off button.

Rachel liked Dakota. She liked Gavin, too. It wasn't his fault they'd based their marriage on one night of mediocre passion that led to their boys.

It wasn't hers, either. It just…was.

Molly was still making gagging faces in between cookie bites. She didn't understand this part of things.

Gavin and Rachel had tried. Tried-ish.

But, despite his mother's proclivity to shoving them together, guilting them together, and offering to pay Rachel to ensure they stayed together, their marriage was as dull as their kitchen knives.

Let's just say, if their marriage were an entrée, it had no seasoning at all.

No one really understood what had happened on that one night eight years ago that had changed their lives. The night she hand-selected Gavin from a group of guys for her first ever supposed-to-be one-night stand.

The evening had resulted in one of them climaxing. (Spoiler alert, it wasn't Rachel.) He'd called her a few times after, but she hadn't returned his calls because that would've totally ruined the point of having a one-night-only curtain call.

Then—and oh boy, was it a big *then*—were the words, "Congrats, it's twins."

That part did not suck, because Rachel loved the hell out of her boys.

Besides the children, she and Gavin had shared a marriage that lasted a few months before they both came to their senses and recognized they made much better co-parenting friends and partners than co-parenting spouses who slept across the hall, because he snored like a freaking freight train on fire and she, so he told her, hogged all the blankets.

They were excellent…friends. Friends who had two kids together and eventually lived separate lives because it was just more comfortable for everyone.

"What did they want?" Molly asked, the dislike of Gavin apparent in her tone.

"Long story." Rachel grabbed the keys on her way to the door. "I'll fill you in on the way."

Where Rachel and Gavin got along fine, he and Molly despised each other. Which Rachel didn't understand.

"He's not coming to the game," Molly correctly guessed.

Phone stuffed into her pocket, Rachel flicked on the slow cooker so dinner would be ready when they arrived home. She tossed the extra cookie in a zip-top bag so it would be safe in her purse—once her boys discovered she kept tampons in the interior pocket, they avoided the thing at all costs.

"I guess that means Travis will attend instead," Molly mused.

She had been working to convince Rachel to practice her flirting skills with Travis Frank for the past four months.

The idea was so far beyond ridiculous, so off the beaten path that it didn't even show up on Google Maps.

But flirting was Molly's job, so she looked for opportunities everywhere. Rachel didn't blame her because Molly literally taught the basics of dating and had to keep her skills sharp for her clients. She used her inability to take no for an answer and her YouTube channel to teach others the intricacies.

"Dane might come," Rachel said, hoping it was Dane who would attend. Gavin had two brothers. She got along fabulously with Dane. Not so much with Travis.

For a lengthy list of reasons substantially longer than Molly's meddling.

"It'll be Travis," Molly said, a small, knowing smile teasing the edges of her hot-pink-painted lips.

"Probably." It usually was Travis who filled in when Gavin couldn't make it. Rachel started the mental prep work for dealing with him. "Do not start up about him again."

Molly bit at her bottom lip, apparently refusing to respond.

Rachel could literally feel her matchmaking friend brewing an idea to push Rachel and Travis together. Last time he'd been to a game, Molly manipulated them into sitting thigh-to-thigh on the bleachers. The time before that? Her car broke down and she asked Travis to drive them home. Then Molly caught a ride with the umpire's wife instead.

Oh, to be sure, Molly didn't *believe* Rachel and Travis had any business being together. She just wanted to piss off Gavin.

It was her way.

"I like Travis." Molly bit at her bottom lip, saying the words with the caution of one merging onto a road littered with construction. "I like it when he comes to the games."

When Gavin couldn't make a game, one of his immediate family members always showed up to—and she was quoting him here—"represent the family."

Like they were mafiosos or something. They weren't.

They were, however, loaded beyond belief because Great-Meemaw Frank had created the first Puffle Yum and sold the shit out of the toaster tarts.

Rachel paused, setting the purse strap onto her shoulder. "Travis is a fantastic *uncle.*"

She made it a point to enunciate that last word. Because any idea of flirting with Travis or doing anything beyond friendly chatter with him was an absolute nopers.

"Is that new?" Molly gestured to Rachel's bag. She may have been a black belt in flirting, but her distraction techniques could use some work.

Rachel knew how Molly operated and, in her mind, as long as she didn't verbally commit, she would weasel her way out of an implied agreement later.

"I grabbed it at the Coach outlet in Loveland last week," Rachel said. The rose-colored over-the-shoulder bag was the last on the shelf, and Rachel had fallen in deep lust with it on first sight.

"I think I need at least two of these," Molly mumbled, examining the stitching.

"Too bad, I got the last one." Rachel grinned, nabbing the bag away with a smirk.

Molly shook her head. "There are always more online."

"Dinner's cooking, I have my keys, shoes, purse, go bag, sunglasses, boys are going straight to the field after school."

Rachel inventoried everything she needed for the game.

"You ready now?" Molly asked.

"Let's go." Rachel dropped her sunglasses into her bag and held the front door for her friend.

This week was Molly's turn to drive.

Which meant Molly would be busy driving the vehicle and Rachel would spend the thirty-minute drive to the baseball field calling Cassie back and then chatting about everything but her least favorite Frank brother. So perhaps, just perhaps, Molly would leave it alone.

Maybe.

CHAPTER 2

RACHEL

Rachel had her resting mom face firmly in place. The one she'd learned from her mama, and her mother had learned from hers. The one that showed just the correct amount of interest but covered the fact that she wasn't 100 percent listening.

The late-spring sun pelted them with rays while they entered the baseball field. Thanks to Molly's extra-fancy, extra-fast driving, they'd arrived with a few minutes to spare.

"I'm telling you." Molly led the way along the walkway toward the bench where they would wait for the Little League game to start. "Men who shop for groceries are excellent stepdad material."

Wait. What?

That was not the criteria single moms should use as the litmus test for future husbands.

Dear future husband, please be funny, be excellent in bed, take care of me and my kids, and above all else, pick out the best watermelons.

No.

As *Sesame Street* once pointed out, one of these things is not like the others.

Besides, guys rarely enjoyed grocery shopping. At least, in Rachel's experience, that was a no-go. Not that she had an abundance of experience with grocery shopping members of the male species, but she had enough secondhand experience people watching to know that the handsome ones were in and out and on their way.

In and out of the grocery store, that is. Other things, too, but that wasn't a place she wanted to allow her mind to wander, because her body hadn't wandered there in years, and she was pretty sure it was resenting her and would turn Team Molly on this one.

"The produce section is ripe for all sorts of subliminal messages, all ready for you to exploit." Molly did the bouncy walk that was her signature. Molly walked like she lived— happy and always moving.

Rachel's walk was more just-get-me-where-I'm-going efficiency.

"Whatever you say," Rachel said. This reply was all-purpose and evergreen.

"You show you are confident in the way you push the cart," Molly continued. "Show that you understand how to select and handle an eggplant. Things like that."

This whole thing was a no for Rachel, *thank-you-very-much*. But Molly could do whatever Molly wanted—which was good because Molly did that anyway.

"Whatever you say," Rachel said, again.

"Well, I say that you and I are going produce shopping later." Molly bumped Rachel's arm with hers.

Rachel slid her gaze to Molly. *Ha. No.* "I'm not doing that with you. Not when you're in dating-Molly mode."

"You haven't been listening at all, have you?" Molly tsked. "I'm in dating-Rachel mode."

Rachel stiffened. She appreciated she had someone to

hang out with at the games. Especially when that someone was her bestest best friend. Even if that friend was filled to the brim with ridiculous ideas about the dating Rachel should do, and the calisthenics her downtown lady bits should take part in with members of the opposite sex.

"A guy in the produce aisle is not in the headspace for becoming an insta-dad," Rachel insisted, looking to where her boys warmed up on the field. "He's there to select lemons or broccoli or whatever, not pick out a future life partner."

"Orrrr…" Molly stopped mid-stride, turned her body toward Rachel. "Maybe he's there to squeeze a few oranges while watching potential mates stroke zucchinis to test for firmness. Thus discovering the future mother of his children." Molly waggled her eyebrows, as though all of this made sense and wasn't whack-a-doodle.

For the record, it made little sense and was, in fact, totally whack-a-doodle.

"I refuse to meet a man by subliminally encouraging him to ask me on a date because I stroked a banana or a zucchini or any other girthy produce." Rachel rummaged through her handbag to search for her sunglasses as they walked. Damn, she knew she'd dropped them in there before she left the house.

"It's not happening. If I need company, I'll just adopt a puppy or something," she continued. Coming up empty from the inside pocket, she turned her attention to the oversize beach bag, the one that had never seen a beach but was her own personal "bug out" bag where she kept all the things she might need for herself or her kids.

"If you don't want to be so obvious, just squeeze a couple of cantaloupes." Molly shrugged, clearly oblivious to Rachel's search for eye protection and her extreme disinterest in the suggestion.

"Are you equating cantaloupe to breasts, because men like

breasts?" Rachel asked, even though she knew she shouldn't have continued engaging in Molly's dating cray-cray.

"See! You're catching on." Molly nodded enthusiastically.

Rachel shook her head. She would not be doing *that*.

"If you use two lemons, it's a totally different subliminal message."

"For guys who like small breasts?" *Stop. Asking. Questions. Rachel.*

"No, silly. Guys love having their"—Molly tipped her sunglasses to the edge of her nose and looked pointedly at Rachel's crotch area—"*ahem* squeezed."

Molly further illustrated this point by making two fists and squeezing.

Rachel didn't have the equipment Molly referred to, but she still felt the urge to cross her legs. See, when life tossed lemons at Rachel, she found a recipe on Pinterest and squeezed a pitcher of lemon martinis for an impromptu girls' night soiree. Sometimes, if she was feeling bold with her lemons, she'd mix up a pitcher of whiskey smash instead. She didn't squeeze them to make a sexual point.

Rachel twisted her lips, paused her stride, and shook her head. "We're done. Change of subject."

Then she stuck her head back into the depths of the beach bag filled with snacks and extra gear and just-in-case bandages and water bottles. Where the heck had she put those damn glasses? Gah.

"Good call, Rach. Because that's the worst advice I've ever heard." A throaty male voice with a hefty dose of southern drawl came from behind them.

Rachel paused. She knew that voice like the inside of her handbag.

Don't get her wrong. The southern accent was nice. Sometimes if he said the right thing with extra southern mixed in, it made her tingly and her tummy twist in ways that weren't bad. Not bad at all. Actually, the twisting was sorta good. Which was bad.

Blurgh.

Of course, it would be Travis.

"Don't go around squeezing a guy's nuts. We don't like that." Travis knew where his sunglasses were because he pulled them from the bridge of his nose, folded them carefully, and tucked one end into the front of his shirt.

If he kept up that look, pretty soon he'd be wearing loafers with no socks. He could probably pull off the look, though, and still knock all the ladies out with his brand of handsome.

Travis was a hottie. The worst kind of hottie—the kind who knew it, embraced it, and owned it. He was also untethered, immature, and irresponsible.

Short blond hair with a bit of an unintentional Supermanesque wave, muscles because he embraced his hotness, worked out, and apparently didn't eat Puffle Yums, and the kind of symmetrical features that probably turned on even facial recognition software. Yes, the symmetry of his face was *that* good.

Rachel did not like Travis's brand of hottie knowledge, preferring the kind who had no clue they were attractive. They were so much nicer to her.

Rachel ignored him, shoving her face back into her bag on her sunglasses search.

She didn't have to look up to see him shaking his head; she knew intuitively that's what he was doing. Probably closing his eyes in a half-lidded what-the-fuck, this-is-ridiculous eye roll he did so well.

"Some of you do." Molly laughed, lighthearted, the subtle hint of flirt in her tone that Travis ate up. "Like the squeeze thing, I mean."

Travis laughed. "Rach, you know how you say I never take anything seriously?"

Yes, she did.

"I take my stance here extremely seriously." He gave her a smolder and a wink that made her nearly—only nearly—forget who he was, where they were, and why he was a bad idea.

Between him and Molly, it was like a big ol' flirt bomb had decimated the Little League field.

Molly was dancing the dance to hand deliver Travis right to Rachel.

Which was…blah.

Of course, Molly wouldn't try for Travis herself. Rachel had suggested it, but Molly said that would be, and Rachel was quoting here, "weird."

Rachel mentally batted Travis away like the unreliable annoyance he had proven over and over to be.

"Tell Rachel and me more about what you'd prefer squeezed," Molly said, right on cue.

Rachel extracted her head from her bag, wishing that Molly had not just asked that. But, oh boy, she had. "Or you could, you know, *not* do that."

Travis grinned. "I'd love to tell you what to squeeze."

"I just said not to."

"But did you mean it?"

"Yes."

"You sure?"

"Travis." She turned to face him, squaring her shoulders.

"Yes, Rachel?" he drawled.

"Knock it off." She used her mom tone. The one that, generally, got her what she wanted.

Molly smiled. "You two, this is great."

Rachel scowled. She gave up on her sunglasses search and went back to marching toward the benches.

Molly let well-timed laughter tumble over the thick air among them. "What would you suggest, then?"

"I suggest we go be adults and watch the baseball warm-ups," Rachel said. Fine, it was more of a huff.

Travis stood, thoughtful. Too thoughtful. Travis didn't do thoughtful. This was new.

"There are so many other things you can do down there—don't go squeezing around. Do you want me to start a list of things men enjoy?" he said to Rachel with another hefty dose of charisma.

Rachel's stomach did the flippy good, but also bad, thing. "I know what men enjoy."

She didn't, not really. But she could probably make a few good guesses.

"I'd love to hear what you think Travis would enjoy," Molly said.

"I can start at the waistband and work my way down?" Travis continued.

Gah. This, right there, was why Travis drove her up the wall.

"I think I'll stick with the squeezing thing Molly suggested." Truly, Rachel just wanted him to stop talking about it. "Hard. With fingernails."

Did she imagine it or did he cross his legs just a touch?

"Nope." Travis pinched his lips closed and shook his head. "Don't squeeze the boys. I can speak for all men when we say 'no' on this one."

"You speak for all men on this subject?" Rachel asked without adding even the thinnest coffee filter to her thoughts before they vocalized right from her lips. "Literally, all of them?"

"Of course not," Travis said lightly. "Just every man I've ever met and every one I'll ever meet."

"The produce manager will get upset if I lick the lemons." The words tumbled from Rachel's lips before she fully processed their meaning.

She couldn't help it, her cheeks burned, and she was pretty sure she'd turned the color of the red accent wall in her living room as her mind played a film reel of licking Travis's lemons.

Yikes. No. Nada on a banana. That would not happen.

"Rach." He grinned, the slow way he drawled her nickname making her cheeks burn brighter. "You never cease to surprise me."

One-hundred-percent inappropriate, that's what this was. Because, first of all, his brand of irresponsible didn't just land on the playboy square of the game. His misguided style landed every-freaking-where. Taking nothing seriously was literally his thing.

What was the second of all? Oh, right, right, right, he was *Gavin's brother*. Okay, fine, they were only friendly co-parents who shared a couple of kids, but he was *Gavin*. Her ex Gavin. She was Rachel. His ex Rachel. This definitely went on the list of reasons.

The fact was, *this* was Travis, and he drove her bonkers 99.9 percent of the time, and that was plenty of reason for her to force her mind to not think of his lemons or zucchini or… you know what? Rachel was going to go full carnivore and just avoid the produce aisle from here on out.

If she needed vegetables or fruit, she'd just hit up the frozen variety in the freezer section.

"You can't just walk in here and say something's a bad idea without a suggestion as to what *would* be a good idea." Molly's eyes danced in the way that Rachel just knew she was plotting yet another not-so-subtle shove in her direction.

"I promise, any suggestions I give will have nothing to do with produce," Travis said, slow and deliberate. "I shop at the supermarket, too. I don't want to have to explain to my nephews what their mama is doing to the pineapple."

"I'm not doing anything to the pineapple," Rachel said, her voice raising before she quickly caught herself and hissed, "*that's* my point."

Here he was stealing her point without even so much as a *please may I have it?*

Travis leaned closer, so only a foot of space separated them, enough that it should've been plenty. Yet even though it was a full foot of space, it felt like only a fraction of that. Like it was just the two of them there at the baseball field. His eyes held hers, her heart beat faster, her stomach twisting itself into lemony, whiskey-flavored knots.

"You make lewd gestures with a mango, we'll have to have a private discussion about appropriate uses for groceries," he said, utterly serious.

Blurgh. Gah.

She scowled at him.

He didn't seem to care, settling in stride with her as the trio continued toward the bench.

"So she sticks to obviously sexual fruits and vegetables." Molly nodded with her train of ridiculous thought.

What the hell was an obviously sexual fruit?

"No tropical fruits," Molly tossed in, continuing. "Stick to the basics."

Rachel stared openly at Molly like she was fresh in the act of molesting produce.

"I cannot believe I'm participating in this conversation," Rachel said under her breath.

Travis's eyes glimmered. "I don't know, the conversation keeps getting more and more interesting. Makes me wonder where it's going next."

"Nowhere, it's going nowhere," Rachel mumbled, tripping a little over a crack in the sidewalk.

The stumble was slight, barely there, but Travis's hand hovered at her elbow, apparently ready to save her from biffing it.

That was *nice* of him.

He rarely did nice with Rachel. Not really.

He dished out the critical and sarcastic just fine, however. Then she doled it right back at him.

Truthfully, it became exhausting.

"Feels like it's going somewhere," he said, as though he knew this for certain.

Blood flowed to her cheeks, and she would bet money soon she'd have hives. "Please, stop."

He took her in for a moment, studied her with those deep blue eyes—like he really saw her. The feeling made her shiver all over.

"Maybe we should start over. Say hello and pretend we never had this conversation about groceries," Travis suggested.

"Excellent," Rachel said, eyes focused straight ahead so she didn't trip again or get caught in his eyes once more.

"Trav!" Molly bounced along the path with them. "Good to see you here. What are you up to these days?"

"Not a thing other than watching my two favorite nephews win this here ballgame," he replied, laying on his southern accent thicker than necessary, letting the full twang hang out.

If you asked Rachel, he should have to have a license when he wielded that thing. Some unsuspecting woman might just get smacked upside the head by the sheer sensual sounds he could produce.

His brothers didn't wield their accents like that. They both seemed to cover the twang, to blend in with the other Coloradans.

Not. Travis.

Rachel paused mid-step when Kellan threw the ball across the field with remarkable precision for an eight-year-old. The kid lit up when the ball made it home.

His brother, Brady, wasn't so into baseball, but he played because his brother wanted to play. Rachel hadn't yet been able to extract from him an extracurricular activity that he would be truly excited about. He seemed content to do whatever Kellan wanted to do. Contentment, however, didn't bring him joy.

If there was one thing Rachel had learned from watching Marie Kondo, she needed to find something that sparked Brady's joy.

The joy Kellan had on the baseball field.

"Rachel, how are you doing this fine afternoon?" Travis asked, his words low like he meant them for only her, even though Molly was right there with them.

Rachel slid her gaze to him. He was staring at her, and not like she was funny. Not like he'd been staring before.

She cleared her throat. "Great. I'm great."

"Gavin couldn't make it," Travis said, his voice low and, God bless the man, sympathetic.

"I know. He called. I guess you drew the short straw?" she asked, her gut plummeting.

The boys didn't get to see their dad as often as she'd have preferred—Gavin traveled a lot for the work he did with the family company. He'd taken over management of the Puffle Yum foundation, charitable work that he seemed to approach the same way Brady approached baseball. Like it was just something to do to pass the time.

"Are you kiddin' me?" Travis asked, feigning insult and refocusing on the field. "I came to watch my nephews kick some ass on the field."

Used to be, the boys would trip all over themselves for Gavin's attention. Lately, they seemed to have resigned themselves to the fact that he had other priorities. Rachel did her best to fill their lives up so much, they didn't notice when Gavin couldn't be there.

Rachel took the last steps to the park bench where she usually watched the games—away from the stands, but still with a full view of the game.

"Good thing I got here when I did." Travis looked straight

ahead, his eyes moving from Kellan to Brady and back again. "I consider it my civic duty to save men's balls from the vise grip of the mommy brigade."

Oh, look, the rest of the mommy brigade. Rachel waved to her other friends already in the stands. Maybe they'd come to her rescue.

Happily married, perpetually chill April was their yoga-loving friend who also managed a blog, a podcast, and a web community. Brown hair always in a low ponytail, light complexion, and a smile that seemed to make a person relax on contact, April was the real deal. The Calm Mom, her brand, was popular all around the country. Her reach made sense, because April's abundance of tranquility was impressive.

She sat next to Kaiya, their resident multilevel marketing salesperson. With black hair cut in an A-line and flawless gold-toned skin, her words held a perpetual kindness that made everyone want to support her business. She sold all-natural skin care products she'd discovered while visiting family in Japan two years ago. The company was huge in Asia and becoming bigger and bigger every month in the States. The overnight serum was the most kick-ass cream Rachel had ever tried. Not to say that a serum could change a woman's life, but Kaiya's was just that good.

"How do you meet women, Mr. Frank?" Molly asked, getting down to business.

"Well, I'm glad you asked, Ms. Molly." Travis settled in beside Rachel. "Because I meet women the old-fashioned way."

Don't ask. Don't ask. Don't ask.

"What's the old-fashioned way?" Rachel asked.

Dammit.

He paused, looking from Rachel to Molly and back to Rachel. Something curled in Rachel's belly and she couldn't quite figure out what it was. The same feeling she always had when Travis was around. One part curiosity and two parts stay the hell away because, danger, danger. Player, player.

"They come to me." He grinned then, and that grin made Rachel seriously consider swiping right on his profile picture.

"I suggest clients show off their strengths," Molly said. "Do the things they're good at. Attract a potential partner that way."

"Then I guess I'd be doing the laundry for him on the first date," Rachel said. Laundry was one thing she was exceptionally good at. "Since I can get anything out of cotton, maybe we should meet at the laundromat. Offer to separate his colors. Bonus, if it doesn't work out, I'll still have the laundry done."

That was some seriously mommy logic going on right there.

"You could tell him how much you like your laundry good and *wet*," Molly said, the last word coming out on a sultry breath.

"It makes sense. Besides, if you're equating meeting a man to sex, then laundry is totally like sex," Rachel added, apparently rolling with the nonsensical bouncing around the ball field.

"I think you might have sex with the wrong people, if you're comparing it to laundry." Travis held up his hands. "I'm not judging. I'm just sayin'."

"Oh, come on. You're telling me you've never thought of it like that?" Rachel asked.

"Like a chore I have to do?" He seemed to take a mental inventory of his past partners. "Nope."

"It's not *that* much of a stretch." Rachel threw up her hands.

Molly looked as unconvinced as Travis felt. She stayed silent, though, clearly letting Travis take lead on the inquisition.

"Maybe you should explain it?" Travis asked, his expression unreadable.

Rachel nodded, ready to dive in. "Okay, it's like…"

"This ought to be good." Travis settled in.

Rachel's palms started to sweat, but she sallied forth. "It's like, you have to do things in a specific order."

Rachel was all confidence as she did her best to explain the unexplainable.

"And on certain days," she continued.

"Uh," Molly started to speak.

Travis apparently elected not to.

"There's a lot of bending over," Rachel continued, because that much was true.

This time both Travis and Molly remained totally silent. Rachel kept on going. There was a point here. She simply needed to get to it.

"The first time, you don't really know what you're doing. It takes practice. You should always pretreat so it works out for all the garments involved." Rachel didn't even stumble over the words as she said them. "If you don't, somebody's going to be unhappy."

Travis's eyes went a little wider, but other than that, his expression didn't change.

"When it's over, the buzzer should go off," she added, like this entire conversation made sense.

Travis and Molly hadn't moved at all during her tirade on laundry sex. They both stayed still.

Because laundry sex made no sense at all.

"Well, this episode of *Find Rachel a Man* has been real, but I've got a game to watch," Rachel mumbled.

"I guess more of the lecture on laundry sex has to wait," Molly replied.

"Or…" Travis said.

Rachel paused at his voice. Molly turned toward him.

"Or," he started again. "You could use this as a learning

experience. Let's just call it the latest episode of *How* Not *to Meet Men*. We've covered the basics here today."

"You're impossible." Rachel turned her body as far away from him as she could. Which, unfortunately, wasn't that far.

"I'm reasonable," Travis whispered so only she could hear.

She turned, glared at him, but the look he was giving her made her want to ask him to do a load of his extra dirty… clothes.

No. She shut her eyes. Rachel absolutely refused to think about Travis's laundry. Or stroking a pineapple. Or anything else. She opened them again.

"You're the least reasonable person I know," Rachel said under her breath.

Travis kicked back, getting comfy on the bench. "I think if we've learned one thing here today, it's that we need to expand your horizons."

Molly's cheeks stretched wide with her smile. "Now we're talking."

"No, we are absolutely not." Rachel huffed.

"I think we might be," Travis murmured softly.

Dammit, Rachel's stomach did the flippy, floppy goodness oh-so-good acrobatics at what sounded like a Travis declaration.

CHAPTER 3

Travis preferred to live in the realm of fact. Hey, don't judge him by his past. This was true now. He'd learned things were easier with data backed up by indisputable evidence. He'd just taken the long way coming into that knowledge.

Now, he understood there was fact and there was opinion.

For example, it was a *fact* that the boys won their baseball game the evening before, after the uncomfortable squeezing conversation. No one, not even Rachel when she was on a tear, could dispute their win.

It was, however, Travis's *opinion* that his brother, Gavin, was the favorite of their parents. He based this on years of observation.

Another *fact* was that Gavin didn't regularly make his children a priority.

The evidence? He flew to Boston for the summer instead of bringing his kids on the family summer sabbatical—the one that always took place during two full months at the Puffle Yum Twin Lakes retreat. The summer residence was a twelve-thousand square foot lakefront monstrosity with nine bedrooms, eight bathrooms, a pool, a buttload of open space, and a private dock for a couple of boats.

The entire Frank family held a two-month family vacation together there every year. It made them appreciate any time they spent apart the rest of the year.

"Do you think he told Rachel he's skipping out?" Dane, his other brother, asked.

Gavin should've talked to Rachel. But Gavin was Gavin and he didn't do the hard things. The evidence pointing to Gavin's asshattery was as vast and wide as the Puffle Yum brand's popularity.

Travis's stomach wound around itself like a twist tie for bakery bread. He shook his head.

"Nope." He did not believe Gavin had told her.

"That's what my money says, too." Dane kept his gaze forward, but the little tick happening in his jaw belied his outward calm.

Travis's gut tightened further. If this continued, he'd need a whole bucket of intravenous antacid. This is how it went when he was around Rachel—he wound himself up in knots, especially when there was not-so-great news to share.

Usually, this resulted in him teasing her or matching her sarcasm bite for bite. Even when he tried not to.

"I'll let her know." Travis steeled the words and gripped and ungripped his fists. "If Gavin didn't."

Dane pulled into Rachel's driveway, right behind the SUV she'd gotten in the divorce. "It'll go better if I do it."

Travis didn't disagree, but Dane sometimes took the back roads during a conversation when there was a highway right freaking there and the highway version took half the time and half the effort.

Travis opened the car door and stepped out into the sunny day on the quiet street in front of Rachel's house.

His heart did the plummeting thing that it did when he

knew Rachel was facing disappointment. Usually, he ignored it. Today felt…different. Scratchy. So he turned his attention from his feelings to the well-kept pots of flowers around her front steps and the wreath on the door he knew she made herself by somehow weaving twigs together.

She'd given one to each of them last year for Christmas.

"I'm going to shove him in the lake," Dane said as he headed toward Rachel's front door.

"Kinda hard to do when he's not going to be there," Travis said under his breath.

Rachel's house looked like it came from one of the *Country Chic and Charm* magazines—whatever the fuck that meant. They were magazines at the checkout line of The Home Depot, and he'd noticed them because they reminded him of Rachel's digs.

Her home had been a cookie-cutter house when first built, but she'd repainted it light blue with white trim and added a porch swing next to the all-weather storage bins for the boys' shit. The fancy kind that didn't look like storage bins, but looked like benches instead. Bins that were not of the bargain variety.

"My money says Gavin will show up at some point because without him, how would any of us know the exact correct way to grill a burger?" Dane paused on the front step, turning back to face Travis.

"Or drive the boat," Travis added.

"Or do the backstroke in the pool."

"Or make Saturday morning toaster tarts."

Dane chuckled. "Like there aren't instructions he personally wrote on every single package."

Gavin had it in his head that he could do anything better than the rest of them, and he took a lot of pride in showing them exactly how to manage it.

"Three seconds in the fucking microwave." Travis grinned

a wry smile. "Takes longer to pull them out of the wrapper than to cook them."

"Which is why God invented the pop-up toaster," Dane said, the mood finally light.

Travis smirked. "Not thinking that was God."

"Can't tell me He didn't have a hand in it, so we didn't have to use the microwave for three fucking seconds."

Travis's foot stalled midair as he considered the possibility that he and Dane could roll Gavin in the mud pit that was the east side of the lake, instead of pushing him *in* the lake.

Mud would be harder to get out of his pants. It'd take longer than three seconds to pretreat all those stains, and that thought had Travis grinning like a kid.

Yeah, Travis and Dane could pull that off.

Travis reached to press the doorbell, careful not to bump Rachel's wreath or the handmade wooden sign that announced, *Welcome! Did you bring margaritas?*

He didn't get invites to the house unless it was for a birthday party or something for the boys, so he'd never brought her booze. Once, he'd tried to bring Gavin beer when they'd lived at their old house. Turned out, according to his mother, it was inappropriate to bring alcohol to children's birthday parties.

The door flew open and Kellan gave a whoop.

"It's the uncles," he shouted, flinging himself at Dane.

Kellan's twin, Brady, took in the scene, a grin on his face but the slightest bit of concern etched around his eyes. The kid seemed seriously older than his years.

"It's the nephews," Dane replied, ruffling the kid's hair even as Kellan released him and bolted past, checked the street, and ran back inside.

"It's not here yet," Kellan yelled, still on a flat run through the entryway back up the stairs. "Uncle Dane and Travis are, though." He yelled the last part loud enough that Travis assumed he was alerting his mom to their presence.

"Hey, Uncle Trav." Brady grabbed Travis's hand, hanging on tight. "What do you think it is?"

"What what is?" Travis kneeled so he was eye to eye with his nephew. He didn't have a favorite, but if he did, it'd probably be Brady. He couldn't say exactly why, but he and Brady? They just understood each other.

"The birthday present from Dad." Brady didn't let go of Travis's hand. "He couldn't bring it today. He had to go to Boston again."

"I'm sure whatever is in Boston is important," Travis said, instead of what he wanted to say. Which was that Gavin should show the fuck up for once.

"He's having it delivered. Do you know what it is?"

Brady's hand was getting sweaty in Travis's, but he didn't make a move to take it away.

"No idea, kid." Travis shrugged. "Hope it's good, though."

Knowing Gavin, the odds of it being spendy were 100 percent, but the odds of it being good? Well, those were more fifty-fifty.

"Hey." Rachel emerged from the office she kept near the dining room. Her office was mostly a desk she'd set up in the alcove under the staircase so she could hear upstairs and downstairs at the same time. "I got a two-for-one deal on the uncles this time."

Rachel pulled the elastic from her hair and the long, blond waves fell around her shoulders.

Travis loved her hair. The way she pushed it behind her ear, flicked it over her shoulder.

And why the hell was he thinking about her hair? He shook his head.

It's not like he didn't like her. He did. Except her uncertainty about him.

He didn't care for that part.

She smiled a genuine grin at Dane before turning a

quizzical stare to Travis. That quizzical stare made him swallow harder and turn on what he hoped was charming sizzle. The smile, the extended eye contact—it worked on most women.

Not on Rachel.

She rolled her eyes at him. Legit, she rolled her eyes like he was an eight-year-old friend of the boys—and not one she particularly liked.

"We need to talk to you about this summer," Travis said, using the smooth tone that sounded like a good takeoff felt in a small aircraft.

"It's important," Dane confirmed.

"If it's about your family's summer pep rally, the answer is—"

"Don't say no right away this time," Dane said before she could continue.

"Evelyn sent you." She observed Dane and crossed her arms under her breasts. The movement lifted them a little and —*Eyes are up there, buddy.*

Rachel didn't catch his wandering gaze because she was all eyes on Dane.

"Of course she sent us," Dane replied, the answer not nearly as smooth as what Travis would've delivered. "She knew you'd say no to her, so she sent us."

"She sent you?" Arms still crossed. Not a good sign.

"Yes, she asked us to formally request that you join us on the family summer sabbatical." Dane sounded so much like their mother when he gave the formal request, Travis nearly broke a stitch in his side trying to keep from laughing.

"That's why you're here, too?" Rachel turned her attention to Travis, using that look of hers that could make him spill any secrets he'd ever thought of keeping. She'd perfected it with the boys but wielded it like a sword. The slight tilt of her head, eyes turned to slits, and the raised eyebrows that made his collar itch.

The principal at his elementary school used to have a similar expression when he'd gotten hauled in there on playground candy-trafficking charges.

She cleared her throat.

Right. What was the question again? He nodded because he probably would've nodded to anything that she said right then.

"No." She smiled at Travis this time. Not just Dane. That was nice. Even if the word coming from her lips was no. "Thank you for the invite. But, no. That's Gavin's family time."

"But we like you better," Travis said, clearly still under the spell of the Rachel attention, since the vortex of Gavin's mention hadn't sucked the happiness from the room.

"You should tell him that. He'll be back for the party on Saturday." Rachel grinned at Travis, but this wasn't a cheery grin like Dane usually got. This was calculated. Purposeful. It was…Travis stepped back because, man, it felt like an invitation.

Rachel never gave him any looks that were inviting.

Maybe he was coming down with something, because nothing felt right.

Thus another step back.

"Travis?" Rachel asked, the question drawing his gaze to hers. "You okay?"

"Fine. I'm fine," he replied. The sweat he felt forming in his hands had everything to do with Brady's persistent grip, and nothing to do with Brady's mother.

If he took another step back, he'd bump right into the Shut the Front Door sign.

She arched an eyebrow and pressed her lips into a line. She didn't believe he was fine. Rachel was intuitive like that. He'd say it was a mom thing, but, really, it was a Rachel thing.

When Gavin and Rachel had first gotten together and

Rachel was pregnant with the boys, Travis wasn't around much. Gavin spent way too much time back then arguing about Travis's choice of work hours, the women he dated, the cars he bought.

And whatever Gavin had said to Rachel about Travis, it had stuck, since she also wanted the bare minimum to do with him. And, yeah, it'd taken a little longer for him to figure himself out than other adults, but his choices hadn't hurt anyone. Well…anyone but him. He'd broken the shit out of his ankle in a Tijuana dune buggy.

In the meantime, Rachel hadn't just erected a wall between herself and Travis, she'd dug a trench the size of the Grand Canyon around all sides.

The distance worked, because Rachel put the "string" in high strung.

"Uncle Trav?" Brady asked, startling him and stunting his self-imposed escape.

The kid pulled on their linked hands, so Travis turned his gaze from Rachel to his nephew as his back hit the sign.

"Why are we going backward?" Brady asked, lifting an eyebrow in what, on any other day, would've been a comical parody of his mother's expression.

Travis licked his lips. What was he supposed to say? *I'm running away from your mother.*

"Your mom scares me," he whispered, like that was so much better.

"Me too," Brady whispered back, all serious eight-year-old.

Now that? That was fuckin' funny.

"That's enough, Brady." She said the words with her certified mom tone, but the look she gave her kid had the soft love that wrapped around a person and didn't let go.

Rachel dropped her arms from under her breasts. Travis did not look at them.

"Rach, Travis and I would like to discuss this further,"

Dane said, totally breaking up the moment like he was a bouncer in a rowdy night club.

Rachel shook her head. "That's unnecessary."

"It's about Gavin," Dane said, for once getting to the point and not taking the back roads.

"Can I talk too?" Brady asked.

Travis looked to where Brady held his hand. He couldn't be sure anymore if he was clinging to Brady's hand or if Brady was clinging to his.

Travis shook his head. "Not until you can grow your own mustache."

Dane laid his hands against Rachel's shoulders, turning her toward him. He could do that. She let him. Because he was the good brother. The one who went to the office during the day, every day, and probably fixed her sink.

She liked Gavin well enough, but it was clear the two had never been in love. Whatever they'd had, she never looked at him with that soft love she gave her kids.

Sometimes, if the lighting was just right, she seemed to look at Dane that way. Probably because she adored Dane. *Adored* him.

Travis hadn't asked, but he was pretty certain Dane got invitations to dinner with the boys and Rachel that didn't include the rest of the family. He probably even brought over margaritas because the sign on the door suggested it.

"That's unnecessary. They asked me the grown-up things, and I said no," Rachel volleyed back.

"We have some more Gavin things we need to discuss," Dane said.

Now that got Rachel's attention.

"Head upstairs, Brady." Rachel gestured up the stairs and winked as though both uncles showing up at the same time was standard operating procedure for their family. "Grown-up talk is about to start."

Brady looked at the adults, searching for something. The

kid might've been a kid, but he was one of the most percep-tive people Travis knew.

"Now," Rachel said to him when he didn't move, her tone kind and firm and undeniably in charge.

"See, she's scary," Brady said out of the side of his mouth before he ran up the stairs.

"As I mentioned before, we're issuing your formal invita-tion." Dane mimicked their mother's voice, tone, and inflec-tion, as he delivered the message.

"We covered this. I am, regretfully, declining your invita-tion," Rachel replied, her impression of their mom not nearly as good as Dane's. Then again, she hadn't had decades of practice with it.

"Gavin isn't coming this year." Travis peeled off that bandage. Yanked it clear free. "Did he tell you?"

Judging by the shocked expression crossing her face—the way her eyes got bigger, her mouth dropped open, and her eyebrows fell together, Gavin hadn't told her. Because of course he hadn't.

Before Travis could count to three, Rachel slapped on that expression she used to appear totally impassive before dishing out punishment for her boys. He'd seen her brandish this weapon and, frankly, thought it was sexy as hell.

Except this time she directed the look straight at Travis, hitting him directly in the solar plexus.

"That can't be right." She glanced at Dane for confirmation.

Dane, whose jaw was ticking with apparent irritation. He nodded. "It's true. He should've mentioned it to you, so we could invite you up, and you might say yes."

Travis shook his head to knock out whatever jar of moths had taken up residence in his brain and made himself speak.

"Trav?" Dane asked, yanking Travis back to the present. "Thought we agreed I'd do the talking."

They had. That was before. This was now.

"You were taking too long." Travis took three steps forward. Yeah, Travis had gone off script. Somebody needed to get things moving.

"Why don't you go check in with the twins?" Dane asked, tilting his head toward the stairwell. Offering an out that Travis hated he wanted to take.

Travis followed his gaze to the staircase.

"Or go fix some grub in the kitchen," Dane continued.

This tactic was their mother's. When she wanted to send someone away, Mom sent them to bake or do a chore. Food fixed anything, in his mother's estimation.

Especially sugar.

"The boys can't go without a parent." Rachel leaned against the stairwell bannister. "I'm not okay with that."

"Yeah. We figured that's what you'd say." Dane held his hands up, palms facing her. "That's why we're here to convince *you* to come."

In truth, they always invited Rachel on the annual family trip. They invited her to the family everything. His mother was on a mission to see Rachel and Gavin happily married again with more grandbabies. She didn't care that Gavin had moved on with Dakota and that Rachel seemed happy with her life.

"You know, Rach—" Travis shoved his hands in his pockets. "We can take the boys with us."

"Without Gavin or me?" She looked at him like he'd suggested they dance naked in the driveway. "No."

"Rach."

"Drop it, Travis," Dane said quietly.

"The boys will just have to miss this year." Rachel's head was already shaking, subtle like. "I'll call Gavin…"

"Heads up that if you say no, Mom will probably visit soon." Travis knew she may not have enjoyed him visiting, but she'd absolutely hate a visit from his mother. "She wanted to come with us and make it a whole thing."

"There's no way I can take two months off to come play at the lake."

"Is there anything we can do to lighten your load?" Problem-solving Dane was in the house, ready to take on the weight of Rachel's world.

"Work doesn't take a holiday," she said.

"Still, Trav and I can help you out." Dane was practically giddy with his willingness to sniff out a solution. It's what he did because it's what he was good at.

Gavin told everyone what to do. Dane figured out solutions. And Travis? Well, he had the gift of ensuring everyone had a good time.

"I can't even manage today." Rachel threw her hands up as though their surroundings were proof of that.

The house looked like the boys had fought a war in the living room and the other side won.

"I'm still getting through today. I'm not thinking about the summer yet," she continued.

"What can we do to help?" Dane asked. "Today. To make things easier for you. We can talk about summer later. Let's deal with today first."

Travis might as well hop up on the bannister and watch Denver's king of solutions at work.

"Well, first I need someone to count up the calendar sales for the PTA and submit the order." Rachel started a countdown on her fingertips. "Then I have a new client who needs updates done for his website, but we're still trying to track down the login information from his former assistant. I have four ad accounts to check. Two bookkeeping files to update. And about two dozen phone calls to respond to." She kept her voice neutral, as though reciting a grocery list. "Somewhere during that I'll be figuring out how to explain the lake vacation situation to my boys without causing too many questions about why their dad won't spend time with them. Oh, and I'll need to get everything set up, managed, and torn down for the party." She lifted her chin in that take-no-shit way of hers, but her lower lip trembled a touch and fuck it, he knew, she was barely holding it all together.

She needed a massage or something.

Dane had clearly been thinking more like: take the boys to Chuck E. Cheese for dinner. That's what Travis would've offered up, anyway.

"Rach." Travis did a slow walk toward her. He shoved his hands into his pockets so he wouldn't reach out and do something ridiculous like try to comfort her. "Has Gavin helped with any of the stuff for the boys? The PTA, the party?"

She got the lip wobble under control as she said, "He offered to hire a party planner."

Dane whistled a low sound that somehow came out like the word "fuck."

Which was apt. Even Travis knew what a blow that offer must've been to Rachel. She wanted help, yes, but she didn't want it done for her.

Gavin helping was one thing. Gavin hiring someone else to help? That was a big ol' middle finger to the way Rachel liked things done.

"Dane and I can help with the party. Mom and Dad, too. We mean it, whatever you need," Travis said as Dane looked like he was still percolating on the summer solutions. "Same thing for the summer. I get it, you want the boys to be with their parents. You come along with us. Whatever you need. We've got your back."

Rachel shook her head. He could practically see the mental gymnastics she was doing in her mind to sort out the summer without Gavin and the family sabbatical, which he guessed was a break she looked forward to. Even if she wouldn't admit it. "This summer is out. I'll keep the boys here, find them a day camp or something while I'm working." Well, that was going to make Meemaw very unhappy.

First, she lost Gavin at her summer summit. Now she was losing her only grandchildren, too.

"Can you work from the lake house?" Dane asked. "Built-in childcare with a twenty-four seven Meemaw, Pawpaw, and the uncles. There's a big office in the library you can have all to yourself when you need to work."

Where Travis was clipped and brusque and to the point, Dane was smooth and calm and logical.

His tone got Rachel to pause.

"Free WiFi," Travis added.

Dane glared at him as though this was precisely why he didn't invite Travis on sales calls.

Before Rachel could answer, the doorbell chimed. Kellan and Brady barreled down the stairs like the house was on fire, and if they got outside, they could meet a real-life firefighter.

Color Travis impressed that even with their enthusiasm and the abundance of elbows thrown to the other, neither took a header into the railing.

"Mom!" Kellan bounced toward the door, screeching to a stop as he ran smack dab into her chest. "What did he send?"

Rachel placed her hands on Kellan's shoulders as though to make him stop bouncing. It didn't work, but she tried. "I don't know. The door is still closed."

He skirted to the left and around her, not even pausing for her to answer as he threw open the door. Brady cautiously followed.

Travis held the door as Rachel and Dane trailed after the boys. Rachel paused. Dane kept walking.

Travis stilled behind Rachel as the driver of the van removed two animal crates with a puppy in each one.

A golden retriever puppy in each one. Purebred if Travis had to guess.

Travis glanced at Dane. Dane, who now got to figure out what the hell to do with two puppies at the very-specific puppy-free Twin Lakes residence.

The only animal allowed there was his mother's fake cat.

"I didn't know you guys were getting dogs," Dane murmured.

"Neither did I." Rachel looked over her shoulder at him, her skin the color of ash and her eyes huge. She was grinding her teeth so hard, he could practically hear her dental bill increasing by the moment.

Uh. Damn. This was not good.

"Rach?" Travis asked. "You okay?"

"No," she said. And he totally believed her.

The identical twins removed the identical little beasts. Travis grabbed leashes from a pouch on top of the crates and helped snap the leashes to their collars.

"There are two of them," Rachel said to no one in particular. "Of course each kid needs his own. Because, of course."

"I'm going to name mine Pete," Kellan announced, hefting the squirming puppy into his arms and heading into the house. The blue leash dragged on the concrete walkway behind him.

"What about you, Brady?" Dane asked, handing out puppies like they were cotton candy at the Cherry Creek farmers market.

"Re-Pete, I guess," he said with a shrug, lugging the second pup through the front door.

Rachel gaped as the boys rolled with the puppies like they were practicing for a jiujitsu match on Rachel's pristine carpet.

"You both should say goodbye to Gavin," she said, so only Travis and Dane could hear.

"Why?" Dane asked.

"Because I'm going to murder him," she replied, her expression frozen.

Well, fuck.

She pulled out her phone and pushed a bunch of buttons before holding it to her ear.

"You think she's ordering a hit?" Dane asked out of the side of his mouth.

Travis was 85 percent sure she was not. He gave a subtle head shake. "Nah. Too messy. She's more creative than that."

"Gavin?" she asked, the tether on her temper barely there, given how her voice wobbled and her cheeks reddened. Gavin must've said something in response, because she was intently listening. Travis caught Dane's gaze and they shared a brotherly moment of silence for the wrath their sibling had brought down on himself via puppies.

"Great. So glad it's going well," she said, totally normal. "Hey, I have a quick question." She paused only a moment before shouting, "Have you lost your mind?"

The riot act she read Gavin was remarkably well prepared, given that she'd found out about the dogs only a few minutes before. That did not matter, because her points were both concise and effectively maneuvered into her tirade.

Travis couldn't help it. He smiled. He leaned against the exterior of her house and watched the show.

Sure, pissed-off Rachel was kinda scary, but also oddly adorable.

Man, he ran his thumb over his bottom lip, he could just listen to Rachel yell at his brother for days and not get tired of it.

CHAPTER 4

A birthday party was not the time for losing her shit.

"Everyone's outside. Have fun." Rachel shooed the latest kiddo into her backyard to contain and entertain them until their parents showed back up in two hours to remove them from the premises.

The party had started. Gavin hadn't shown up.

Again. As his wedding inched closer, the slacking on his dad duties had gotten worse. He was practically becoming Travis. Rachel was *so* done with covering for him.

See, Gavin was Rachel's ex for lotsa reasons, all of which had become abundantly clear when he had two additional live beings hand delivered to her front door. Without. Asking. First.

This was the second time *that* had happened.

The first, the twins, was also her fault. She'd consented to the activities that led to their conception—even if she hadn't meant for that outcome.

But no one even tried to give her an orgasm before twin puppies showed up at her front door.

Gah, there were puppies *in her house*. Puppies that were now hers to tend.

God, she wished someone would read her sign and bring her some freaking margaritas. Don't get her wrong, she adored dogs. Was, in fact, totally a dog person. Her family had always had a pup or two living with them during her childhood.

But there were six kids in her family, and a mom, and a dad, and the dogs they brought into the home were from rescues—older, with adequate bladder control.

So, yes, she loved dogs. However, there were no hours left in the day for her to manage two more living beings under her care. Keeping them fed and watered, veterinarian appointments, picking up after them...

Puppies were an exponential exercise in both adorable bouncing and what-the-hell-have-I-gotten-myself-into?

She needed sleep and she needed the two months she'd been counting on to focus on her business. Her to-do list last night hadn't shrunk. Even with Travis and Dane taking pity on her—or maybe just sticking around to prevent her from flying to Boston to cause bodily harm to their brother—she'd made only minimal progress on her to-do list.

The dogs were up like four times each. Add to that her Down Under client's emergency wardrobe malfunction on YouTube needed Rachel's immediate help to fix the video, and Brady woke her with a tummy ache. So she hadn't had over sixty solid minutes of shut-eye before something, some-one, or some canine needed her attention.

All of that probably contributed to her lack of fucks left about Gavin's feelings when he was late to his kids' birthday party.

This was their birthday and it would be goddamned perfect.

Perfect after she got everything finished up. She had an eight-year-old mad scientist party plan, and that plan included watermelon slices shaped like the number eight. By God, she'd serve this watermelon in eight-shaped slices, unless she gave in to her baser desires and beat the shit out of it while pretending it was her ex-husband.

Her puppy-delivering, twin-producing, going-to-Boston-sans-children ex-husband.

"It's Rachel," Evelyn said, like she did every single time she walked up to her former daughter-in-law. She popped into the kitchen like a Meemaw fairy godmother. "Can I help?"

Oh, yes. Yes, yes, yes.

"Can you tie the ribbons on those?" Rachel nodded toward the gift bags she'd stayed up until two a.m. packing make-your-own slime kits, DIY rock candy, and all the necessities for a marshmallow catapult. That last one wasn't really a mad scientist thing, but it looked super fun on Pinterest.

"Of course." Evelyn started tying ribbons. "What else do you need?"

"I need to see if one of the uncles will supervise the games outside, someone needs to add the figurines to the cake, punch needs refilling, puppies need let out to do their business—supervised—and the watermelon needs cutting into slices that look like the number eight." Somehow, she said all of that in one big breath.

Evelyn's expression didn't change, thanks to her latest facelift, but she did not start tying ribbons. Instead, she threw open the door to the backyard and called, "Bob. We need your help."

Bob was one of Rachel's favorite Franks because he smiled all the time, respected that she and Gavin would never reconcile, and sometimes brought her chocolate. He strode through the door to the kitchen and didn't even get to say hello before Evelyn had him tying the bows.

"Which do you want done next, dear?" Evelyn asked.

Um.

"Punch bowl." Rachel decided on the spot.

"Of course." Evelyn went right to work.

Huh, this was new. Evelyn hadn't mentioned Gavin or his whereabouts or how he'd spent the week before telling her all about Rachel and the boys and what they were up to.

"The party can start," Dakota announced, stepping through the foyer, Gavin on her heels. "We're here!"

"I dislike that woman," Evelyn said, not under her breath, as she scurried out the door with the punch refill pitcher. She didn't even turn to acknowledge Gavin or Dakota.

Now, this? This was odd.

Apparently, Gavin and Dakota were both in the doghouse.

Rachel would say Dakota wasn't so bad, but she had clearly been part of Operation Puppy 2.0, so she was not on the list of Rachel's favorite people at the moment. Actually, she wasn't even on the list of people Rachel would tolerate today, and after one puppy peed in the hall for the fourth time, Dakota was very close to being put on the list of people who were not getting a Christmas present.

She'd already decided that Gavin wasn't on the gift list. Rachel gave excellent presents. Everyone said so.

Sometimes, she even helped others shop for presents—she was that good.

"Dakota, Gavin, so glad you could make it." Rachel slashed the watermelon, cutting it clean in two with one quick slice of the butcher knife.

"Rach, hi," Gavin said as he and Dakota moseyed into the kitchen holding two giant gift boxes.

Travis came through the back door and tipped his paper cup toward the boxes the two lugged into the kitchen. She got co-ed Travis today with a black and gold University of Colorado T-shirt and twill cargo shorts. He seemed to have been wrestling with the kids in the grass, given the bits of her lawn falling from his hair and the grin attached to his mouth.

"There better not be anything alive in there." He gestured to the box in Gavin's hands.

If whatever was in those boxes was alive, Rachel might have to lock herself in her room to scream.

"Mom said you need help," Travis said, turning to Rachel, more of her lawn falling to the floor. "Somethin' about taking the dogs out?"

Rachel nodded, giving a chin jerk to indicate the dining room. Travis went to spring the puppies from where they were sequestered away from the chaos of the children and the science experiments Rachel wasn't entirely sure were puppy safe.

"What else can I do?" Evelyn asked, and you know what? Rachel decided right then that she liked the woman after all. Two presents this year for her holiday season.

Sure, Evelyn may have had unhinged hopes of a Rachel-and-Gavin-kiss-and-make-up fiesta, but she also offered to freaking help and didn't offer to just hire someone to do it.

Rachel gestured to the fruit and vegetable baskets she kept near the fridge. "Would you—"

"Puppies!" Molly shrieked, cutting straight through Rachel's request. Apparently, she'd caught sight of Travis with a puppy under each arm.

The sight of Travis with two puppies? Whooo boy, it nearly dissolved the solid mad Rachel had been nursing since the canine arrival. Nearly. And she was definitely not going to evaluate *that* further.

"Evelyn, would you hand me that zucchini?" Rachel pointed at the zucchini on the counter next to Gavin. The zucchini looked mighty comfortable nestled in a brown wicker basket filled with other produce. Rachel didn't need a produce aisle to make her point on this one. She had her ex-husband, a girthy vegetable, and a knife.

Without a question, Evelyn extracted the zucchini and handed it over to her. If she didn't know better, Rachel would've thought that Evelyn knew what she planned to do with the vegetable. Knew and approved.

Huh.

Travis handed one of the dogs over to Molly. "Let's take these guys outside and let the weird vibe of the kitchen continue on without our presence."

Rachel held the zucchini in her hand, inspected it, set it carefully on the cutting board next to the watermelon, and made eye contact with Gavin.

He looked to the produce, then back to her. "What's going—"

She slashed through the zucchini with the knife, quick and with precision.

For the first time in a long time, Rachel felt a little better. Not quite so wound up. Maybe she should take up zucchini chopping as a stress reliever.

Oh, or there was that place where she could go and throw axes. That could be fun, too.

Already feeling lighter, she deftly continued chopping until the entire vegetable was well and truly diced.

Gavin stood unmoving, totally pale. He did break their locked gaze, his moving to the sliced zucchini before sliding it back to her.

Bless her heart, even Dakota's mouth opened the tiniest of inches.

Good. Rachel had made her point.

"You and I are going to chat." Rachel hung on to Gavin's gaze a moment longer.

Gavin took a step toward her. "Rachel, I know you're upset—"

"What did he do?" Molly apparently hadn't made it outside before Rachel's zucchini slicing demonstration.

Rachel glanced at her best friend, who was covering Pete's eyes with her hand.

"What are you doing?" Rachel asked.

"I didn't want him to see the massacre," Molly whispered.

"Come outside and I'll tell you all about what Gavin did." Travis held the door open for Molly.

The party was hopping in the backyard, Kellan, Brady, and all their friends bouncing on the trampoline Gavin had bought for them last year.

That present hadn't sucked, even though there had been an initial concern about broken bones and trampoline-related accidents and how it would fit. Eventually, she'd let it be, because Rachel could handle a lot. She rolled with it, rearranging the backyard furniture so it would fit.

The trampoline didn't require food and shelter and love and...

She set the knife carefully on the cutting board, then worked to untie her apron.

"I think it happened," Travis said to Molly where he probably thought Rachel couldn't hear, but she could totally hear.

"*Seriously*, what is happening?" Molly melodramatically stage whispered.

"He pushed her last nerve," Travis said, deadpan.

They had no idea. Nada. She was *so* done.

Rachel started toward the dining room. "Let's go have that chat, Gavin."

Gavin, however, didn't follow.

He seemed to be in some state of shock. Probably because of the zucchini sitting there diced up nicely next to two slices of watermelon shaped like the number eight.

"Now." Rachel used the tone that always worked on the boys, hoping her take-no-shit tone covered her utter distress at her ex-husband and what he'd pulled with the puppies, not showing up in time to help with the birthday party set-up, and sending his brothers to ambush her into taking their kids on the family vacation that lasted two-freaking-months.

Seriously, what kind of family vacation lasted two whole

months? Four days was plenty. Her family managed to do all the socializing they needed to do each year in four days.

They'd all get together. They'd have some dinners. Maybe hit the beach. Then they'd all go home.

That was how family vacations should go.

Not with the Puffle-Yum Franks. Oh no. They had to well and truly drive one another up the wall for sixty full days.

Rachel did her best attempt of a saunter out of the kitchen to the dining room.

Gavin, thank goodness, finally followed her.

Unfortunately for him, he started to speak before they reached the dining room. "Rach, you're being un—"

"Do not." She whirled on him, shoving her pointer finger in his face. And yes, it was kind of comical, but no, she didn't care. He had pissed her right the hell off.

Given that before Dakota, and before the puppies, they'd had a lovely co-parenting relationship, he was ruining everything.

"We are going in there"—she moved her pointer finger from his face to the dining room—"to discuss your hare-brained idea about giving our sons puppies that will live at *my* house."

Dakota decided it was her place to say something. For the record, it wasn't. "Rachel—"

"No." Rachel turned to Dakota. "If those dogs were your idea, then they can go live at your house." Rachel brushed by Gavin's fiancée. "But we both know that won't happen, because you travel too much," Rachel said to herself. The pettiness felt indulgent for a change.

Once in the dining room, she pushed the French doors closed, shut the blinds, shoved her hands on her hips, and paced from one wall to the other.

"Rachel," Gavin said in that placating way he had. The one she'd thought was cute the night he took her home and knocked her up. Before the exhaustion of twins. There wasn't time for Gavin's cute anymore. She had a birthday party to get back to, and she had two kids, and two dogs, and an ex-mother-in-law who—

Fine, Evelyn was getting a pass, since she was totally helping. But the rest of them needed her.

"You gave them dogs," she said finally, tossing her hands wide.

Gavin didn't say anything.

"Do you want to explain to me why you sent our children animals?" She expanded on her previous statement.

Gavin didn't sit. Instead, he pulled out one of the high-backed dining room chairs that looked really nice but stained really easily, crossed his arms over the back, and stared at the seat. "You always said you loved dogs. Golden retrievers, as I recall, are your favorite."

Wait. Oh damn. Dammit.

She took in a quick breath. Her heart pausing for three solid seconds.

He'd remembered that? Even she'd forgotten that.

She let out a long breath of air.

He was not wrong, and, apparently, he had been paying some attention to her when she spoke.

"I do love dogs. And yes, on the golden retrievers." She crossed her arms, but most of the anger fizzled away as she began to understand that he hadn't gone off half-cocked. He'd apparently listened to her the one time she'd said something without thinking it through. "But this is the type of thing we talk about before you go balls deep and have *two* of them delivered."

He raised his gaze to hers, his eyes pinning her. They were the same brown as Dane's, but his were darker.

"I thought you'd like the surprise," he said. "You've always loved surprises."

Dammit. Correct again. Except...

"I love it when people bring me margaritas unannounced.

I love it when your dad drops random chocolate deliveries. I love it when—"

"You said you love surprises, Rach. All the time." He pressed his hands against his hips. "I thought you'd love this surprise. I mean, when we were together, all you talked about was getting dogs. Two of them. One for each of the boys."

"I didn't mean…" She thought back on that first year with the boys. She'd wanted so much back then. That was before she learned the motherly art of settling for what she could get. There was a conversation when the boys were really little, she started talking about dogs, and… "Shit."

"I should've talked to you. That's on me." He didn't apologize, but his tone said it for him.

"You should've talked to me about the summer sabbatical, too." She held his brown eyes with her blue ones and felt… nothing.

He stood straight. "Did Mom talk to you? I asked her to wait until you and I could find time to communicate about it."

Rachel pulled out a chair and sat. "No, your mother sent your brothers."

"Fuck." He sat in the chair he'd been leaning against, their knees nearly touching but not quite.

"When were you going to tell me that you aren't taking the boys this summer?" she asked.

"As soon as we could have a conversation alone." She waved an arm around the room.

"We're alone."

They were. Funny thing, she couldn't really remember a time when they'd been alone since he'd proposed to Dakota.

That was odd. *It was odd, right?*

He pinched the bridge of his nose. "Dakota has a four-week gallery thing. I'm going with her. It's important to her and it's important to me."

Rachel's blood cooled. For herself, for Evelyn, for her boys. "What about what's important to your kids?"

The kids who looked forward to going to the lake house with their dad each summer? Who talked about it nonstop starting in freaking *February*?

"I'm trying here, Rach." He looked up then and she saw it, saw the man who was genuinely trying and somehow managed to screw it all up anyway.

She wanted to hug him. But that was no longer her place. Not anymore.

"Then try harder," she said instead of offering comfort.

She wasn't his wife anymore. Her priorities were to her children and herself.

"The kids can't go without one of us. Your mom will fill them with sugar, your dad will teach them to smoke cigars, and Travis will teach them how to tree surf. Even Dane will get in on *that*." She ran her hands through her hair, gripping the strands at her skull.

"Can you go for me, Rach? Just this time?" Gavin asked. "You can work from anywhere. And you deserve the break."

Break? This was not going to be a break.

She looked up, turning her eyes to slits she hoped would have the right effect on him. "Seriously?"

Gavin ran his hands over his hair. "If you can help me out this time, I'd be really grateful."

Just what she needed—Gavin's gratitude. It filled her up and made all the sarcasm come right out.

"Gavin, there's no more of me left to give," she said, because there wasn't.

He said nothing in return because...dammit, she was going to go to the lake.

"I'm not saying yes," she added quietly. "Yet."

He grinned his Gavin grin. "But you will."

"I'll figure something out." She always figured something

out. Which, they both knew, meant, yes-but-I'm-not-willing-to-admit-it-yet.

The French doors squeaked, and Travis gently set one puppy and then the other on the hardwood.

How long had he been there?

"Don't mind me, they were just…uh…they finished their little project outside." He flashed Rachel and Gavin a grin and then, for what seemed like good measure, gave them two thumbs up. Gah, did he ever take anything seriously?

Thankfully, he left as quickly as he'd shown up, pulling the squeaky door closed behind him.

"Rach." Gavin lifted Re-Pete when he tried to climb his leg. "I want to be here for the boys."

"Then be here."

He studied the puppy, not lifting his eyes to Rachel's. "But I also want to respect what you need and what I need."

Look at this, communication was the bomb. She told her clients the same thing all the time. Communication opened pathways you never knew existed.

"Then help me out sometimes," she said. "Even when it's not your weekend for them to come to your house."

Gavin nodded and set Re-Pete back on the ground. The pup immediately whined for him. "Can the boys come hang with me tonight? I wanted to ask, but then I wanted to ask in person and then the whole puppy thing and you being pissed thing…"

Yes, they could totally go spend the night with their dad but, "Where the boys go, the puppies go."

"Fair enough." He nodded, a barely there smile at the corners of his mouth. "You don't mind them spending their birthday night with me?"

Did she mind? No.

Did she care? Of course.

Their birthday was important to her, but if Gavin was

willing to try, she could use a break from the puppies. It might mean a lot to the boys also to be with their dad.

Bonus, if they were at their dad's house, then she could sleep.

Sleep sounded wonderful. Maybe it'd even be uninterrupted, and she'd turn off her cell phone and forward client calls to her answering service. It'd practically be a momcation.

"I think the boys would really like that," she said.

That got her a Gavin grin. The good kind. The full kind. The kind that had the power to make a woman change her mind about (nearly) anything.

"We good?" he asked.

"You're going to take the dogs frequently." It was both a question and a confirmation. Mostly a confirmation.

"I'll even come by and walk them." He made an X with his finger over his heart, just like she often did.

She held out her hand. "It's been a pleasure doing business with you, Mr. Frank."

"Likewise, Ms. Gibson." He took her hand and gave it a shake, studying her. His expression reminded her of something that had made sense once upon a time, but now it didn't quite click.

That expression was not the stuff of happily ever afters, and the realization smacked her in the chest like a full-grown golden retriever chasing its ball.

"How many people do you think are at the door listening?" she asked, hopefully distracting him from whatever he was thinking that made his eyes warm like that.

She released his hand and gestured to the closed doorway.

"All of them, if I had to guess," he said, seriously.

She smiled. "Should we give them a minute to scurry away?"

"You're too nice, Rach." He gave her a smile that made her glad he was the father of her children because, maybe, they'd inherit an ounce of his magnetism.

Without further comment, he pulled open the door.

Evelyn was wiping down the picture frames in the hallway, a bottle of Windex in one hand and a microfiber cloth in the other.

"Everything okay?" she asked.

"Things are great." Gavin showcased his charisma-soaked smile. The one that somehow made Rachel experience a solid bout of nostalgia. Not in the romantic way. More like reminiscent of the girl she'd been before kids, before the mortgage, before clients, before responsibility ran smack over the top of her.

"You convinced Rachel to come to the lake?" Evelyn asked, hope clear in her tone.

"Don't push it, Mom." Gavin patted her arm as he started to move past, but with an ease of obvious practice, he herded his mother along beside him.

That was nice. Really nice.

The smile. The nice. Together they nearly had Rachel wondering why on earth she and Gavin hadn't worked.

Then her toe was wet. She glanced at her foot. Her big toe was being munched on by Pete as though the red nail polish were super delish.

Right. That right there was why they hadn't worked.

Gavin never really understood who Rachel was. How an offhand comment about puppies didn't mean she wanted them delivered seven years later.

She picked up the culprit currently licking her feet. Apparently, not wanting to be left out, Re-Pete quickly bounded toward her. She picked him up, too.

"I guess you boys are staying," she said, stroking their fur while keeping her focus on Evelyn and Gavin as they moved to the kitchen.

The dogs were staying and she was…well, whatever this was, she wasn't sure she liked it.

CHAPTER 5

TRAVIS

Travis happened to know firsthand that Gavin worked out-of-control hours and traveled on business every weekend he didn't have his kids—sometimes even when he *was* supposed to have them. The one thing Gavin did not do was apologize.

Travis could remember maybe three times when he'd heard an apology from his oldest brother. All three of those times were hoisted on him by their mother's insistence. And as soon as she left the room, Gavin took them back.

So it made no sense when in the middle of the ground-beef, mad-scientist, taco-palooza snack bar Rachel had put together—Gavin apologized. But there he'd been apologizing to Rachel. Mom, Dad, and everyone else heard what sounded to be his sincere apology for administering an unexpected dose of canines the night before.

Gavin didn't even take it back when Mom went inside. Which meant...something was up with his brother.

Maybe Rachel's agreement to go to the lake struck some kind of hole in the always-right façade of his older brother.

For the record, it wasn't eavesdropping on his brother and his ex if a guy was returning puppies.

Travis decided to noodle on that later. First he had a party to enjoy. And now he had some retribution to dish out— Frank style. He moseyed right up to the twins' bedroom and found the kid he was searching for.

"You know what you should take to your dad's?" Travis asked Kellan.

He could've gone with Brady, but Kellan was probably a better bet once Travis planted this particular little seed.

Brady had a lot more *people pleasing* in him. Kellan was more about doing what pleased him.

"What?" Kellan glanced up from the overnight bag he was filling with birthday presents and other related loot.

"Those recorders you showed me last week after your baseball game. I happen to know your dad loves music. He'll think they're fun." Travis chucked his nephew on the shoulder.

Rachel emerged from the boys' closet with a couple of pairs of pajamas. She blinked hard at Travis, as though trying to figure out where he'd come from.

"I know he particularly likes music right when he wakes up. So be sure you play them first thing in the morning. Bonus points if you manage to do it before he's out of bed." This was not a fib. Gavin would think the recorders were fun —for five seconds—because, damn, the screeching noises those so-called instruments let off would make him pull his hair out just enough, but not so much that Travis felt like a jerk for suggesting it.

Besides, served him right for showing up late. And for cutting down the tree Travis had been climbing when they were teenagers. And for dumping over Travis's canoe last summer at the lake. Twice. The first time could've been an accident. The second time definitely screamed malicious intent.

"Oh, and you should take that sand stuff." Rachel handed over a bucket filled with multicolored sand packets meant for layering into plastic jars. Travis had a hunch the boys wouldn't be filling jars with the sand but would probably wind up in a sand war, stuffing it in each other's clothes, on bedsheets, and in various other annoying crevices.

At least, that's what Travis would've done with his brothers when they were that age. Bonus points if you could manage to get the sand wet first. Double bonus points if you got it stuck in the other guy's shorts.

He had a hunch Rachel knew the sand thing had that kind of potential. Sending it to their dad's house held a note of brilliance.

"Uncle Travis is right, Dad loves music. The puppies would probably love to sing karaoke with you, too," Rachel suggested, catching Travis's gaze with a wicked gleam in her eyes. "You should take that with you."

Kellan nodded with all the enthusiasm of a kid given permission to shove sand down his brother's shorts and wake everyone up to his rendition of the best of Justin Bieber.

Travis smirked.

Yeah, Rachel knew exactly what she was doing.

He gave her a subtle go-on-ahead nod. The knowledge that his little recorder idea might cause a little sand in Gavin's shorts warmed him like he was sitting on a beach in summer.

"Great idea, Mom." Kellan scrambled to put everything into a pile.

"I've got your number on this one," Travis murmured to Rachel from the side of his mouth.

She lifted a shoulder and nibbled at her bottom lip. "You inspired me with the recorder idea."

"I have a unique set of skills." Travis leaned against the doorway so he wasn't in her personal space. They were getting along great, and he didn't want to fuck that up.

"I've heard about your unique set of skills." Rachel crossed her arms. "Gavin told me all about them."

Travis just bet. He studied her face, searching for details, but none emerged. His back teeth set on edge.

"Which particular skills are you referring to this time?" Rachel asked.

He filed away a mental note to quiz her sometime about exactly what Gavin had told her and when and why.

"Not only can I come up with unique ways to drive my brother nuts, I also have the ability to help the boys forget some of this shi—" He caught himself, since Kellan was possibly within hearing distance. "Stuff at Gavin's place."

"If you make it so those recorders stay at Gavin's house, I'll totally owe you."

"How big are we talkin'?" Travis asked.

The wicked gleam was back, and he liked it. A lot. "Pretty big. I mean, *that* would be quite the feat."

"Big enough you'll come along to Twin Lakes?" He couldn't help it. Rachel *should* come and, as a bonus, if she agreed here, he could take full credit for getting her to tag along.

Everyone would end up a winner, except Gavin would be dealing with recorders, puppies, sand, *and* karaoke.

Rachel rolled her eyes. "You're so much like your mother, it's scary."

"You mean I adore your children and don't want them to miss the best summer ever?" he asked, hoping she understood that he was being totally serious with this insistence. "Then, yes, I'm exactly like my mother."

Without the penchant for wearing hot pink and sleeping with his hair in curlers.

"To be clear, there will be no tree surfing." She crossed her arms.

He huffed. "You take things way too seriously."

"And maybe you don't take anything seriously enough." With that parting shot, she shooed her boys down the stairs.

He did so take things seriously. All the time. Just not the things she did. Frowning, Travis grabbed their duffel bags and followed.

"Call me tomorrow when you wake up." Standing in the doorway, under her Shut the Front Door sign, Rachel pressed a kiss to Brady's forehead.

Travis crossed his arms and grinned as she practically had to tackle Kellan to get him to slow down long enough for a hug.

He would've helped out but, since *he didn't take anything seriously*, he held back. Rachel didn't need his help, anyway. She managed the Frank hooligans like a pro.

Not that Kellan wasn't affectionate. Travis just happened to know that he usually saved that for when he didn't feel well, wanted something, or when Brady was the object of their mother's affection.

There was no time for cuddling, thank you, there was a whole rainbow of things to do in the world.

The whole crew—Rachel and all the in-town Franks— spilled out onto the porch.

"Thanks for helping Rach out today." Gavin pulled their mother into a hug. "I'm sorry, again, that I couldn't be here when I should've been."

Two apologies in one day? Over the same thing? Travis looked to the sky to see if there were pigs flying.

Seriously, what in the Sam Hill was going on with his brother?

There was something up, Travis could smell it like three-day-old salami left in Rachel's SUV over a long weekend.

He thought he understood Gavin's modus operandi in life. Then the guy went and started apologizing and Travis wasn't sure what to do with the curveball. So, he figured he'd do what he knew best, exploit the situation. If Gavin was in a giving mood—

"Hey, Gav." Travis smacked his brother on the back and spoke when he was certain the boys couldn't hear. "Kids have a game this week. You gonna make it?"

Gavin paused, thought for a brief second, and finally said, "Planning on it." Then he added quickly, "I'll be there."

Travis wasn't squinting at his brother; he was squinting at the situation.

Huh.

The first part of that phrase meant that Gavin could have an out if something came up. Travis understood how he worked, and Gavin always said some shit like that because plans could, and often did, change.

This was standard for Gavin.

The second part, *I'll be there*, that didn't leave any wiggle room as far as Travis could figure.

Which meant? Huh.

"Let's go, boys." Rachel continued shooing the boys toward Gavin's Escalade. Each of them had a puppy on a leash.

Gavin loaded the dogs first, then the boys hopped into the backseat.

"Wait," Kellan shrieked, just as Gavin nearly shut the door.

"Three dollars says he forgot something he hadn't planned to take until right this second." Rachel stood on the step just below.

"I forgot Mr. Pretzel." Kellan scampered out of the vehicle toward the house.

"I need Chewy." Brady followed his brother, leaving Gavin standing at the waiting vehicle with only Dakota and the two puppies loaded.

Scratch that. One puppy.

There was an escapee chasing after the boys, his leash trailing behind.

No. Another puppy followed, and then there were none. Gavin rubbed at his temples and Travis would bet his trust fund that wouldn't be the last time that happened before morning came around.

Travis rolled his tongue over his bottom lip and wished he had a beer and one of those travel chair things to sit back and see where this was going to go.

Finally, the boys returned with their stuffed animals and real animals and climbed back in the car. This time, it seemed to stick, because Gavin managed to get the door closed.

"Hey, Rachel?" he called from the driver's side window of his SUV. "Thanks."

Rachel mouthed something to Gavin that Travis didn't quite catch and gave a wave to her boys.

Perhaps—and Travis wasn't ready to call this one yet—Gavin was not quite the jerk that Travis and Dane thought he was. Jury was still out, no verdict yet.

"I want this, you know?" Rachel said to no one in particular but, since it was just Travis out there—everyone else had gone back inside—he figured there was a solid chance she was addressing him. "But I also wish they made breathable Bubble Wrap for eight-year-olds."

"Kids don't need Bubble Wrap, they need a dose of falling on their ass to learn from their mistakes." Falling on his ass taught him the most effective life lessons.

That sentiment, however, earned him a teeth-gritted glare.

What? He wasn't wrong here.

"I think he's sorry about the puppies," Mom said, coming up behind Travis on the porch.

Funny, he'd thought she went back inside with the rest of them. Someone should put a bell on her; the woman managed to be everywhere at once.

"Agreed," Rachel said, the Travis glare melting a little. "If he's not sorry now, he'll be sorry by tomorrow morning."

Mom gave a chuckle. "Serves him a bit right, you know?"

"Maybe I don't feel so guilty after all." Rachel started back into the house. "I mean I've got a whole night just for me. Maybe I'll curl up with a book, leave my work cell in the office, and get a solid four hours of shut-eye."

"You deserve it, dear," Mom said as she hustled to the back yard, probably to figure out where she'd lost his dad sometime during the party.

Four hours? Of sleep? And that was "solid?"

Was Rachel a cyborg? With the kids gone, she should raise her expectations and go for a full nine.

He'd be happy to help out with that. He was just that nice of a guy. "I'll get started on cleanup."

"It's okay." Rachel seemed to fight a yawn as she waved him off. "I'll deal with it."

"Nah." Travis didn't exactly have plans. He'd probably even go home, sleep, and hit the office tomorrow. For a bit, anyway. Then he'd go flying. Not the corporate jet; that thing was a beast.

"It's really fine." Rachel yawned and pressed the back of her hand to her mouth. "I'll leave most of it for tomorrow, anyway."

"I'm here now." Travis looked over the mess that seemed as though the third-graders had gone to war with a bunch of slime-wielding wombats...and the wombats won.

"I don't need help." Her gaze traveled around the mess, and her face fell. Clearly, she needed help.

He reached for a puddle of slime chilling out on the end table. The slithery mess fell through his fingers. "I can scrub slime."

"I said—" She shook her head. "I've got it."

He let the slime fall to the glass-topped wood. "You sure do like to do things yourself, don't you?"

"Yup." She wiped the slime into her hand, sauntering to the nearest bin and dumping it. It stuck between her fingers.

"Why?" He grabbed a Kleenex and handed it to her for the residual slime.

"That way I know it's done right." Two swipes and she tossed the tissue into the bin with the slime.

Mom and Dad slid open the door from the yard. Mom stilled, clearly—for the first time—taking in the gravity of the mess.

"How can I help?" Mom asked, rolling up her sleeves.

"I've got it," Rachel replied, wiping up another puddle of goop. "Seriously. You all can head out."

"Rachel likes to do things by herself." Travis pressed his lips together.

"We should call Gavin, make him get his tush back here and help with this." Evelyn looked at Bob. "Call your son."

Rachel pointed to Bob. "Do not do that. I finally got the kids in his car; I don't know if I can do that twice."

Mom heaved a sigh, grabbing a waste bin and tossing empty cups and plates in. "You know, Rachel, Gavin talks about you all the time. Why you can't make things right between you, I'll never understand. The amount of stubborn in the lot of you stresses out my cat."

Travis rubbed at his forehead. Things never went well when his mother brandished the feelings of her nonexistent feline.

"You don't have a cat," Travis said from the side of his mouth.

"Don't tell me what I do or don't have." Mom huffed, puffing up like she did when she wasn't getting her way and Dad probably wouldn't step in to remedy the injustice.

"Gavin talks about the *boys*, Evelyn," Rachel supplied emphatically, putting her hand out for the trash can. "And as I've said many, many times, Gavin and I are great friends, and that's all." The point would have been well made, except Rachel yawned again.

Travis gave her extra points for the certainty with which she spoke, but the yawn totally mucked up the delivery.

Hell, if she weren't careful, she'd fall asleep and tip right over on the porch.

Mom released her grip on the bin, letting Rachel take it.

"Talking about the boys is talking about you." Mom ignored the rest of what Rachel had said, like the pretend cat she liked to go on and on about.

"It's really not," Rachel said.

Travis shuddered at the look on Mom's face. Rachel clearly needed to make this point, because usually she just stepped aside when Mom was on a tear.

Mom wasn't used to being challenged. Hell, she'd been talking about the pretend cat since before Travis could remember.

"Gavin and I were never meant to be," Rachel continued as though she hadn't seen Mom's expression or what that meant for everyone's evening. "We were an accident, and we became friends. I'm grateful for his friendship. Grateful we share kids. You have to know that we're not going to get back together, though. He has Dakota."

"Pssh." Mom steeled her expression. "You both need to give the other another chance. It hasn't been easy for Bob and me, either. We make it work."

"You and Bob love each other," Rachel said, doubling down on her willingness to stand strong against his mother. He had to give Rachel mad props. Engaging with his mother like this never went well. But Rachel was going all in.

"And you don't love my Gavin?" Mom arched an eyebrow.

See, now *that* felt like a trap if a trap ever was. Mom was the queen of spinning webs, and anyone who spent time in her life had to learn to avoid them.

Travis hoped Rachel had learned how to do just that.

Rachel paused, thoughtful, clearly selecting her words carefully. She opened her mouth, shut it, opened it again, shut it, and finally said, "No, I don't love him."

Travis winced on behalf of his brother. Ouch.

Mom's expression fell, and her lips slipped into a deep frown.

That frown hit Travis right in his gut.

"Well," Mom said. "I guess that's that."

There was no way that was that. His mother's traps were always incredibly inventive. The web on this one was barely a thin string, and yet Mom let Rachel bat it aside with hardly a fight. Impossible. Impossible that this was done.

Plus, he'd be sorely disappointed if they ended on that note. So dissatisfying for the bystanders.

"I really do care about you," Rachel continued. "If you'd consider dropping this preoccupation with Gavin and me, I'd reconsider hopping on a plane to the lake house."

Look at Rachel, manipulating her agreement in her favor.

Mom clearly thought so, too, because she stilled.

And, maybe, just maybe Travis was the only witness to the most impressive battle of wills in the history of the planet.

Although, that might be a bit of an exaggeration.

Probably.

Mom swallowed visibly. "That's what keeps you away from our family functions?"

"Honestly?" Rachel asked, rocking from foot to foot ever so slightly. "Yes. It makes me uncomfortable, and Gavin and Dakota can't possibly be comfortable with it, either. No matter what you think, they're getting married. It's happening. I've been helping her pick out mini tuxedos for the twins. So if you want me to attend these things, that type of passive-aggressive has to stop."

Travis's jaw slipped open. Rachel had just said...to his mother...

What world was he living in? Gavin was apologizing and not taking it back, Rachel was standing up to Mom, there were puppies… Nothing was as it should be.

CHAPTER 6

RACHEL

Negotiations were most certainly not Rachel's strong suit. She held her own when it came to the boys, but Evelyn had her number.

To be honest, Rachel wasn't sure who had won this round. It seemed to be a draw. Which probably meant that Evelyn won, because Evelyn always won.

Now everyone had left, and it wasn't even eight, and Rachel was ready to collapse on the sofa and watch something mindless. Clicking on HGTV, she did just that. Her eyelids started to drift closed as Joanna Gaines helped remodel an already lovely home in Waco. Then the doorbell rang.

Because of course it did.

The only thing that had Rachel rising to see who it might be was the hope that it could be a tag team of Girl Scouts with cookies ready for purchase.

She pulled back the curtain. Travis stood there, a glow of porch light illuminating his broad back, since he had turned toward the street. She frowned. What on earth was he doing here?

Unlocking the door, she tugged it open.

"Travis?" she asked.

Well, wasn't this just unexpected? Also, not entirely desired. Sofa, television, then maybe a Matthew McConaughey flick to get her in the mood for a little special alone time. The kind that involved her imagination and her hand.

"Hey." Travis turned back to her, bashful, which wasn't the usual for him. He held out a paper bag. "I thought you might appreciate some refreshments after the party."

She opened the bag, looked in, and then glanced back up at him. He'd brought her tequila, limes, Grand Marnier, simple syrup, and the cute salt that came in a special plastic container with the sombrero lid.

Her heart squeezed, in the good way.

Gavin was right, she liked surprises—when they weren't of the *alive* variety.

"You read my sign?" she asked.

He grinned, the bashful gone and his persistent charm taking its place. "I did. And I also figured you deserved a little present for standing up to my mom the way you did. She's not used to that. It's good for her."

She liked the bashful better. The bashful was vulnerable, and Travis didn't generally do vulnerable. To be totally honest, the charisma put her on edge and made her wary of his intentions. Most women probably fell all over themselves when he turned on that dark magic of his, but Rachel wasn't most women. That part of him was so polished, so determined…it wasn't authentic.

The conversation stalled when Rachel didn't say anything further. The vulnerability seeped back into his expression as they stood there together at her door—her inside with all the fixings for margaritas, him outside… alone.

"Come in," she said immediately, like an idiot who became incompetent around a guy who sounded like a young Matthew McConaughey and had around the same build—the athletic kind that she admired.

Travis, however, didn't move.

She'd invited him in, and he hadn't moved. Crap.

The seventh-grade awkwardness had nothing on the way she felt right then.

She gestured into the house. Internally she warred with herself for overextending the invite. On the one hand, he'd brought her the makings of drinks. On the other, he was Travis.

"I mean…" The decision became easy because…tequila. "You're welcome to come in, if you'd like."

He stared at her for a moment, then a wry grin spread across his mouth.

Oh dear. That was nice.

She had to stop comparing Travis to movie stars just because he was being a good guy.

"I'd love to come in." He followed her inside, latching the door behind him.

He pulled off his shoes and set them next to the sign she had made up that read, Shoes Off, Please and Thank You.

"It's quiet." She moved to the kitchen to unload the bag. No one had ever taken her margarita sign seriously. She hadn't, either, when she first made it, but then as time went on and the boys got bigger and the intensity of life weighed heavier—she'd wished more than once that someone would leave her a basket of margarita fixings.

"It is," he said, his deep voice seeming out of place in the quiet space of her home. "Quiet."

"It's never quiet." She set the limes aside, finished unloading the bag, and folded it carefully before sliding it into the cabinet under the sink.

"Even when the boys sleep?" Travis pulled two glasses from the cupboard.

"You have no idea." She did her best to keep her eyes open. It was hard, but she managed it. She snagged a cutting board for the limes and the cocktail shaker she wished she got to use more often.

"Do you want one or two?" Travis popped the top off the shaker and filled it with ice from the fridge. "Or a pitcher for later?"

Uh, a pitcher for later, duh. She pulled the shaker back into her grip. "I can mix them. You don't have to."

"Nope, the sign says margaritas, not the ingredients. I'm fixing them up for you."

She looked at him from under her lashes. "I won't ask you to do that."

"You're not asking." He took the shaker from her.

"Before you start in on telling me how you can make them better, I'd like to point out that I do know how to do this. As a matter of fact, I take margarita making seriously."

Oh, ouch. She'd definitely touched a nerve.

"On the rocks"—he held the shaker—"or in a blender? I should've asked that first."

"Do you know how to use my blender?"

"I bet I can figure it out."

"I don't know. It's one of those special Pampered Chef ones that can make soup or margaritas or whatever blended concoction you want as long as you press the right button."

His eyes heated with an intensity Rachel hadn't felt from a man in…wow, it'd been a while, huh?

"Then I'll make sure to press the right button," he said.

"Let's go with the shaker kind." Rachel decided immediately.

Travis Frank seemed to maybe, might be, hitting on her with margaritas, and those dimples, and that grin. And she was tired. And her boys were out for the night. And sometimes if she squinted while he was talking, he kind of looked like a superhero version of McConaughey.

"Thank you," she announced when he started mixing. "For the margaritas."

Yes, she was thanking Travis. Miracles could happen. It couldn't have been the tequila, because she hadn't had any yet, so probably just fatigue.

She wasn't positive, but she was pretty sure that as he squeezed a lime into the container, he said, "You're welcome."

Life had exhausted her, and she had the night off and Travis Frank was making her margaritas and then she was going to sleep. She was going to sleep the hell out of this Friday night.

* * *

TRAVIS

Fun fact, Rachel was a lightweight. One and a half margaritas and she was an open book.

"My mama told me it was inappropriate to bring beverages of this sort to a child's birthday party," Travis said, holding up the remnants of his first, and last, margarita in a mock toast. "I take her guidance on social customs as gospel."

"That's ridiculous. You should bring margaritas whenever you want." Rachel's face filter had dissolved about halfway through her first margarita, so she looked appropriately appalled.

He held back a smile. Tipsy Rachel was a hoot.

"When, precisely"—she waved her fingertip in a circle—"did you first read my sign?"

"I don't know." His southern-boy senses prickled, telling him he was about to get in trouble. He itched at his collar. "Probably around the time you put it up."

"That sign has been there for two years." She set her margarita on the coffee table to more fully talk with her hands. "You're telling me, I could've been having these margaritas this whole time?"

Well, yeah, he supposed so. He nodded.

"You should always read the signs and do as they request," she said on a huff, falling back against the sofa cushions. "When you're driving in traffic, you don't just *not* stop because your mother told you the signs are optional."

No, he always stopped. She had him there.

"You know, every time I come over, I *do* shut the front door." He ran his thumb along his bottom lip. "As requested by that sign there."

That got him a full Rachel smile.

He leaned forward, elbows on his knees. "You know that Mama has lots of thoughts about lots of things."

Rachel glanced to the ceiling, flopping her arms to her side. "She ruins everything."

"It's her gift," he replied, his lips twitching at Rachel's margarita-induced melodramatics.

The television murmured low in the background, the only light in the room coming from the screen—some show about houses that Rachel had turned on—the hallway, and the small bulb over the stove.

This, this was nice. She was Rachel. There were no expectations. They were friends. Maybe. Maybe they could be friends. Stranger things had happened that day—Gavin had even apologized.

"I'm coming to the lake," Rachel declared.

He had a feeling that she was half-past drunk and into blitzed territory, but he was a gentleman, as per his mama, and didn't say anything about that. Also, he'd provided the liquor, so it was his responsibility to ensure she didn't do anything too ill-advised that night.

"I heard," he replied. "It came through on the family text chain. Mama is thrilled."

When his mama was thrilled, everyone could breathe a little easier.

"I have to get work done, so I'm going to need your help," Rachel said. "Dane's, too."

Wait. Hold the fucking phone. Did blitzed Rachel ask for help? This was good intel. Still, sober Rachel probably wouldn't want his help, so he'd need to tread carefully.

"Figured as much," he said. "You know we've got you covered while we're there. You can get all caught up."

Rachel laid her head on the pillow, and her eyes started to drift closed. He didn't say anything further, instead watching the show she'd left on the television. Now some beefy guy was attempting to build a house.

When he'd glanced back at her, she was snoring softly with her hands up under her cheek.

It was adorable. Shit.

Was he allowed to think of Rachel as adorable?

The woman was made of steel. The wind tried and tried to blow her life over, but she held steady. She was a force of her own. The problem was, he had a hunch that if the wind got too strong, she'd need a net to catch her if she blew over. He wasn't sure that she had that net, and that made his chest ache. He'd been able to fuck up all the time when he was younger because he had the Frank family safety net.

Maybe if she didn't try so hard to do everything herself, she'd see that there was a ready-made group of people happy to catch her in her life.

He couldn't quite say what came over him, but he reached for the green, fringed blanket folded over the arm of the sofa and covered her with it.

"Rach," he whispered softly. "What's the code for the door so I can lock up?"

He could've texted Molly for it, or Dane, or Gavin, but he

figured it was easier just to see if she was awake enough to answer.

She was. She did.

Then she settled again.

He set his hand against the blanket covering her back and smiled. Then he frowned. Gavin was such an idiot. He'd had this. Had her.

He'd let it slip right through his fingers.

Travis shook his head. Everyone always said Trav was the idiot of the family. And, sure, maybe he'd earned that title. But it was his "responsible" brother who let his family slip through his fingers.

Travis sauntered into the kitchen, washed his glass, and fixed up a full pitcher of margaritas for Rachel.

He left them in the refrigerator with a note: *Read the sign lots of times, apologies for the delay.*

Because that was the truth.

CHAPTER 7

The one constant in Rachel's life over the past nine years had been change.

Change in her relationships with her family—her parents hadn't been happy she decided to move to Denver permanently so the boys could be closer to their dad. Her siblings hadn't been thrilled, either.

Change in her body—the postpartum phase should've lasted a few months, she figured, but eight years in and her metabolism was still messed up.

And change in her goals—it used to be she wanted to be a big shot like her brother Jack, work in a Los Angeles high-rise, and make lotsa money. Now, she settled for her own personal office under the staircase, the kitchen table, sometimes even her bed…wherever her laptop took her.

Life changed. Things flowed in different directions. She got that, embraced it most times.

But Travis bringing her margaritas? Yes, she would embrace it because they were delicious.

She could admit his margaritas were better than hers.

However, they'd spent time together last night like friends. Like she was hanging out with a male friend. A male friend who showed up late with an extra helping of five o'clock shadow that sometimes made her tummy flip and… other things.

That could not happen again, because if it did she might start to feel things more than a tummy flip, and she didn't have time for more than a tummy flip. Especially not with someone like Travis. If she was going to have tummy flip time with a man, he needed to be a helluva lot more stable.

Filled coffee mug in hand, she opened the refrigerator to grab milk for her coffee and cereal. She stilled.

Travis had left her a whole pitcher of margaritas.

With a note. In bold handwriting slashes from a black ballpoint pen in all capital letters, he apologized for not bringing cocktails sooner.

What did she do with that?

Her lungs released a shaky breath.

Yes, life changed, but would it really be so hard for it to freaking at least try to fit into some semblance of the design she endlessly had to adjust?

The alert chime on her front door beeped. She looked up.

"Just us," Molly said, letting herself in and striding through the living room to the kitchen with her son Oliver. "I came early to help you clean up." She pulled the tablet from her purse and handed it to Oliver. He grinned like it was Christmas morning, since Rachel happened to know that Molly was stingy with screen time.

Which was odd, if you asked Rachel, given her profession as a YouTube personality.

Sunday mornings were for their "special" working mom meeting at the neighborhood park. Special because they all brought mimosas. Also, the moms each owned a business of some sort, but this was not a work meeting. This was a let-the-kids-play-while-the-moms-catch-up-on-all-the-things-that-happened-that-week meeting.

Oliver settled on the sofa and Molly turned her focus to Rachel standing in the kitchen.

She paused, probably because the kitchen was clean. Not just after-party-exhausted clean, but *Rachel* clean. And Molly knew Rachel well enough to know that after the party she'd have crashed and left the details for the next day.

"Did the house-cleaning, margarita fairy visit your house last night?" Molly eyeballed the half-empty remnants of Rachel's last-night cocktail. "Or do you have a new best friend you forgot to mention?"

"How could I possibly replace you? You'd never allow that." Rachel grinned.

"So it was a margarita fairy," Molly said.

"Yes. Well, mostly." He'd cleaned up after himself and even used the special spray that Rachel liked because it smelled like lavender.

Not that he'd known it was her favorite—it was the only cleaning spray in the kitchen—but what kind of guy even used cleaner? Didn't they usually just go for a wet paper towel and call it good? Or was that only her experience?

"He?" Molly's eyes turned to slits. "Like a mystical man creature who fills your cup with cocktails?"

Well, that was one way to put it.

"Something like that." Rachel poured a dollop of milk into her coffee.

"Who…" Molly placed both palms on the counter, totally serious. "Is he?"

"Pretty sure he's like the Tooth fairy, and he'd prefer to stay anonymous." Rachel shrugged.

Molly pursed her lips like she did when she was thinking too hard. "Was it Dane? I bet it was Dane."

Rachel poured cereal into a bowl. "It wasn't Dane."

"Gavin?" Molly didn't seem certain about this guess, but

she tossed it out anyway. "Did Dakota keep the boys so your ex-husband could bring you drinks because they realized they take advantage of your awesomeness and therefore don't deserve your goodness?"

Rachel sipped her coffee. Fine, she chugged her coffee. "Travis."

She wasn't good at keeping secrets. Why would she in this case, anyway? Molly needed to help her dissect why he'd returned after everyone had left. Why he'd come bearing gifts. Why he'd cleaned up the rest of the kitchen when Rachel fell asleep. And why he'd covered her with a blanket before he left. Why? All the whys?

"Travis?" Molly stared. "Is this a joke?"

Rachel gave her head a slight shake and said, "Have I ever joked about Travis?"

Molly's mouth fell comically open, then she used the back of her hand to push it closed. This was Molly and her flare for dramatics and propensity toward slapstick—both of which made her YouTube channel so popular.

"Stop, it's not a big deal." Rachel spoke with certainty. "He felt bad because I'd had a rough week."

Molly lifted the cocktail from where Rachel had set it beside the sink. She examined it.

"That's from last night. I wouldn't—"

Molly took a slug of the cocktail.

Clearly, Molly had no issue with day-old cocktails first thing in the morning.

Her eyes widened, nearly as soon as the margarita had hit her taste buds.

"Travis gives good margarita," she said.

He did.

"He left a full pitcher of them in the fridge." Two hands around her favorite yellow FiestaWare mug, the big kind that held a solid two cups of Joe, Rachel nodded toward the refrigerator.

Molly marched across the kitchen, flung open the door, and if her eyes were wide before, this time they got so big, they resembled that of a Molly-inspired dragonfly. She closed the door, turned, leaned against it, and said, "Marry him or I will."

Ha. No.

"I'm not getting married." Again. Ever. Done that.

Hated it. Wouldn't repeat.

Rachel did try to learn from the mistakes of her past, the marriage one being a biggie.

Even if she considered it, Travis would absolutely not be in contention.

"Well, we're taking this with us to the park." Molly grabbed the pitcher from the shelf and immediately started rummaging through the cupboard, pulling out Rachel's stock of to-go coffee cups one by one. "Who needs Sunday morning mimosas when we have Sunday morning tequila?"

Rachel sat at one of the kitchen barstools and ate her cereal while Molly ransacked the cupboards for travel mugs.

"Works for me," Rachel said. "I need it out of the refrigerator before the boys get back this afternoon, anyway. They'll think it's punch and that won't end well for any of us."

She shivered.

Molly gave the pitcher a stir and dumped the liquid into the waiting to-go cups she'd already, and very efficiently, filled with ice.

Rachel hurried to finish her cold cereal and warm-ish coffee so they could head to the park and Oliver wouldn't have to wait.

She glanced at Oliver lounging on her sofa. He'd been born around the same time as her boys—a few months earlier. The difference? Molly and her ex had never even tried the marriage thing. Once Ollie was born, his dad disappeared, and Molly sued him for substantial child support. She won and never looked back.

She also never seemed quite content, despite all of her theatrics.

If anything, Rachel guessed the theatrics hid how badly Molly wished she could find a someone to love.

Rachel did not have that same desire. She had two boys to shower with adoration, and that was enough.

"Let's roll," Molly announced after she'd loaded the travel mugs into a cooler with wheels Rachel kept in the pantry.

Placing her bowl in the sink and rinsing it before loading it in the dishwasher, Rachel grabbed her park bag, and they headed out.

CHAPTER 8

"Oh my gosh, this is amazing," April announced, holding up the stainless-steel travel mug as though they were holding royal court. "Did he sprinkle these with some kind of special margarita man-candy dust that only hot guys have access to?"

Sometimes she'd bring yoga mats, but they definitely didn't do yoga. No, they'd all sit on them while they drank mimosas. It was way more fun.

"He's not a hot guy." Rachel sprawled out on the blanket they'd laid on the grass, turning her head to focus on the clouds in the blue Colorado sky above. Fine, he was a hot guy. But she was trying desperately not to fixate on the curl of his hair, the muscles in his arms, the way he filled out those cargo shorts…

"Uh." April waved her hand in the air over Rachel's face.

Rachel turned her head to her friend.

"He pretty much is," April said slyly. "Don't tell Kent I said that. Actually, you can. We're secure in our relationship."

"I have to agree with the hot thing." The newest member

of their mom brigade, Sadie, was not actually a mom, but she was awesome enough to join the brigade nonetheless. With a tawny complexion from her mother's Venezuelan roots, black hair, and a seemingly unflappable warmth in her eyes, Sadie had become a regular at their Sunday morning mom meetings. "You can tell Roman I said that, too. He'll probably agree if you show him a pic of Travis."

"Gahhhh!" Rachel tossed her arm over her eyes. "Travis is just *Travis*. He's not allowed to be hot Travis."

Rachel flopped her arm back to the side, staring up at the clouds again.

Sadie appeared in the view above her. "It's okay if you find a man attractive. You know that, right?"

"Travis is not a man. He's Travis," Rachel muttered.

This got her a Sadie smile. "Whatever you need to tell yourself."

The other moms all allowed a bending of the rules of their Sunday mom group to accommodate Sadie's attendance because, first of all, they never wrote down any rules. They were all pretty flexible about the whole thing. And second, Sadie was a ton of fun *and* an attorney.

Everyone knew a mom group needed at least one attorney and one medical professional. They were still on the hunt for the medical professional.

Not to be left out, Sadie brought her nephew on Sunday mornings so his parents could have a bit of a break and sleep in, which every mom in the group knew meant Sunday was their morning for a booty call.

Some people went to church, some people…

"Hey ladies." Kaiya hurried toward their meeting on the blanket. "I brought samples." Kaiya gave each of them a small gift bag with samples.

"I freaking love your samples." Molly dove right in to her bag.

Well, if it was sample Sunday, Rachel hoped she'd hit the

jackpot with the lavender-scented facial cleanser. She loved that stuff, and the squat purple bottles were so stinkin' cute.

April gestured to their circle. "Rachel brought margaritas."

"Oh, I'm so in." Kaiya looked to where her daughter dangled from the monkey bars, then settled on the blanket next to April. "We need to get together for momtinis soon. Cory's heading to her dad's for a few weeks this summer. I'm going to need serious distraction from the quiet that's about to hit when she leaves."

Like Molly's ex, Kaiya's was not in the picture. Unlike Molly, Rachel had never even seen Kaiya show interest in anyone as a relationship possibility. She seemed more interested in all-natural skincare products.

"It'll have to be after Rachel gets back from her big summer trip," Sadie said.

"Shhh," Rachel said, savoring the unwrapping of her sample. She rarely got gifts that came with wrapping and bows, so she took her time with it. Then she hit pay dirt. "Lavender." Rachel held up the bottle like she was on a game show with Pat Sajak.

"Woot." April gave Rachel a high five.

"Is that Gavin?" Molly asked, shielding her eyes from the sun.

Rachel turned and the excitement from lavender samples disintegrated as a weight seemed to be placed squarely on her shoulders. Yes, that was Gavin. Gavin with their two boys, the two dogs, and a couple duffel bags of stuff.

He was heading straight toward her.

Her limbs seemed to get heavier with each step he took in her direction. Still, Rachel stood. But she didn't move forward.

"Do you want to take him some moisturizer samples?" Kaiya asked.

Rachel shook her head. "Don't waste them on him. He doesn't know how to moisturize."

"That freaking guy," Molly said, under her breath. "I don't like him."

"I'm reserving judgment." Sadie had secured her lawyer mask of neutrality in place. She nodded, doing that attorney thing where she focused her entire attention on a situation. She'd make an excellent mom someday, if she decided to have kids. Her children would be just the right amount of terrified when she used that expression on them.

Rachel started toward her kids. They paused only briefly, each letting out an individual, "Hi, Mom," before letting out a *whoop* and bolting toward Ollie and the other kids playing on the playground.

A drippy, oozy feeling settled inside Rachel at the expression on Gavin's face. The boys weren't due back until the afternoon, but that wasn't the part that made her feel icky. He looked like he had something to tell her, and that something was not going to be enjoyable.

"Gavin?" Rachel asked as he wrangled with the two leashes holding the pups.

"I know. I'm early." The guy looked beat. Like he'd not had Travis bring him evening margaritas.

He held out the leashes for the dogs and Rachel took them.

"I..." He shoved his hands through his hair. He had dark hair like Travis, but Gavin's was a bit longer around the ears. The kind of haircut that took extra maintenance to make it seem like it didn't.

"Are you okay?" she asked, because he didn't really look okay.

"Last night was..." He studied the grass.

"Two-kids-and-two-puppies hard?" she responded.

He glanced up then. "I fucked up with the whole puppy thing."

No kidding.

"It is what it is, Gav." She held the leashes so the dogs couldn't run off, and they settled at her feet.

A long pause descended over them. He had something he wanted to say, she could feel it. For some reason, he wasn't spilling it. And, since she had no idea what he wanted to share, she didn't speak either.

"How are we going to tell them?" he asked finally.

She shifted the leashes so they rested more comfortably in her hands. "Tell who what?"

"Tell the boys that the dogs have to go back to the breeder," he said.

Um, that was not happening. No takesie backsies when you give puppies to a couple of eight-year-old boys.

"Gavin, that's not how this works. You gave the boys a gift. It was a ridiculous gift. Now we have to make it work."

Gavin stared at the grass surrounding his feet as though he were holding the conversation with the individual blades instead of Rachel. "Dakota asked that the dogs not come back to the house."

Say, what? Rachel didn't say anything because she couldn't get her mouth to move, such was the shock running through her bloodstream.

Her mind made several suggestions as to what she could say to him…

She should've made that call before you both purchased the dogs.

Yes, I totally agree, what's the number for the breeder? That's not her call to make.

The boys love them and we're not messing that up.

"I'm sorry, I think I misunderstood you." She settled on those words, since they seemed the least confrontational and, presently, she wasn't trying to be a jerk.

The pups were done holding still, and they started to pull on the leashes toward the mommy picnic ten feet away.

Rachel held tight.

To be honest, holding on tight when things were falling apart was what she did best.

"They peed on the rug." Gavin looked torn between good intentions and the bad outcomes of making not-so-good choices. "Ten times. They peed more inside than they did outside."

"Did you contain them to a small area?" Rachel asked. They had been doing better at her house once she sequestered them in the dining room.

"Dakota said they can't come back."

Dakota did not get to take this away from her kids. They had something they loved, and Rachel would fight for their right to hang on to it. Even if the thing they loved was actually two things that enjoyed peeing on the carpet.

"I didn't know Dakota paid your mortgage." Rachel happened to know that she didn't. Even since their engagement, Dakota kept her separate apartment on Speer Boulevard downtown.

"Rach."

"Gavin."

Yep, that was a touch of snark coming out in Rachel's tone, which wasn't the usual, since she normally liked Dakota. Sometimes she had to say it over and over again to convince herself, but there were all kinds of people and all types of friends. She and Dakota weren't the kind of friends who would hang out at the neighborhood park on Sundays drinking margaritas together, but they'd say hello and swap stories if they saw each other at the grocery store.

Unless it was the produce department. Rachel probably didn't want to watch how Dakota picked out vegetables, so she'd definitely have to hightail it to the dairy aisle.

Dakota didn't eat dairy.

"Rach, I'm in need of a little help here." Gavin adjusted his stance, and she waited not-so-patiently to see which direction he'd be taking this.

Her guess was that he'd either go with a giant heaping of the Gavin magnetism, also known occasionally as the Frank charm because all the brothers employed this technique, or he'd go with the sad, puppy dog eyes. Which, she would be remiss not to note, would be total bullshit, given he was trying to convince her they needed to re-home the puppies that *he'd* saddled their family with.

"Okay, look, here's how it's going to go, because I'm not bending on this," Rachel announced because Gavin was seriously eating into her Sunday morning girl time. "I didn't want the dogs to begin with, but they're here. The kids love them, they've already had enough instability in their lives, and so we're not taking them away. *I'm* not taking them away. And I still stand by my previous assertion that where the boys go, the dogs go. If Dakota has a problem with that, she's going to have to sort that out with you."

"Hey, guys." Molly bounced up beside Rachel. Deftly, she snatched the leashes and, somehow, simultaneously slipped Rachel's travel mug into her hand. "I'll grab these two so you guys can chat without getting *peed* on." Molly continued under her breath, "Like Gavin's carpet."

Normally, Rachel would've told her to be nice. But today wasn't a normal day.

"Thanks," Rachel said, disentangling her feet from where the dogs had gone this way and that, thus creating a medley of leash tangle around her legs.

Molly hauled the mini-mutts away. Gavin said nothing.

Rachel toyed with the lid of her margarita mug, flipping open the top, then snapping it closed. Open. Closed. Open. Closed. Click. Click. Click.

Gavin still said nothing. He stood there looking perplexed and staring at the dogs.

"Okay, good chat," Rachel finally said, because whatever was going on between Gavin and Dakota was seriously interfering with her morning. "See you later this week?"

"What?" he asked, pulled from whatever trance he'd fallen into while watching their boys round up the entire playground for some kind of game on the grass.

"At the baseball field," Rachel said. "I'll see you later this week. You said you're coming."

It seemed pertinent to remind him of this promise he'd made.

"Right. Yes." He nodded. Looked at the boys, then at Rachel, finally turned and walked back toward his car.

Rachel didn't know a lot of things. But given that her reality never went as planned and she'd very much like to have a break from chaos, she felt confident in asserting that something was up with Gavin. Something that, if she had to place a bet, would wreck her plans.

The question now was, which ones were coming up on the chopping block?

CHAPTER 9

Rachel marched back to her friends. Not that she was very far from them, but sometimes a girl just felt better after a good march. Control and the confident stride gave a subtle reassurance.

As Rachel approached the blanket, April, Sadie, and Molly all stared at her with large, round eyes.

Rachel plopped onto the fabric and crossed her legs, criss-cross-applesauce.

"Rachel." Sadie laid her hand on Rachel's shoulder.

Rachel picked at the pilling of the blanket, not able to meet Sadie's gaze. Even a whole bottle of lavender cleanser wouldn't make her feel better.

Sadie sucked in a breath as the only crack in her typical lawyer-inspired neutrality. "Not that I heard anything, because I'm really good at not hearing anything. Most days. That point is definitely arguable, but I stand by it. But if I *had* heard something, I'd say maybe you and I should talk about the parenting agreements you have in place with Gavin.

Because I'm wondering if he might be violating a few of them?"

Ugh.

Technically, he was. Not with the dog thing, but with the constant working thing and how often he wasn't able to fulfill the timelines he'd agreed to.

He worked a lot, though, and he did provide for the boys, so Rachel shook her head. No, she wasn't going there.

A shuddering breath escaped from her lungs. *Get yourself together, Rachel.*

Gavin didn't intend to violate the orders and, honestly, most of the time it was easier this way. Rachel was more in control when Gavin wasn't around so much. That control allowed her to prevent everything in their lives from going totally sideways. They all just tilted a little with the chaos.

"I don't want to do that; everything's fine." Rachel replied, because it was always fine. She just, sometimes, wished that things could be easy for a minute. Even a few seconds.

The baby Sadie was watching that morning got a little too close to the edge of the blanket, so Sadie reached for him and pulled him back into the center. He immediately went to work at edging toward the grass again.

Sadie patted him on the back as he started past her, then pulled him to the middle of the blanket. "If everything stops being fine, you know where to find me."

April's one-year-old was unloading a package of Goldfish crackers onto the blanket. "You did a great job of taking a deep breath over there."

Rachel sighed. She had a sinking feeling down to her toes that the dogs were not going to be going to Gavin's anymore because Dakota decreed it.

"You know your boys are going to rule the world someday, right?" Molly asked Rachel, pulling her glasses down to the tip of her nose as she glanced in the direction of the sounds of children.

Rachel had no doubt that this world domination was what they plotted late at night in their room. She'd overheard enough of their breakfast conversations to know her boys had the potential to either lead the free world or find themselves in deep, deep trouble with their shenanigans.

"They'll figure out how to be co-presidents or something. My munchkin will be their vice-president," Molly announced brightly.

Rachel allowed her gaze to trail to the field next to the playground where the twins had begun to coordinate a soccer game with several of the other kids from the playground area. They'd incorporated the dogs but kept them on their leashes. At least they were being responsible dog owners. Unlike their dad.

This version of the game didn't seem to follow any of the traditional rules, but the other kids all looked to be fine with the scenario, if she were to judge by the enthusiasm with which they shouted new regulations to one another and Kellan and Brady approved or vetoed those ideas.

Her boys were tough; she gave them that. They always bounced back whenever disappointment hit. Heck, they didn't even seem to register it most times. They just roared into the world with rose-colored glasses.

Dad can't make the game? No worries, they got to see their uncles.

Mom burned dinner? It's fine, they preferred cold cereal, anyway.

Her parents didn't have a substantial relationship with them? Eh, who needed two sets of grandparents?

She blew out a breath and gnawed at her lip, hoping they'd hang on to this kind of resilience. Hoping *she* could be enough for them.

The children ran back and forth between two small orange cones—she had no idea where they'd found the cones and did a quick scan of the street to ensure there weren't any missing from a construction project.

There weren't.

"Where'd they get the cones?" Rachel asked.

"There's a stack by the bathrooms." Sadie gave a pointed look to the aforementioned stack. "They asked first."

"I said it was okay," April added.

The children began kicking and spiking, yes, spiking the balls.

Yes, balls. This version of the game came with four balls. A soccer ball, of course. A volleyball because, why not, and two tennis balls.

God help her if her children did decide to become politicians.

"I'll be their campaign manager when they run for co-presidents." Sadie said, offhandedly. "That way they don't wind up in prison."

"Can we go back to talking about the margaritas?" April scooped up a handful of Goldfish crackers and placed most of them back in the single-serve package so her daughter could dump them again. "The Travis margaritas."

She kept a few and tossed them into her mouth.

Rachel shrugged. "He read my welcome sign. It's not a big deal."

Though it was the nicest thing anyone had done for her in a while.

"Except he makes you blush," Molly replied. "All the brothers are handsome—even Gavin, though I hate him and wish tonsil scabs on his throat."

"Why do you hate him so much?" April asked. "I mean, aside from the whole buying the dogs and then refusing to let them come to his house, he doesn't seem *that* bad on the big scale of jerkwad."

"Honestly?" Molly looked at the women. "He doesn't treat Rachel with the respect she deserves. She does the work.

He reaps the rewards. She keeps doing the work and he's still over there reaping. *That* pisses me right off."

"And Travis and Dane don't piss you off?" Sadie picked up the baby and did the sniff test on his bottom like a pro. Yeah, she fit right in with their group.

"Travis and Dane step up for Rachel and the twins whenever she asks. Even when she doesn't ask." Molly stared pointedly at Rachel. "She should ask more often. Especially when it comes to all things Travis."

Baby still in her arms, Sadie turned to Rachel. "I don't think she's going to let up about him."

No, Rachel didn't expect she would.

"Maybe you're right," Rachel said, falling back onto the blanket to study the sky, thinking of the game she and her mother used to play when they'd search for shapes in the clouds.

"Of course I'm right," Molly said, perky as ever.

Sadie snickered before blowing a raspberry against baby Luke's tummy.

"Maybe I need to meet someone. Have someone to look forward to seeing." There. That cloud right there looked like a lopsided version of Chris Pine with an extremely long… right…yeah…she was a mother and should not be evaluating the cloud version of Chris Pine's… ahem…

"I recommend it," Sadie said, giving the baby's neck kisses that made him laugh like an unhinged hyena. "Roman's the best thing that ever happened to me."

"You think you two will have kids?" Rachel asked, checking out another cloud that looked like Blippi…again, with the third leg thing, which she was heretofore going to pretend was simply an extraneous cloud that Bob Ross had painted in the sky and accidentally placed in an unfortunate locale.

"I hope so," Sadie said. "Roman wants kids and so do I, but we're also really happy just being us."

Rachel closed her eyes. *Happy just being us…*

She wasn't even happy right now just being her. How could she be happy as an *us*?

"That's the key, I think," Molly said from Rachel's left. "The being happy when it's just the two of you thing."

"Then Kent and I are screwed; we hit our stride as a couple once we had kids." April winked at Rachel. "But everyone's different."

Rachel turned her head and opened her eyes to see her best friend lying beside her, also studying the clouds.

"Don't you want to meet someone?" Sadie asked, directing her query to Molly.

"Of course I do. I'm just waiting for perfection in a male specimen," Molly said.

"In other words, she'll be waiting for-eva," Rachel said, refusing to acknowledge the cloud that had an uncanny resemblance to the Blue Wiggle…with that damn Bob Ross extraneous cloud.

"Maybe you can fix me up with one of your male divorcees, Sadie?" Rachel asked, closing her eyes and letting the wind whisper over her skin instead of searching the sky. "Someone with a really awful ex-wife, so he'll fully appreciate how nice I am to him."

"You don't want my divorcees," Sadie hummed lightly after she spoke. "These days they're all being charged with one crime or another. You know, since I started working in criminal law, too."

Rachel cracked an eyelid, watching Sadie as she held baby Luke close to her chest and made the low rolling noise in her throat.

Sadie was so going to let her fiancé knock her up. And soon, by the look of it.

"I'm glad my practice is moving away from family law and into the realm of defense." Sadie pressed a kiss to Luke's temple. "Do you know how much easier it is to defend a serial arsonist than an unfaithful husband who will not give up dibs on the VHS player his brother bought in 1987 and left in the attic of the home where he and his ex lived?"

"I literally have no idea, so I'll have to take you on your word," Rachel said, crossing her eyes when Luke looked at her. She stayed that way until he laughed.

"Does the VHS guy need me to find him a match?" Molly asked, suddenly serious. "I think I may have a viewer who would be perfect for him."

"Molly." Rachel tsked. "No."

"I'm going to side with Rachel on this one," Sadie added. "Just say no to men who cannot see the ridiculousness of clinging to a VHS player that stopped working in 2002."

"Rachel!" an all-too-familiar voice called from behind her.

She knew that voice. Gah. That voice, though only a sound, made a fifty-pound weight settle in her gut.

Rachel closed her eyes. "Oh my gawd, it's Evelyn."

"I freaking love this woman," Molly said, her words giddy. "Two times in two days, it's my lucky weekend."

Then Molly could just adopt her as *her* mother-in-law.

Rachel sat up, adjusting her white cotton button-down shirt so the buttons lined up straight in the middle.

"It's Rachel," Evelyn said, like she hadn't been stalking her to find the Sunday morning mommy group.

"Evelyn," Rachel said, feigning happiness and pretty sure she was doing a really crappy job of it.

Rachel stood, looking to Sadie, Molly, and April for the reassuring Evelyn's-out-of-control looks she'd hoped to receive.

None of the women provided such reassurance. Instead, they grinned like they were at a matinee at the Denver Center for the Performing Arts and the show just got started and it was a comedy and they were just oh-so-happy to be there.

Evelyn wrapped Rachel into one of her Estee-Lauderscented hugs, and Rachel let her. Because, despite everything, Evelyn did give good hugs.

"I stopped by the house to chat about lake plans," Evelyn said into Rachel's hair, just above her ears. "You aren't there."

Clearly.

"So how'd you find me here?" Rachel asked.

The lake. Blurgh. The lake. Summer vacation with the Frank family. Her heart semi-stuttered and halted because, apparently, that's what dread felt like.

"I asked Gavin, of course." Evelyn's high heels sunk into the grass as she continued forward. Somehow, she managed to make the trek look easy in heels. Rachel happened to know that it could not be easy, since they'd watered late that day and the ground was extra soft.

"Gavin cares deeply for you, we all know it, so of course he knows where to find you."

Wasn't that just creepy?

"I thought we agreed that you wouldn't be pushing the Gavin agenda if I agreed to come along?"

Evelyn laughed. "I'm not pushing any agenda. I'm only explaining why I'm here."

Uh-huh, and the sky was purple, not blue.

"Ladies, it's so nice to have a little girl time." Evelyn sat on the edge of the blanket and baby Luke crawled right to her. Meemaw was, most certainly, a baby magnet.

She removed three boxes of a new flavor of toaster tarts—Rachel couldn't read the flavor, but the box was bright blue—and handed them out to Rachel's friends.

"You have the best friends, my dear." Evelyn patted the blanket beside her, indicating it was time for Rachel to sit. "Who would've expected that?"

"Can I offer you a margarita?" Molly chimed in.

"Or any non-binding legal advice?" Sadie offered with a laugh as baby Luke grabbed Evelyn's pearls and shoved them in his mouth.

"Yes on the margarita," Evelyn said in her thick drawl. "That answer is always yes." Evelyn then caught Rachel's gaze and trapped it with her own. "I'm not in need of any non-binding legal advice presently, but I'll keep you posted."

"What did you want to talk about for the trip?" Rachel sat back down, giving a bit of space between her and her former mother-in-law.

"I've already directed the staff to set up an office for you," Evelyn announced. "Bob used to work all the time when our children were smaller. Dane still does. The work ethic is wonderful, isn't it? So I suppose it's to be expected that you can't take time away for family."

Don't engage, Rachel. Don't engage. Not when she'd used all of her built-up frustration engaging with Evelyn yesterday.

"A real office will be significantly better than your cubby at home," Molly said, all perky like this was a good thing and Evelyn hadn't just built Rachel up and put her down in the same sentence. "Or Starbucks."

"We have a cappuccino maker," Evelyn assured, as though this was one of the reasons Rachel would want to attend. "But if you have any special requests for espresso brands, let me know. I'll ensure they're provided. And skim milk, of course."

Well, that was nice. Rachel did enjoy espresso. She tended to live on caffeine lately. She also preferred her milk of the whole variety.

"Anything else?" Rachel asked.

Evelyn held the baby with one arm and the margarita with her other. "We just want to be sure that nothing comes up to change your mind about joining us."

"I already said I'd go." Rachel sipped from her cup. "You can stop selling it now."

"Consider it done." Evelyn took a cautionary sip from her travel mug. "This is wonderful."

"Isn't it though?" Molly said.

"Have a sample," Sadie handed an extra gift bag of Kaiya's samples to Evelyn.

"How'd you get two?" Molly's forehead scrunched.

"I guess Kaiya trusted me to give it out for her." Sadie's eyes glimmered.

Molly huffed, because they all knew—even Molly—that if she'd been given two, she'd probably have used both.

Evelyn pulled open the bow on the bag and pulled out a sample bottle. "I just love mint."

"I've never tried that one," Rachel said as Evelyn opened the bottle to give a good sniff. "I got lavender. It's my favorite."

And, come to think of it, nearly every time she got a sample from Kaiya it came with a lavender bottle. She glanced to where Kaiya was helping her daughter across the monkey bars. Huh.

"Oh, lavender is my favorite, too." Evelyn held out the mint bottle and did a quick swap to try the other.

Rachel gave the mint a go and...oh, it was lovely. Not lavender lovely, but still nice.

"Skin care samples, toaster tarts, margaritas, and friends," Molly said on a sigh. "The perfect Sunday morning."

Evelyn popped the entire lid off her cup and peered inside. "I didn't know margaritas would taste so good this early in the day."

"Travis made them," Molly-the-freaking-traitor announced without giving any thought to present company.

"Travis brought you drinks?" Evelyn eyed Molly, clearly surprised. "I didn't realize you two were close." That last part held a subtle note of concern.

Shit.

Molly's eyes widened at Evelyn's tone. Evelyn's not-sure-I-like-this mama-bear tone. Rachel had a similar version she used when Brady had brought a frog to live in their shower and neglected to mention it to her until she went to clean the shower and found a giant bullfrog lapping up water from the drain plug.

"No, not me..." Molly nibbled at the side of her lip. "He didn't bring them to me. We're...um...only friends."

Crap. Rachel rubbed at her hairline.

Evelyn's gaze traveled around the circle of women, taking stock of who else might have been Travis's mysterious margarita mama.

Sadie raised her eyebrows at Rachel.

"He made them for me," Rachel said, to end Evelyn's awkward perusal. "Last night he brought them over, since the party was kind of rough, and the sign on the door mentioned them."

Well, that didn't quite sound right, either. April started to speak. "What she means is—"

"Travis isn't good for you." Balancing the baby in one arm, Evelyn grabbed Rachel's other hand and squeezed. "He shouldn't be bringing you drinks. That's not entirely appropriate, is it, now?"

"It's really nothing." Rachel studied her tumbler. Why did she feel like she'd been hauled into the discipline office at work? "I mean, it's not nothing because it was really nice of him. It's just not what you're thinking..."

Evelyn's expression darkened as Rachel spoke. She looked practically fit to be tied.

Molly sidled up next to Evelyn. "Travis was being kind to Rachel only because she was having a bad day."

"You have to know," Evelyn said, her tone more serious than Rachel had ever heard it, "Travis and Gavin have always had a bit of a rivalry."

Yes, Rachel was aware of this. Gavin had been clear about his frustrations with his brother. He hadn't been a jerk with his remarks, but there was always an undercurrent of discontent there. It didn't help that Travis sometimes didn't show up to work and left Gavin taking up the slack.

"They always tried for the same things. Wanted the same things." Evelyn situated herself so she leaned toward Rachel. "You don't want to get tangled up in that."

"Of course I don't," Rachel assured her. "We shouldn't even be having this conversation because it wasn't what you're thinking it was."

"Do you think my intuition is faulty?" Evelyn asked, apparently turning on the full mother-in-law effect.

"That's not what she's saying," Sadie chimed in, and thank goodness she was all fired up to go attorney on the situation. "She's simply explaining that Travis brought them to her only to be friendly. As a member of the same family. He didn't bring them to her so she'd get all liquored up and take off her top."

Rachel's mouth dropped like Molly's did when she was trying to be comical. Rachel was not, however, going for comedy. "Sadie..."

"I assure you, she didn't take off her top," April said, trying to be helpful, Rachel was certain, but her friends needed to stop talking about her taking off her clothing.

"Family is a funny thing," Evelyn said. Rachel could totally be on board with that.

"Amen to that." Molly raised her travel mug.

Evelyn smiled, but it was of the variety that didn't reach her eyes.

"Sometimes family bonds are the strongest thing there is —harder than granite, tighter than woven silk." Evelyn paused. It didn't seem like it was for dramatic effect, but rather so she could pick her words carefully. "But sometimes when pressure hits just the right spot, a small fracture forms."

Rachel knew all about family fractures. She'd experienced it firsthand in her own when she'd found out she was pregnant and hers practically disowned her.

She'd learned two things from that experience. The first,

she'd never do that to her boys. Ever. And the second? Always use caution when it came to family.

"That is not what Travis was doing." Rachel crossed her arms because she didn't have the energy to defend Travis's kindness to Evelyn. Even with a full night of sleep under her belt.

"Hear me out," Evelyn said.

Rachel nodded because she had a feeling Evelyn wouldn't give her a choice.

"The crack, the frayed stitch, it's tiny, but it threatens the integrity of the entire thing." Lost in her own thoughts, Evelyn drew along the seam of the blanket with her fingertip in illustration. "When relationships are tested, or promises broken, it's our job to ensure that we do everything we can to prevent those teeny tiny imperfections. Because with a small, frayed stitch, it takes only one quick tug for the entire fabric of the family to pull apart."

Oh yes, Rachel knew all about that kind of tug. That kind of damage. Which was why she kept her distance and held tight to her boys.

"I'm promising you, there's no crack. No fray." Or whatever mixed metaphor Evelyn wanted to go with. "Travis didn't make a crack by being kind to me." Of that, Rachel was certain.

"I don't doubt that." Evelyn passed off the baby to Sadie and stood, brushing the wrinkles from her slacks. "But the fray has been there for a while between my boys. I'm just asking that you aren't the one to tug it free."

CHAPTER 10

They were leaving later than they'd originally planned, having to make accommodations for all the schedules involved. By the time everyone made it to the airport, the sun was starting to edge over the Rockies as the Franks loaded up the Puffle Yum corporate jet.

The boys had already boarded with their grandparents, while she did a final mental recheck of their suitcases.

Children's Tylenol, swimsuits, socks, antacids, moisturizer…

She continued running through her mental list of items to keep her mind off the fact she was about to board.

Uh-huh, Rachel was getting on a plane. And, she was pretty sure, the only thing that could make this family vacation more intense was adding puppies to said plane.

Actually, they *were* doing that—the puppies and plane thing—so it was about as intense as it could get.

Rachel's nerve endings had been mainlining bolts of anxiety straight into her bloodstream in the weeks since she'd agreed to the trip. She'd had to rearrange her summer schedule, and avoid any Frank who didn't go by the name Gavin—all while wrangling clients, kids, and puppies.

Though she held firm that the puppies followed wherever the boys went. Gavin had learned to deal with it. The boys mentioned a baby gate in Gavin's kitchen to keep the dogs away from his carpet.

As a bonus of Gavin being around more often for the boys, Evelyn hadn't brought up anything about Travis's cocktails. After Evelyn took off from the park with the lavender cleanser—Rachel hadn't noticed Evelyn never swapped it back until Evelyn was long gone—she'd been utterly beside herself that Gavin and Rachel were in the same room more and more often.

Even if that "more and more often" was totally platonic, and Dakota had been there, too.

This trip was happening, though, and it included Travis. Rachel really hoped her ex-mother-in-law wouldn't get weird about things and start ranting about fraying blankets. Rachel had a hunch, though, as she walked up to the perfectly innocuous Puffle Yum corporate jet sitting on the tarmac at Centennial Airport, that Evelyn was going to get weird about things.

Travis moved behind her as they approached the steps leading to the aircraft.

He didn't say anything, but she sensed him walking there. She somehow knew instinctively it wasn't Dane's footsteps.

She didn't need to turn to confirm his identity.

"Kids, dogs, three suitcases, purse, house keys, laptop, charger, cell phone, charger, and sunglasses." She continued her final inventory of everything under her breath.

"Would you feel better taking the car?" Travis asked, stepping beside her, the little creases between his brows deepening.

"Yes," Rachel said, quicker than necessary. The answer to

that question was simple because, fine, yes, she did not like to fly.

Also, fine, yes, she had a perfectly running Toyota Highlander with an abundance of room for herself and her children and their puppies. But the drive was a solid seven hours when she factored in multiple bathroom breaks, eating breaks, and one son who had a penchant for tossing up anything he'd eaten if he spent more than three hours in a moving vehicle.

Therefore, the corporate jet option with only forty-five minutes of actual flight time seemed like a natural fit.

Except.

The whole hating to fly thing. She didn't have a fear of flying, per se. She just happened to hate doing it because it was scary. Call that whatever you'd like.

She took in Travis. He dressed remarkably fancy for the flight. Her mouth went dry.

Had she ever seen him in pressed slacks before? Truly, she couldn't say she had. And a button-up white shirt? Travis knew how to do buttons. That was good to know.

He looked…okay, well, the first word that came to mind was yummy. But she nixed that thought and went with professional. He looked professional.

"I'm a great pilot." Travis cracked a smile, the charming one that stretched his lips and showed a pop of teeth and probably got most women in his vicinity to drop to their knees and start unbuckling his pressed slacks for him.

Gah, she was not allowed to think things like that. Bad Rachel.

Also…wait.

"You're not the pilot," she declared.

Travis was not a pilot. He didn't even play one on television, as far as she knew. Unless he had some secret life she didn't know about.

That was totally possible.

"I am a pilot, and I'm today's pilot," he said with the confidence of an actual pilot.

Rachel started to step backward but stopped herself, instead turning toward Travis the pilot. "I didn't agree to this."

"Rach, it's fine. I fly this bird all the time." He gestured to the aircraft.

Oh, hell no. Not Travis. Anyone but Travis. She preferred her pilots to understand the significance of flight in a metal box.

"Why didn't I know you're a p-pilot?" she asked… stammered…whatever.

"There's a lot about me you don't know," he said, and his words sounded remorseful.

She wasn't going to evaluate that remorse further than the basic acknowledgment of its existence.

"I have no doubt," she said. He could be the bestest best pilot in the world, but it didn't change the way her lungs seemed to fill with fluid at the thought of being in the air with him at the helm.

There was something about knowing the pilot of the plane you were going up in, several tens of thousands of feet in the air, had stopped attending his college classes because he preferred taking body shots off co-eds at the campus pub.

"Hey." He stepped forward, studying her face. "If you'd prefer to drive, we can take the boys and the dogs and meet you there."

Her boys? On this plane? Without her? Hell. No.

His assurance did nothing to assuage the plummeting feeling in her body about the fact that Travis was piloting this beast of a plane.

"The boys can't go up without me." And just like that she got lightheaded again.

"They'll arrive in one piece," Travis had the creases between his eyebrows again. This time, though, his gaze was soft. Like a caress. Like he cared.

Ugh. This was Travis. Travis did not get to stroke her with a gaze.

"It's not that I don't trust you." She swallowed. That was mostly the truth. She trusted him to drive her kids to the park or take them to Empower Field at Mile High. "It's just that I prefer the pilot in command of my children's futures not be—"

Him.

"Me?" he asked.

She said nothing. Sometimes it was the best choice.

"I decided somethin'," he said. Well, mostly, he drawled.

"What's that?"

"You're going to be my copilot." Travis nudged her arm with his own.

Not freaking likely. That was a no from her.

She stared at the plane—a metal flying box of anxiety made only of sheet metal, bolts, and jet fuel.

Travis stared at it with that caressing gaze, like it was to be cared for and revered. Cherished. Polished.

"No," she said. "And please tell me you have a copilot with the appropriate credentials."

He didn't respond. He just asked, instead, "Can I tell you the best thing about you being my copilot?"

She didn't really think he was asking, though. More like he was going to do what he wanted.

"We both know you're going to say it, so you might as well get it over with," she mumbled. He was like his mother that way.

"If you're *my* copilot, then I'll be *your* copilot," he said, turning that gaze back on her, letting it lightly graze over her skin, the fine hairs along her arm seeming to stand right up and take notice. Sheesh, it was like her body thought he'd brought her margaritas again.

Maybe Molly was right. Maybe Rachel needed to get laid. Good God, not by Travis and his caressy-caress looks, because that would apparently rip the seam of the family structure irrevocably, but there had to be a male in the Twin Lakes region of Colorado who might be interested in a booty call.

She'd figure out a strategy if they landed. *Once*. Once they landed.

Like a good pilot, a one-night stand should be someone you didn't know outside of the situation.

Although…in rolling that thought around her brain… the last time she'd done *that* she'd ended up with a set of twins and a man who had a penchant for disappearing from his fatherly duties more often than not.

"Let's just let the licensed pilot fly the plane." Forcing her feet one in front of the other, she stepped up the staircase and into the cabin.

Two balls of fur barreled into her.

"Crates," she said, the word shrill. "They have to stay in their crates on the flight."

"They don't like their crates." Kellan caught Pete around his neck and lifted him against his chest. "Meemaw said it's fine."

Rachel chanced a glance at their grandmother. Evelyn raised a thin, penciled eyebrow at her. It didn't raise very much because of the filler she used in her forehead creases.

Rachel didn't judge; she had every intention of Botoxing the shit out of her face once her wrinkles got deep enough. Though, Kaiya's products were helping to delay the process.

"The dogs won't hurt anything," Evelyn assured.

Except, they'd probably defecate on the pristine leather chairs, chew the armrests, run into the cockpit and force the plane into an emergency landing. An emergency landing of the hard variety that might even involve flames. Which meant…

"They need to go in their crates, please and thank you." Rachel leveled Kellan with her don't-mess-with-me-about-it stare. He took note, working with his brother to get the dogs back in their cages.

Dane secured the cabin as Travis made his way to the cockpit, a small metal clipboard in his hand, aviator sunglasses wrecking his otherwise perfect blond hair. Even though the guy was definitely not a superhero, he had a bit of the Clark Kent vibe right then.

"What do you think, boys? I'm trying to convince your mom to copilot." He focused on her boys, doing an abbreviated round of roughhousing with them that did nothing to allay her worry over the flight. She closed her eyes and mentally checked the list of items she'd needed to pack, ticking each off one by one in her head.

If this didn't work, she'd grab her phone and earbuds for the meditation app April recommended. Rachel used it sometimes when she got really nervous. Fine. She used it once. There wasn't a lot of time for meditation apps lately, what with the full-time parenting, impromptu family vacation for the summer, and a full client load.

"Mom, you have to do it." Kellan pulled her eyelids open with his thumbs and absolutely no regard for her personal space or mental stability.

"As I explained to your uncle, I want to make it to Twin Lakes in one piece," she said. "I went to business school, not flight school."

Come to think of it, she was pretty sure Travis had gone to business school, too. That thought made bile rise up a little in her throat because *he* was going to be piloting the aircraft, it seemed. Although, no one else questioned his credentials.

"It'll be so cool," Brady announced. "Then we can tell Dad you aren't scared of flying anymore."

The cabin went silent. Too silent.

"You're scared of flying?" Evelyn asked. "Gavin never told me that."

"I don't think Gavin tells you a lot of things." Rachel forced herself to smile but it felt weak. "Let's leave the piloting to those with training. My experience with playing *X-Plane* with the boys never ends well for my virtual passengers."

"You play *X-Plane*?" Travis asked.

"She's super bad at it," Brady announced, substantially louder than necessary.

Could the seat just open up and swallow her until they got to the lake house?

"Sometimes being a copilot is rewarding," Travis said, but it felt like he was talking about a lot more than the flight to Twin Lakes.

He could just go on talking about rewards and she'd just go on pretending that she didn't know him.

Kellan somehow managed to wear his seat belt and still get up on his knees in the seat beside her. Rachel immediately adjusted the strap to prevent so much freedom.

"I know myself," she said. "Therefore, I do not *trust* myself to fly anything larger than a kite."

The edges of Travis's mouth twitched. "Fair enough."

"That's it?" Rachel asked.

Because with Travis that was never it.

Travis shrugged. "I'm not going to force you to do somethin' you don't want to do. I'll just give you a little crap about it and move on."

"I wanna sit in the cockpit." Brady bounced in his seat, raising his hand like he was volunteering for the first round of chocolate cake instead of sitting in one of the first seats to go down in a crash.

Absolutely not. She opened her mouth to figure out a way to say that without breaking the kid's heart. "I don't—"

"He loves airplanes," Kellan declared. "He never stalls on *X-Plane* like you do."

"This plane is a Gulfstream G550," Brady said, still bouncing even though the seat belt remained clipped across his lap. "It has dual Rolls-Royce engines, but not the Tays. Those were phased out after the g-four."

Airplanes? For real? That was going to be his *thing*? No. This was a phase. That's it.

He could just like soccer or join the math club. A hobby that wouldn't kill him. Fractions never killed anyone.

Rachel's mouth parted as her son continued—

"This plane can go up to fifty-one thousand feet, but we won't go that high, since we're not going too far. Twin Lakes is close." He leaned back in the chair, kicking his feet against the edge. "I hope Uncle Travis will take me someplace farther someday, so we can go higher."

Rachel glanced at Bob and Evelyn, whose expressions of shock must've mirrored her own because, apparently, her son was an aviation savant and she never—literally never—suspected it.

Yes, he loved flight simulators, but they were video games, and he seemed to be an equal opportunity video game enthusiast.

She flipped through the memories she had of his games, searching for whatever she'd missed.

"What else do you know about airplanes?" Travis asked, resting his arm against the back of Brady's chair. Nonchalant, like this was not a big deal.

"I know lots." Brady shrugged, still kicking his feet against the edge of the chair. "What do you want to know?"

"What else do you have in your noggin' about the trip today?" Travis asked.

"The airport we're landing at is the highest commercial airport in North America," Brady replied immediately. "The approach is one of the hardest to manage, but you did it last year without any problem, so I think we'll be fine."

Hold the phone, Travis flew them last year and Gavin knew about it? He'd have had to because he was on the plane.

Travis grinned at Brady. "Thanks for the vote of confidence."

Seriously, about that…

Brady scrunched his face. "I probably shouldn't have said that in front of Mom. She gets weird about aviation."

"I don't get weird about it," Rachel said before thinking. Brady raised his eyebrows at her in a move that reminded her remarkably of his uncle. She shook away the thought. "I just don't care for flying. Like you don't like cauliflower."

"You don't need cauliflower to get from one place to the next," Kellan chimed in. "You don't need cauliflower for anything."

"Preach it, kid." Dane headed toward the cockpit, and was he about to do what she thought he was about to do?

Rachel's stomach plummeted and hit her toes like a super hard landing. "Is *Dane* the copilot?"

"He is," Travis replied.

Rachel grabbed Travis's arm. "Is he qualified?" she asked, ready to grab her kids and dogs and get off the plane altogether.

Travis extracted her fingers from his forearm. "He is."

Rachel bit at her bottom lip. Hard. "Are you sure?"

"I signed off on his license, so I'm pretty confident in his abilities."

"You can do that?" She gripped her purse to her chest instead of grabbing Travis again. "Sign off on other pilots? Is that a thing? One pilot just says another is good enough and on they go?"

That seemed like a remarkably bad idea. This, right here, was why she didn't like flying.

"I'm a flight instructor." Travis kneeled so they were eye to eye. He spoke calmly, like she would if she was explaining to her children that cauliflower wouldn't murder them in their sleep.

"I thought you worked at Puffle Yum," she said.

"I do that, too."

Oh.

"The flying is more of a hobby, but it comes in handy." He patted her knee. Patted it. Like *he touched it* in front of his mother.

She was pretty sure she heard Evelyn growl.

"And you're good?" she asked. "A good pilot and instructor and all of that?"

"So I'm told," he replied, confident and cocky.

She swallowed the uncertainty that had wiggled its way into her throat.

"Rach?" Travis asked, tilting his head toward the front of the plane. "Can I talk to you alone for a second? About Brady?"

She nodded, standing on wobbly knees. She set her purse in her seat.

Her eyes caught Evelyn's and Bob's as she passed. Bob winked. The man had charm—gobs of it that each of his children had inherited.

Evelyn pursed her lips and mimed tearing a thread from her sleeve.

Rachel followed Travis to the cockpit where Dane sat in the seat to the right.

Travis set the metal clipboard on the console next to the seat on the left before turning to Rachel. They were so close. Really close. Practically touching close. Too close.

She tried to step backward, but the closed door stopped her.

Who closed the door?

Travis's eyes dimmed at her movement. She did her best to ignore it.

"Do you mind if Brady hangs out up here with us during the flight?" Travis jerked his chin toward the jump seat.

"Yes." She nodded. "I mean, I mind."

She did. He was eight. What if he touched something?

He should stay in the cabin with her and the rest of the family and leave the piloting to the actual…pilots. Or whatever these guys were.

Travis's jaw ticked, but he didn't say anything more. "I'll watch out for him," Dane said, not looking up from whatever he was doing with his own metal clipboard. "Once we're in the air, Travis can handle the bird on his own."

"I can handle the bird on my own before we're in the air," Travis said.

"If you'd feel more comfortable, he can come in after takeoff and go back to the cabin before we land," Dane suggested, not acknowledging Travis's comment. "Gotta be honest, though, those are the best parts of the flight."

He looked up at her, then, and something in her expression made his lips turn down. "I guess that's only if you like to fly."

One could say that. She bit at her bottom lip, glancing between the two of them.

"Rach," Travis said, his tone entirely too serious. "The kid clearly loves airplanes. Let him have the chance to see what it's all about up here."

No. Just no.

"Please," he added, before she could say anything.

"I'm sorry, I'm not comfortable with this," she said, her tone the one she used when she was through negotiating with her kids and it was time to move on to the next subject.

Dane and Travis shared a look that she was not going to read further into because if she did, she'd probably take her kids and their dogs and stay on the ground in Denver forever.

Instead, she turned to leave, pulling on the door. It didn't open.

She pulled harder. Still didn't open. Harder.

Still nope.

Her heart rate was spiking, and where the fucking hell was April with her meditation app when Rachel needed it? Before she could kick the damn thing, Travis was behind her, his chest to her back and his scent surrounding her and making her stomach do the unacceptable flippy thing it did sometimes when he was there. He reached around her shoulder and pushed the door open.

Push. Not pull. Good to know.

Not that she'd need to know because she had no intention of coming back into the cockpit again.

"Rach," Travis said, low enough so only she could hear.

She turned and, hoo boy, he was really right there, just ready to rip at the seams of his family structure.

She started to step back, but he beat her to it.

"I know you're not comfortable with the plane, but I'll keep your family safe."

Her throat didn't seem to be capable of swallowing all of a sudden. She had to force it.

"You can't promise that," she said.

She was pretty sure she was the only one capable of it.

Sometimes Gavin, but he was sure iffy lately.

"I can promise that I'll do everything I can to keep your kids safe when they're in my plane," Travis said, expression solemn like he was at church confessing to sins that would make the most experienced priest blush down to his toes. "And you too."

Oh.

That was…

Dane had never said anything like that.

He loved them. But…

"I promise *you* that," he said.

Without saying anything else, and leaving her standing

there like a statue, Travis turned to climb into the pilot seat, buckling in before slipping on his headset.

Okay, so that declaration totally did make her tummy do the flippy-do, howdy-ho.

She rolled her lips again and crossed her arms around her middle, holding herself up like she'd done so many times before since the boys were born.

CHAPTER 11

Despite Rachel's intense discomfort, the flight was not awful. They didn't even crash or anything.

The whole group arrived at the Frank residence in black SUVs that waited for them at the little airport. The place hadn't changed since the last time she'd been there when the babies were first born.

Stone and wood with the rock-lined staircase leading to the front door remained the same. The huge bank of windows facing the mountain hadn't changed either. They'd built the house with one thought in mind—make it massive and make it permanent.

Though the house was enormous, precise placement of the trees made it blend right in with the rest of the forest. Green pine and juniper trees everywhere with crisp mountain air that smelled amazing—clean and bright—but tended to make her light-headed, what with the lack of oxygen this high on the mountain.

Travis disconnected from a call and strode next to Rachel, where she stood at the base of the staircase leading to the enormous front door. The boys were going bananas running through the trees, kicking up the gravel of the driveway on their way across and making enough noise that it sounded like there were substantially more than two of them. She figured she'd let them get it all out of their system and blow off some steam with the dogs before they went inside.

Less opportunity to break Evelyn's stuff, and all that.

"I've been thinking about Brady," Travis said as chauffeurs from the service that had picked them up at the airport unloaded bags and hauled them inside the house.

Rachel closed her eyes. Damn. She didn't want to talk to Travis about Brady. Because she'd already used her quota of nos that day, and she had a hunch she was about to use a bunch more.

"What have you been thinking?" Rachel asked, tilting her head to indicate they should probably go inside.

He clearly wasn't ready yet, because he didn't head that way. Instead, he glanced at her sneakered feet.

What was up with that?

"Are you up for walking and talking?" he asked, pointing toward the copse of trees with an opening and a path leading through.

Oh. Okay. Sure. She could walk and say no at the same time. Except...

Rachel looked to the stairs leading to the entry arch, then to her boys screaming up an entire hour of pent-up third-grader energy. "I'm on duty."

"I've got the boys," Dane said from the top of the stairs. He waved Travis and Rachel away. "You two have a nice chat."

Rachel turned a bit of side-eye toward Travis. He squirmed.

What could she say? She was a pro at side-eye. It came with being a mother.

"He's in on whatever you're going to want to talk to me

about, isn't he?" Rachel asked, not thrilled about the idea of taking off with Travis or having him and Dane tag team her on parenting choices.

"He is." Travis apparently succumbed to the tug of the wilderness and moved toward a trail at the east edge of the property.

"The boys need to run around for a while longer before they go inside," she said to Dane.

He nodded. "Got it."

"And no sugar before dinner."

He nodded again. "You're the boss."

"Don't let them unpack the suitcases until I get back. I have a system." It was a good system that ensured the clothes didn't get all tossed into one pile in the middle of the room. Which was the way they'd prefer to live.

Dane saluted. "Consider it not done."

Travis paused at the entry to the trail, apparently waiting for her to catch up. She hurried to meet him there.

He, however, didn't seem in a hurry to talk.

They walked in silence for a bit, the crunch of pine needles under their feet, the rustle of the trees, and a bird chirp here and there the only sounds.

The peace was…peaceful. April would totally love it.

She made a mental note to tell April all about it the next time they talked. She needed to check in with her friend anyway, since her husband had been taking extended work trips over the past month. Rachel understood more than most how it felt to manage everything alone. To have the whole world fall on her shoulders.

Travis still said nothing. Of course he didn't. She had his number. He was waiting for her to talk first. Negotiating with her mini-tyrants had taught her a lot about keeping her mouth shut and waiting them out.

The trail opened up to a vast swath of beach along one edge of the smaller lake. A sensation of falling hit her as she took in the view. The jolt of mountain gorgeous seriously knocked the air out of her.

She gasped. A good gasp. The kind of sound that came from witnessing beauty of this magnitude. Unlike the house that was in-your-face enormous, the panoramic view was pure serenity.

Rachel gaped as she turned a semicircle to take in the lake, mountains, and endless sky. "I forgot how beautiful this place is."

A breeze blew light ripples along the surface of the water, and only a few boats in the distance disturbed the scene. Insects made touch-and-go landings on the ripples, risking their lives for a taste of the water.

Risking their lives because at any moment a rainbow trout could pop right up like the Puffle Yum Momster and grab its dinner.

Still pretty, though.

"The new dock is around those trees. We spend a lot of time on the lake during the summer. I'll teach the boys to water-ski this year if you want," he said.

Water-skiing?

"I've never been." Rachel started toward the dock.

Travis shoved his hands in his pockets, like he seemed to always do around her. "Then I'll teach you."

The offer snagged in the air between them. He wanted to teach her to water-ski? What would his mother's fake cat have to say about that?

"We'll see," she said in lieu of an agreement. "What was the thing you wanted to talk to me about for Brady?" Rachel continued her trek in the direction of the dock—away from the trail. The pull of the water was intense.

Back in college, she'd swum on the competitive team. That was long before she'd gotten pregnant. Back then things were as simple as diving into deep water and swimming away her cares.

"I'd like to take him up a few times in my single-engine." Travis cleared his throat. "Let him get the feel for flying in a small aircraft."

Rachel's heart seemed to stop beating.

"Dane liked the idea, too," he continued.

She stilled. Swallowed. Blinked. "I know I'm supposed to say yes, but I'm not going to say yes."

"Do you want me to quote you some statistics about the safety of flying?" he asked. "Because I'd be happy to."

She just bet he would. That didn't change anything, though.

"I know the statistics say it's safe." Rachel grabbed a stick from the ground and broke off small pieces, tossing them aside as they walked along. "But statistics don't help when it's my kid up in the sky in a piece of metal with a single engine."

"But you take that same kid in a piece of metal with an engine down I-70 at seventy-five miles an hour?" Travis asked, trotting to keep up with her pace.

She nodded and tossed the whole stick aside. "I see your point. I acknowledge your point. I even agree with your point." She turned to him. "But the answer is still no."

"You're being unreasonable," he said, crossing his arms and glowering, his blue eyes boring into her.

He couldn't ask her to trust him with her kid. Not Travis, of all people.

"You have no idea how unreasonable I can be," she said.

"I think I have a fair idea." He let enough southern into his accent to piss her off further *and* make her heart beat faster.

Trust was earned and he, he absolutely hadn't earned it.

As a matter of fact—

"Then I guess I'll ask Gavin," he said.

"Seriously?" She shoved her hands onto her waist. "Play the go-to-dad game?"

He stared at the water, seeming to track one of the boats in the distance. "I don't play games. But this is important. That kid had stars in his eyes when he started talking about planes. It's in his blood."

She'd seen the stars, too. They made her throat clog with motherhood-induced panic.

"That doesn't happen for everybody." Travis stood closer to her. A little too close. She could smell his brand of achingly woodsy cologne. It mixed with the low oxygen content of the mountain air, and the combination made her not want to argue anymore. Her traitorous body wanted to do other things with him. Inappropriate Molly-type things.

She moved a couple of inches away.

He seemed to get the point and moved a few inches in the other direction.

"Brady's safety is important to me," she said through gritted teeth.

He turned on her, hands on his hips. "You don't think his safety is important to me, too?"

Not the same way it was for her. He didn't have the same investment.

"Right. Uncle Travis. Understands the significance of safe-ty." She let out a laugh.

"You know, Rach—" Travis took the stairs up to the dock and walked to the edge. "You put too much weight on the wrong shit. You worry about the wrong stuff."

He had no idea what she put weight on or why. Why the safety of her kids mattered more than any other thing on the planet.

"And you don't know anything about it." She crossed her arms under her breasts.

He held her glare with his own. "I know that I'd never let anything happen to my nephews."

Except he wanted to take her son up in the sky. A sky with gravity. Gravity that would pull him back to earth—

fast. "And I know I'd never let you have the chance to hurt them."

The harsh tone of her words seemed to leave a bruise, given his pained expression.

"You think I'd hurt them?" he asked.

"I think you're too invested in *nothing* not to." Rachel stared at her image reflecting back on the water's surface.

God, she missed the water. Missed who she'd been in the water.

Free.

She'd been free.

Travis started back toward the beach, clearly expecting her to follow.

She didn't follow. Just stared at the ripples of the water, counting them.

One, Gavin's not here. Two, Brady wants to fly. Three, Travis can't take him. Four, there is nowhere to cry.

She heaved a breath and turned, ready to step off the dock to the beach. The mountain beaches weren't the ocean kind with small, pebbled sand that stuck to your skin. These were muddy beaches with rocks. Lots and lots of rocks.

Rocks and the pull of the water. She looked back at the lake.

Screw it.

She pulled her top over her head, revealing a black tank top underneath.

"What exactly are you doing?" Travis asked. "My mother could come around that corner at any second."

Instinct seemed to kick in and he did a scan of the beach and trail, apparently to be sure his mother wasn't going to pop out from behind a juniper tree. He could chill. She wouldn't take off *all* her clothes.

"I'm going swimming." Rachel pulled off her shoes, setting them beside her shirt. "I'm having fun. Because, apparently, I take shit too seriously."

And the water screamed for her to let it soothe the ache of motherhood that rooted so deep she thought it would pull her under.

*　*　*

TRAVIS

Fucking hell, was this the moment they were going to deal with *that*?

"You can't skinny-dip in the middle of the day." Travis did a wide wave with his arm. "There are boats out here."

Also, his mother's fake cat would have a whole basket full of kittens. Hell, if he had a fake cat, she would probably have kittens, too.

Rachel gave a sound that sounded like pshaw. "Oh, does me having fun bother you? Make you uncomfortable?"

She frowned and lines around her eyes, that he'd never noticed before, deepened. When'd she get those? And why did she have frowny lines instead of laugh lines? He blamed Gavin.

"Rachel, this is enough." Before he could ask her nicely to reconsider, she turned and did another scan of the water.

"How deep is this?"

Uh. "Deep enough for a speedboat."

They hadn't moved the family boats over yet. Actually, he'd need to chat with the head of maintenance to find out why.

Still wearing only her shorts and the tank top, she dove into the lake like she was an Olympic swimmer.

Her form was spot-on and she hit the water with her freestyle stroke ready to go.

Travis gulped.

Then he turned back toward the trail. Then he turned back toward the water. Trail. Water. Trail. Water.

He decided he should probably—as a southern gentleman—ensure that she did not drown.

"Are you coming in?" She turned, treading water several lengths from the edge of the dock.

He shoved his hands onto his hips. "I am not."

Her blond hair hung around her shoulders, meeting at the waterline to fan around her. Somehow her pink lipstick was still intact.

Pink lipstick that probably tasted like sunshine. No. He could not think shit like that.

Just because he figured she tasted like sunshine didn't mean he was going to go licking her to find out.

Once at Casa Bonita, he'd wondered what the enchiladas tasted like on Kellan's plate. Nope, didn't taste those, just let his mind wonder and moved on.

"Forgot how to swim?" Rachel asked, still treading water.

"I can swim," he called.

"Then you're just a scaredy-cat." She laughed, floating on her back, and her boobs were so right there, two mounds above the water, and he was really wishing she would go back to the treading water thing.

"My mama terrifies me."

Then Rachel, serious as all hell Rachel, did the one thing he did not expect.

Rachel meowed.

He couldn't let that stand. He was not a scaredy-cat. What was he telling his mama about limits and how he didn't like abiding by them?

Rachel laughed like he'd never heard her laugh before. "Your face. You should see your face."

He wanted her to laugh like that. Laugh lines, not frown lines, should find their way into her expressions.

"Get out of the way," he instructed, waving her aside. She did as he asked, doing a side-swim to the north.

"I jump in this lake and you promise to seriously reconsider letting Brady fly." Hell, might as well negotiate with her when he could.

As she moved aside, he was already unhooking his belt and pulling down his jeans.

"No." She shook her head.

The black boxers he was wearing had to count as swimming trunks of some variety. He yanked his shirt over his head and cannonballed into the lake.

It. Was. Fucking. Cold.

He pushed himself up to the surface, sputtering and cussing at the cold.

"You didn't say it was f-f-freezing."

She lifted a shoulder and splashed him. "Meow."

She moved to splash him again, and he caught her wrist in his hand before she could complete the motion. A zing of something that felt like a live electrical wire moved through him when their skin connected.

Suddenly, the lake wasn't really that cold anymore.

Neither of them said anything, and she wasn't laughing anymore. They clearly weren't thinking of cats or airplanes. They were both there, in a lake, and he was holding her… wrist.

Without thinking further, he treaded through the foot of water separating them until there were only a few inches between them. He slid his hand along the inside of her wrist up to her palm until their hands met and he linked their fingers together.

Her mouth parted.

He was hard in spite of the chill of the lake. And he didn't fucking care.

He stroked the fleshy part of her palm with his thumb. "Do you want to meow at me again?"

She shook her head. It was subtle, but there.

"I'm good." He grinned.

"Glad we settled that."

Rachel's free hand skimmed along his side, pulling him closer to her. Any closer and she'd feel… Her eyes went wide.

Yup, she'd felt it. The evidence of his desire was tenting his boxers, and there wasn't a thing he could do about it.

Rachel opened her mouth, closed it, opened it again.

She seemed to be steeling some kind of resolve.

Her leg brushed his as she kicked to tread water, and that seemed to make her decision for her. "Travis, I'd like to—"

"Mom!" Kellan's voice pierced the quiet of their side of the lake.

Travis swam away from Rachel faster than he'd ever moved in the water. He didn't look back, because he really needed to get his body under control.

"Hey, baby." Rachel waved to her son. "Are you coming in?"

"Can I?" Kellan asked.

Rachel nodded, and that's all it took. Kellan stripped down to his Lightning McQueen skivvies and ran down the length of the dock like a hooligan with the police on his tail. Brady followed, but he took his time getting out of his clothes, folding them neatly and setting them beside his mother's.

Dane moseyed along behind the boys, stopping at the end of the dock while they cannonballed into the lake a la their uncle Travis. He, however, did not strip down and jump in.

Instead, he took a look at Travis, then he glanced at Rachel already playing an impromptu game of Marco Polo with her kids, and then he shook his head. "I'll head up to the house and grab you yahoos some towels."

"Towels are for weenies and old people," Kellan yelled.

"Kellan," Rachel admonished. "Use your nice words when someone offers to do something kind for you."

"I'd love a towel," Travis hollered. Giving a thumbs up for good measure.

His erection disappeared, thank fuck, and he had every

intention of getting in on this game of Marco Polo. Back in high school, he'd been known as the Marco Polo prick. That wasn't true, but it could've been because he was *that* good at the game. He did have two brothers, after all.

Rachel was saying something to Kellan, quiet-like, but with intensity. Kellan was listening because Rachel likely wasn't giving him a choice in the matter. Travis had a feeling he was getting an earful about respect, if he had to guess.

Even fun Rachel, in a lake, had her limits, apparently. "No, thank you, Uncle Dane," Kellan hollered with a wave. "No towel for me, but Brady and Mom want one."

"Bring me two in case we need an extra," Travis said, mid sidestroke.

Dane gave a return thumbs up and headed back down the dock.

"Now, boys, I would like to show you how to play Marco Polo." Travis ducked under the water to show them just that.

There was a great deal of scurrying of limbs, and he did not check out Rachel's legs under the water. That's his story, and he was sticking to it.

Travis could hold his breath for an abnormally long time. When he was a kid, it used to freak his mama way the hell out.

He had his eye on Rachel's calf and followed her, careful to stay low enough not to make ripples under the water.

Finally, she stopped moving, and he surfaced in front of her, touching her gently on the shoulder and said, "Polo."

Rachel. Shrieked. Her kids cracked up.

She whacked him in the chest. "I can't believe you just did that. How long have you been there?"

The boys were still laughing and roughhousing and generally having a great time, so he took the opportunity and leaned forward, whispering in her ear, "Long enough to want you to look at me like you did before everybody showed up."

Turned out he could be serious. Serious about playing with fire.

Rachel's mouth parted, and that was all he got because the boys tag teamed him and both climbed on his back. It was the kids against the team they'd elected to call the elderly and, in the end, Dane showed up with towels and Rachel called it a draw.

For the record, it wasn't a draw, and Travis had totally won.

He pulled himself onto the dock, still high on adrenaline from the lake, and the kids, and Rachel.

His mama stood next to Dane. She did not appear thrilled. As a matter of fact, if he had to guess, she'd start talking about her pretend cat pretty soon.

Dane gave him a sorry-she-made-me-bring-her-along look.

Travis pulled each of the boys out of the water onto the dock. Rachel was already climbing the ladder and made it to the top before he could even offer assistance, because, of course, she didn't need help.

She was Rachel.

And as soon as she hit the top step, she wrapped a towel around herself—which was a shame—and helped her boys dry off.

He didn't realize he was staring at her until his mother hissed his name. "Travis."

Mama's tone caught his attention. He turned.

She stepped forward, towel extended like a peace offering. But he knew that look in her eyes. Knew that was not what this was.

"Rachel is Gavin's wife." She said the words softly, but in the tone she used when there was no debate.

His mother had already made her feelings on the Rachel subject perfectly clear.

"They're not married anymore," Travis said, doing his

best to ignore his mama's tone. "They had one of the shortest marriages in the history of marriage. You should know, you were there."

"Messing around with your brother's wife is not what our family stands for." Mama's cheeks were scooting right past pink into red territory.

"No, we stand for toaster tarts."

Past red and into full crimson, her face blazed. "My cat is so disappointed right now."

Her and her fake cat.

Travis took a deep breath and leaned forward to peck his mama's cheek.

"Rachel is off-limits," she said.

"You should know better than to set limits," Travis replied, just as softly as she'd spoken. "I don't pay attention to them anyway."

CHAPTER 12

Travis was in the doghouse.

Not the figurative doghouse. This was of the literal variety, as the puppies were his to watch for the night.

"We need to talk about Brady." Travis held his cell up to his ear as he stretched out on his bed.

"The airplane stuff?" Gavin asked carefully.

The "airplane stuff?" It was never just the "airplane stuff." Travis knew the look in Brady's eye; heck, he'd experienced it himself when he was about Brady's age. The look that meant the kid was destined to be a pilot. That type of desire settled deep in the soul, and there was only one solution—flight.

"Yeah," Travis said, already knowing how the conversation would turn.

"Rachel reached out. She said you might talk to me, too." Gavin's resigned voice came through the other end. "She doesn't want him to fly."

Travis held his palm to his face. "He loves the sky. I can feel it."

"I think he'd be a great pilot." Gavin sighed. "But I won't even attempt to try to overrule his mom. Rachel has her reasons; you'll just have to convince her."

Rachel had made it clear there was no convincing. Which meant, hell. The kid was gonna have to wait until he was old enough to do it himself.

Like Travis had.

And that stuck sideways in Travis's craw.

"You know," Gavin continued, "if you could *not* piss her off while you're there, I'd appreciate it."

Travis sighed. *Fine.* "I'll drop it."

For now.

"And if you might keep Mama at a distance from her, that'd be much appreciated, too," Gavin added.

"Dane and I have it under control." They did. They'd even agreed to a tag-team method that would keep Evelyn out of Rachel's hair.

Gavin sighed. "Mama can just be..."

Travis glanced at the dogs lying on the other side of the mattress.

He knew exactly how their mother could be. His setup that night was his mother's doing, and he had her number on this one.

She acted innocent enough when she'd made the arrangements for him to have two furry bedmates, but his mama worried he'd make a move on Rachel. Frankly, after the incident at the lake when he'd nearly kissed her, he'd worried about that, too.

So his mother had saddled him with the two puppies.

No doubt, she hoped they'd keep him occupied, so he'd have no time to go sniffing around for Rachel.

"She can be Mama." Travis chuckled as he punched the pillow behind his head, willing it into place. "We'll make sure she doesn't go full Puffle Yum on Rachel."

"Thanks." Gavin said something to someone in the background. "I've gotta go, but I'm checking in with the boys again in the morning."

They said their goodnights and Travis turned off the ridiculous lamp made of antlers on the bedside table. But Travis could not close his eyes. Every time he did he saw Rachel's pink lips.

Despite what had happened earlier at the lake, he understood that logically he and Rachel should just stay friends. It kept things simple.

He liked simple.

He liked his privacy.

He did not like having his mama all up in his grill about who he was seeing romantically. Therefore, he should keep his romantic entanglements outside of anyone his mother knew, had known, or planned to know. Unfortunately, Travis was never very good at doing what he should.

A wet nose nudged his cheek.

Travis turned his head. Pete stood on the top of the bedspread, wagging his tail and nudging Travis again with his wet snout.

"I'm trying to sleep," Travis said, adjusting his pillow and closing his eyes.

Pete nudged him again.

Travis rubbed the mutt behind the ears. "Time for bed, kid. Playtime's over."

He'd already taken them out and tossed some balls around with his nephews and the pups before Rachel sent the boys to bed. Then he'd taken them out again for an extra bathroom break before he'd crashed himself.

Travis cracked an eyelid as Pete lay down on his stomach, his face right up against Travis's.

Travis pulled the blankets over his head, and rolled over, willing the dog to go crash on the doggie bed or curl up with Re-Pete at the foot of the mattress.

Pete hopped up and his little paws padded across the bedspread.

Then the distinct sound of a stream of liquid dropping onto cloth had Travis bolting upright. It sounded like someone had turned on a trickle of a faucet.

Given that that there was no faucet in the room and two barely housebroken dogs, Travis flicked on the lamp beside the bed and—with his teeth on edge—he glanced at the dogs.

Re-Pete was still sleeping.

Pete was mid-leg-lift at the edge of Travis's bed, letting it all flow.

Shit. Well, not shit. But that sound Travis had heard wasn't water.

It was piss.

Travis groaned and rolled out of bed.

"Dude." He scrubbed his palms over his cheeks. "I'm not into that. You gotta ask before you try that the first time you spend the night with a guy."

Pete hopped from the bed and ran to the door. He paced back and forth, glancing at Travis and practically broadcasting he needed o-u-t.

"C'mon, you two." Travis stripped the bed as fast as he could—being careful to avoid the puddle—and grabbed the two leashes. Then he nudged Re-Pete awake and hurried with the dogs outside so they could do what they needed to do and not do it on his bed.

He shivered. Damn, it was cold. Mountain air was especially crisp at eleven o'clock at night.

He should've grabbed a jacket or a not-peed-on blanket, because the dogs were in no hurry to finish up.

Re-Pete was now wide awake and sniffing all around the edge of the small lawn, apparently searching for just the right location to leave his gift for Mother Nature.

Pete, on the other end of the spectrum, was peeing everywhere. Lifting his leg on anything not moving.

Which was why Travis shifted from foot to foot and kept his eye on the little troublemaker.

"Your mother asked me to talk to you." Dad's voice came from behind.

Sheesh, Travis hadn't even heard him approach. He blamed the fact that his teeth were chattering.

"I just bet she did," Travis replied. He turned to his dad, then gestured to the dogs. "We're almost done here. You think we can take this inside, so we don't turn into Popsicles?"

His dad had had the brains to put on a bathrobe before he came out into the chill. He watched the dogs for a beat, shook his head, then glanced at Travis. "Meet me in the study."

Dad didn't linger, already heading back inside where it was warm. His dad was a very smart man—no one ever really argued that point.

Like Travis, Dad took the most direct approach to solve an issue or have a conversation. He was decisive but fair.

Travis leashed the dogs and then, all together, he and his new pack headed for the study. At least this was where his dad kept the good hooch.

Travis had barely entered the room, his skin slowly returning to having some kind of feeling.

"You. Rachel. No hanky-panky," Dad said as he poured Travis a bit of amber liquid and repeated the measure for himself. "Your mother is flipping out. She's convinced herself that you're in Rachel's pants."

"This is why you tracked me down?" Travis asked. "In the middle of the night?"

"Have you met your mother? She can't sleep, which means I can't sleep."

"I'm not, how you so eloquently said, in Rachel's pants," Travis said once they settled in. They sipped the scotch as the dogs lazed under the desk.

"All right, I'll tell your mama that." Dad didn't make a

move to get up. He wouldn't, either, not until he'd finished his scotch.

"Mom should just be glad that Rachel and I are getting along and communicating," Travis said, stretching out in the leather armchair.

His dad harrumphed. "Your mother can pull problems from thin air. Problems that didn't exist two minutes prior."

Pete let out a snore, apparently ready for bed now that he'd emptied the entirety of his bladder all over the property. So it was Re-Pete who hopped up to sit on Travis's lap.

Aside from his father explaining why Travis shouldn't consider banging his former sister-in-law, the whole thing had a very Norman Rockwell vibe.

Then again, "banging" was the wrong word. Travis didn't want to bang Rachel.

Well, he did, because she was gorgeous, and he had been feeling some serious chemistry in the lake. He enjoyed the way she laughed, smelled, and he was pretty much desperate to see how she tasted. But there was more to it than that. He couldn't quite put his finger on what that was, but there was definitely more.

Dad turned the cut-crystal tumbler around in his palms. "I'll explain to your mama what we talked about and then maybe we can all get some sleep." He added a, "Finally," under his breath.

"So this is less about me and Rachel and more about you wanting some z's?" Travis asked.

His dad nodded. "Yup. Glad we're on the same page here." He stood and set his now-empty glass back on the tray by the liquor.

"My mama needs to take her own advice and mind her own business when it comes to who I'm spending time with," Travis suggested, hoping that his father would find a way to put a spin on that request that would bring his mother around.

"It's complicated. You know that." Dad shook his head and rested his elbows on his knees.

"What's complicated about me being nice to the mother of my nephews? What's complicated about wanting to make things a little easier for her?" Travis asked. This wasn't rhetorical—he really wanted to know.

His mother had never asked him for a list of his previous hookups, previous girlfriends, previous anything. Everything was fine until Travis started interfering with her perception of happily ever after for Gavin. That's, ultimately, what this boiled down to—Travis couldn't be with Rachel because Rachel should be with Gavin.

Which, given what both of them had said, discussed, and illustrated, was never going to happen.

They'd trusted Gavin to handle her with care and he'd wrecked it. They wouldn't trust Travis because they worried he'd wreck it again.

But he wouldn't.

"Gavin and Rachel aren't getting back together," Travis said. Hell, Gavin was now engaged to someone else.

Dad nodded. "You know how your mother gets when she has an idea that something should be a certain way."

"And she's worried I'm going to screw that up."

"No, not that." Dad wasn't much of a talker. Travis was pretty sure that's why he'd married Mama. Mama was the talker in the relationship, which was why she must've been really concerned if she sent Dad to have this chat.

Dad sat again, reluctantly this time. "She's worried that if you and Rachel get into an…involvement…it'll mean Gavin stops coming around and, eventually, if you and Rachel stop being…involved…then *she'll* stop coming around. Then the boys will stop coming around. At the end of the day, it means your mother doesn't get to see her grandkids."

"I'd just like to point out that the grandkids are here.

Rachel is here. The only one missing is *Gavin*." Travis stood. Paced. "Maybe you should be having a little chat with him."

Dad gave a curt nod. "Not a bad idea."

Travis studied the blue decorations on the rug as his father left the room. But when he did finally look up, he had two golden retriever puppies staring at him like they were ready to start peeing again.

"You two need to knock it off." He pointed to one, then the other for good measure.

Then he sighed. Grabbed their leashes, set aside his unfinished glass of scotch, and headed back toward the linen closet where they stored the extra blankets.

Once he changed out the comforter, they could all get some sleep—just like his dad wanted. Unfortunately, the closet for extra bedding was all the way on the other side of the house, so he had to pass by the second study to get there. Yes, the house had two studies—the one his father had met with him in and the one they'd made into a makeshift office for Rachel's personal use. Mama included it as part of her special let's-get-her-to-come-along package.

The light was on under the door of the second study when he passed by. He forced himself to keep walking. He got his new bedding and refused to look to see if the light was still on when he moved past again.

It was.

Now, he knew a lot of things. One of the things he knew was that he should keep right on going when he realized the light was on. Should take the dogs and go back to bed. Because if the light was on, then Rachel was in there, and if Rachel was in there, then he wanted to stop in and see how things were going for her.

Yes, he should keep moving. But Travis was never any good at doing what he should do. So he knocked against the thick wooden door, and he waited.

CHAPTER 13

Work was not going well. What with Rachel spending a large part of the evening trying to figure out what the heck had happened in the water with Travis.

She knew what an erection was, and that thing he'd been toting around in the frigid lake was *definitely* an erection.

After an abundance of thought, she'd come to the realization that there were two potential reasons for that-which-could-never-be-mentioned-again.

One, he wanted something that was off-limits. Evelyn had been perfectly clear about Rachel's off-limits status.

Or two, he wanted to stick it to Gavin, using Rachel as his latest method in their ongoing sibling rivalry.

Either option was a nonstarter for her.

The tap on the door jostled her from the spreadsheet in which she was elbow deep, creating Cassie's latest social media posts. She scowled at the screen of her computer and the empty spaces that still needed to be filled.

"Come in," Rachel called.

A piece of hair, from the mess of a knot she'd tied it in, fell in front of her face. She blew it away as she dropped in a funny graphic about making nutritious choices. The image involved a side salad having a discussion with a box of French fries.

Unfortunately, it had the opposite effect on her, because she now really wanted fries.

She glanced up when the door opened and did a double take as nighttime Travis strolled right through. His appearance made the mountain air feel even thinner in her blood. She gulped and hoped he didn't notice.

Black, totally respectable pajama pants and an unremarkable black T-shirt that seemed like the extra soft cotton kind. His hair a little messy, and not like he'd tried to make it look that way. He had the just-out-of-bed rumpled thing going on.

She bit at the insides of her lips because she didn't trust what she might say to him. Probably something about the near-meeting of their lips in the lake and what she felt going on below his waistband, even though the water had been freaking cold.

He had both dogs tagging along—they were still awake, but she wouldn't complain about it, since they were his problem that night. He also had a heap of bedding under his arm. She wasn't going to ask about it, because she needed to finish this up.

Rachel was not sitting at the desk. She was sitting on the not-so-comfy-but-it-looked-nice leather sofa. The big mahogany desk made her feel like she was running an evil empire of toaster tart products instead of a tidy, virtual personal assistant company.

She took a second to really look at him and he seemed off —a little grumpier than usual. He was scowling like he also needed to put together a social media spreadsheet.

"Everything okay?" She reached up to pull her hair loose. It fell out of the mess she'd pinned it in.

She liked to tie it out of the way when she focused, but it looked totally ridiculous when she tucked it up into the weird bun that yanked her bangs out of her face and also kept her hair off her neck.

"Everything's fine," he said, but he still frowned. He didn't seem to be scowling at her, mostly at the world in general.

The dogs pulled at their leashes, trying to get to her, but Travis held them firmly. He seemed like he wasn't really sure why he was there. Yet here he was.

She had that feeling a lot in life, so she understood. "I'm just checking out for the night," he said, clearing his throat. "Thought I'd see if you needed anything."

Oh, well, that was sweet of him. Look at him being nice. It was probably his erection from earlier talking. Loss of blood flow to the brain did that to a guy.

She pressed her glasses up against her nose—she didn't wear them often, but she'd already removed her contacts for the night—and tried not to blush, because he was just being nice, nothing more.

Yet, his simple attempt at being nice had her cheeks heating. Go figure.

"I'm good." She adjusted her flannel pajamas—the comfy two-piece kind with a string of buttons running up the front that went all the way to her neck, and the matching pajama bottoms that were one of the least sexy clothing items she owned.

Not that she needed to worry about wearing sexy pajamas when she was on a family vacation. Or ever.

She'd given up on satin and anything with lace because Brady and Kellan had the Frank stomach, and after getting thrown up on one too many times, she'd realized that flannel was much easier to clean. Flannel popped right into the washing machine without having to do anything special to the fabric.

Sure, she loved the feel of satin, but it's not like anyone was around to feel her in the satin, so she settled for the pragmatic flannel.

Flannel was nice, too. Flannel was comfortable, and warm, and very much Rachel.

"We missed you at game night," Travis said.

"I have so much work." She waved to the open laptop. "And I missed a bunch of emails after the flight and then the…uh…impromptu swim."

It'd been way too long since she'd been swimming. Too long since the water had wrapped around her like that.

Until today, she hadn't realized she'd missed that feeling of being enveloped.

Then again, there weren't a lot of spare moments to think about extraneous things like that.

"Sorry about missing out with you guys," she said with a smile, gesturing to the room. "I had to come run my empire." He fidgeted with the dog leashes, not saying anything.

Still frowny. Still just…off.

She squinted at him, trying to see if she could guess what was going on. He was being weird. "Are you sure you're okay?"

"Other than the fact your kids wiped me out at poker, I'm fine." He shifted the bulk of the bedding he carried with him and set it down on the side table next to the sofa.

Wait. Poker? Her children were gambling?

That was not what she'd agreed to. When she'd left the living room, Bob said they were playing cards. She'd assumed —apparently, incorrectly—they'd be playing rummy or hearts.

"Wait. Rewind a second." She made a roll-it-back motion with her hand. "You played poker at game night?"

He lifted a shoulder like it wasn't a big deal. "It's tradition."

"With my kids?" She didn't have any beef with teaching

her kids to gamble, she just figured they should be of a certain legal age first.

"Brady's better than the rest of us. The kid is seriously gifted at bluffing." Travis had relaxed as they chatted, drifting toward the sofa.

Rachel, however, was not relaxing. She gripped the sides of her laptop because it was the only thing she had to hang on to.

"Dad's teaching him to count cards, I'm pretty sure." Travis laughed low.

The low laugh was not helpful.

"He taught Gavin, too," Travis continued. "Dane and I never took to it. Don't worry, he gave the whole safe-poker speech before he started."

"Safe-poker speech?" She made a mental note never to miss game night again.

"How to do it without getting caught."

"Huh." She'd need to discuss that with Bob and with Gavin and, especially, with Brady. "Why didn't you guys play poker when I came last time?"

"We did." He dropped the leashes to let the dogs run free.

They immediately ran straight to her for a quick scratch on the head.

"Where was I when all of you were playing?" she asked, giving the dogs a good rubdown. "Last time."

"I think you were in new-mom-of-twins land."

"That must've been around the time I was delirious enough to tell Gavin I wanted twin puppies for our twin babies." Rachel made kissy faces at the dogs, and they bounced around the edge of the sofa at the invitation to play.

Travis glanced at the dogs. "So this"—he gestured to the pups—"is your fault?"

That interpretation was one option, yes. Although, since she hadn't made the cash transaction, she was taking only part of the responsibility. She gave what she hoped was a yeah-maybe tilt of her hand.

Travis stopped his movement toward her and pulled himself up to sit on the edge of the desk.

Her heart dropped a little. She'd sort-of hoped he'd come sit next to her.

That was ridiculously unacceptable, though, because there was no reason for him to sit next to her or for her to hope that he would.

He started lining up the pens on the desk so they were end-to-end.

She glanced at her computer screen, really needing to get back to it. But Travis was there, and he obviously needed to talk.

If she were being honest, she'd been feeling lonely just before he came in. The kind of lonely that didn't go away. Just standard lonely that happened even when the boys were around, or she was with her girlfriends.

"You're acting strange," she said, making a note of where she was in the file so she could easily pick back up later. Then she balanced the laptop on the edge of her thigh, giving Travis her full attention. "Spill it. I've got to finish this, and I'm guessing you'll need sleep at some point."

"And you don't need sleep?" he asked.

"The sooner I can tie up the loose ends, the sooner I can go to sleep myself."

The air between them seemed to stretch, and she didn't like it. Not one bit.

She waited, not saying anything while he got his thoughts together.

"Dad caught me just now, before I came in," he said, not meeting her eyes. His throat was working as he swallowed hard. If she didn't know better, she'd think that Travis was experiencing a keen set of conflicting emotions.

"Is he okay?" she asked, because Travis was being so odd

that maybe there was something wrong with Bob. She didn't want to even consider that.

"Yeah, he's fine."

"Travis?" she asked, as gently as she could, because worry was starting to seep in. She was getting concerned about what it was exactly that he wasn't saying.

Travis finally held her gaze with his, and that loneliness that she'd had earlier? Poof. Disappeared.

And that made the center of her face go a little numb with realization.

"Dad just wants sleep. He talked to me about it for a bit." Everyone who knew Bob understood the man was not a talker. Even with his kids.

Evelyn was the talker. Bob was the listener. Rachel learned that early on.

"He told me not to spend time with you," Travis said, matter-of-factly.

Well, crap. She did not expect that.

Rachel's eyebrows rose. She did not appreciate her ex-in-laws inserting themselves into a conversation about who she spent time with. That was up to her, and only her. Well, and whoever she elected to spend that time with, too.

In any case, Bob and Evelyn didn't get a say. "Seriously?" she asked.

"Yep." Travis nodded, and he wasn't doing the distant thing anymore. Actually, he was checking her out. The full body scan, the heat of the gaze, the small part to his lips.

He wasn't being obnoxious or anything. More like he was just observing and appreciating. Her stomach flip-flopped, this time with tingles along the tips of her ears.

She glanced down to ensure she hadn't dropped chocolate on her shirt or something, because wouldn't that be embarrassing?

Also, very on-brand for her.

"Your dad told you he'd prefer if you don't spend time

with me? Then you came by here to see me when I'm by myself?" she asked, a little confused by the conversation but choosing to go along with it, since the lonely ache had dissipated.

"Yep," he said again.

"Sounds like everyone wants us to stay apart. First your mom, now your dad..."

"Pretty soon they'll have Dane in on the rotation." Travis slid off the desk and moved to stare into the black darkness at the window. The longing look in his gaze as he stared outside nearly made Rachel jealous. And that was ridiculous, because it was the forest, not a person, but mostly she had no reason to be jealous. None at all.

He turned from the window and speared her with hunger in his eyes.

This time she felt the tingles at the tips of her ears again, and also in another, more intimate location between her legs.

Rachel's computer chimed, and she glanced at the screen. "Give me a second," she said as she typed something out. "The Australians are being needy." Quickly, she finished typing a message. Then she closed the computer and set it aside.

She was feeling all tingly with him, and he was being all weird, and Bob and Evelyn were being extra-invasive.

She and Travis needed to communicate the hell out of this situation. That way they could move on and she could get back to work.

"I think we should talk about what happened at the lake today," she said, folding her legs up underneath herself. The sober way she'd said that made it seem like the near kiss hadn't even fazed her, when in fact, it had. But good for her, for being able to sound so laissez-faire.

"I..." he started to say.

"Because if we talk about it, it won't be a big deal. I've

always found it's the things we don't talk about that become issues."

"That's very deep," Travis said, focusing on Pete, who was now sniffing around the edge of the rug.

Rachel trailed her gaze to the puppy. He usually came to nudge her first before he relieved himself.

"If you want to sit next to me, I won't tell your parents." She patted the sofa. "I also won't deflower you on the sofa," she continued, because for some reason it seemed like the right thing to say. But as soon as the words left her mouth, she wanted to stuff them right back in.

Thankfully, Travis grinned, and his voice went deep as he said, "I hate to break it to you, Rach, but I've been deflowered for a while."

"Good, because that's always such a *thing*," she said, rolling her eyes dramatically.

They'd participated in nearly an entire conversation, and neither of them had gotten defensive. This was…new.

He chuckled, deep and low, and her insides warmed at the sound. She didn't feel like she was wearing puke-flannel right then. The way he was looking at her with that glint in his eyes made the fabric—and her insides—feel like satin.

What were those reasons she shouldn't get in deep with him again? There were two and she couldn't quite remember what they were.

She shifted to make more room for him beside her, hoping that he would sit.

If he sat with her, maybe they'd even touch a little. No big thing, she could brush her hand against him and see if there were more sparks—like at the lake.

It'd be an experiment to determine if there were some kind of enduring chemistry going on. And, since it was just going to be a little observational touch, if the sizzle dissipated, then she could pass it off as platonic. She'd accidentally touched Dane lots of times, and it wasn't awkward.

"I think we should try being friends," Rachel announced, a little too loud. She softened her tone, saying, "We've never had the chance to be friends."

"Rach…" He sat next to her on the sofa. Not close, though. There was a respectable distance between them she was pretty sure his mother would approve of. "I…I don't really want to be your friend."

Her warm, satin insides turned to cold polyester. Oh, well that stunk. "Then what do you want?"

The words came out strong, thank goodness, because inside, the empty ache of rejection sat heavy in her stomach.

He shook his head. "What I want, I shouldn't have." Didn't they all?

There was hardly any room behind her, but she scooched back anyway, until her back hit the arm of the sofa. If she went any farther, she'd fall on her ass and then that really would be embarrassing.

"If I'm making you uncomfortable," she said, "we can be sure we're not in the same place while I'm here."

He scrubbed a hand over his face. "Rach—"

"Do you want to set up a schedule so we don't have to see each other?" she asked, hoping that the light tone was back, and he wouldn't see how this was kind of wrecking her. The lump in her throat was not a good one. She could use a minute alone, to take some deep breaths and prevent her eyes from getting watery.

Which was silly, because she wasn't really sure what upset her.

"No," Travis said. "I don't want to make a don't-see-Rach schedule."

"Then why did you come in here?" she asked. "Tonight, why'd you knock on the door?"

"Honestly?" he asked, turning to her. "I have no idea. I wanted to see you. I saw the light on. I came in." He ran a hand over his hair. "I want to ignore my parents totally on this. I like you. Like how I've been feeling around you."

She sucked in a breath. Oh. Okay. All righty then, that's why he didn't want to be friends. The way he looked at her with the same carnal expression from the lake made the air in the room shift dangerously into Molly-suggested territory.

"How do you feel around me?" Rachel asked.

"Like I'm not flying solo." He had the deep, rumbly, genuine note back in his words.

His nonsense started to make a little sense. And that made no sense, because the heavy feeling in her belly still weighed her down.

"Do you feel that way often?" she asked, because, boy oh boy, did she feel that loneliness creeping into her marrow all the freaking time. Especially at night when the chaos of life finally took a chill pill and things were quiet.

He nodded. "I don't think I realized how often until recently."

She nodded because she could so totally relate.

"Can I make a suggestion?" Rachel asked, hoping she mirrored his sincerity. "Well, it's Molly's suggestion. I called her when we got back from the lake after the whole..." She cleared her throat. "Anyway, she was with April and I told them what happened between us."

"What do you think happened between us?" he asked.

Okay, here was the thing. His knee brushed hers. Like not a big deal kind of brush. It could've been an accidental brush. Nevertheless, it was nice. Really, really nice. Connection nice.

Like jumping in a lake nice.

"I think that there was a moment when we almost kissed," Rachel said, answering his question. "Is...is that what you think?"

A beat of silence descended. Her cheeks heated. What was she thinking? She should be less direct with him. Here she was opening herself up like it was no big deal.

It was a very big deal.

Perhaps communication wasn't totally necessary in this instance.

"That's exactly what I think." He nodded and, honest to goodness, he reached out to toy with the end of a chunk of her hair.

Her hair didn't have the ability to feel, so it made no sense that she felt all buzzy and heady at the touch.

"Molly had a suggestion?" Travis asked, and he seemed unsure about Molly's potential suggestion, but he was still toying with Rachel's hair and he'd moved closer and they were not-really-platonic close anymore.

Rachel nodded, swallowing hard. "She did."

He chuckled, dropping her hair and leaning against the side of the sofa. "Does Molly's suggestion involve a pineapple?"

"Ha. No." She leaned in to him, since he'd touched her, and she figured turnabout was fair play. Except, she wasn't quite sure what to do once she was in his space. His hair wasn't long enough to toy with, he was sitting like he was super comfortable, so he didn't need her to offer a pillow or anything.

Finally, she decided to set her hand on his knee. There, that wasn't weird.

"Am I supposed to guess?" he asked, giving a long look at her hand.

"Guess what?" she asked, distracted by the knee touching.

"Am I supposed to guess what Molly suggested?" His hand covered hers, and for a split second she worried he'd try to push her hand away.

He didn't. Instead he rolled her palm over and linked their hands together.

Oh, that was nice. They were touching and her body liked it very, very much. *She* liked it very, very much.

"Molly thinks we should kiss." Rachel said the words in a

rush. "Just do it. Get it over with. That way we'll both get whatever this feeling is out of the way and we can decide what to do next."

"And you think a kiss is going to do that?" He was now tracing her knuckles with his thumb.

She liked the tracing thing a lot. A whole lotta lot. "Molly suggested that we are at the jump-in-a-lake stage, not necessarily the jump-into-bed stage. So we should just kiss and try that out before we make any other decisions."

"What do *you* think?" he asked.

"I think I agree with her on this one. It's not going to hurt anything." Rachel shrugged but was careful not to move too much and accidentally give the impression she wanted him to drop her hand. Because she didn't want him to drop her hand. She liked the way his tracing her skin echoed inside her. Deep inside in a place she'd forgotten existed, because no one had given it any attention in a very, very long time.

"It's just a kiss," Rachel said. "An experiment. Afterward, we can reevaluate. I mean, most people make the choice to let their bodies do the communication, because it's easy. Maybe we should see what our bodies have to say."

"This is what Molly thinks?" Travis asked.

"Yes." She nodded.

"And you agree?" He pressed a kiss to the back of her hand and released it.

Damn. She didn't like the releasing part. The kiss part was super nice, though.

"I like things structured. That way I know they'll go as I want them to."

"And?"

"The truth is, I'm scared of what might happen if we both like it." She had a feeling she *was* going to like it…a lot.

"Do you trust me?" he asked.

"No." She didn't.

He had that bruised look again.

But his question seemed like an important one. "Should I?"

"That's your call, but I can promise I won't hurt you."

"You can't promise that." No one could promise that. Especially *him*.

She drew in a deep breath.

"So how do you want this to go?" he asked.

"Well, I figure your mouth will press against my mouth. Then we'll see what happens." Rachel shifted on the sofa so their knees touched. Wait, was that what he meant? He probably knew the mechanics of kissing, so she didn't need to provide a tutorial.

He didn't move out of the way, he just let their knees stay there…touching.

"The thing is, as April pointed out, you might be an awful kisser," she said, continuing to speak even though she should've stopped.

"I'm not." The deep timbre was back in his voice and she was really, really into it.

She gestured to herself. "*I* could be an awful kisser."

"I can already tell you that you're not." His gaze attached to her lips.

"You don't know. I don't know. We don't know." She was using a lot of hand gestures and should probably knock it off before she accidentally whacked him. "Let's just do it. Get it over with. Move forward from there."

"Well, if we're doing this by vote, then I guess it's a good thing it's a consensus with your committee."

"Exactly." See? He understood. This was excellent.

"For the record, my committee thinks it's a bad idea." He reached out and toyed with the end of her hair again.

"Who, exactly, is on your committee?" She didn't know many of his friends—they didn't come around when they were in the same place. Mostly because those places were only with his family.

"My parents."

"That's a really crappy committee."

"Yeah, well, it's what I've got."

"Actually, your committee is the worst." Her fingertip itched to reach out. Draw a line along his jaw. "You need a new committee."

His gaze focused on her mouth, and the air between them practically crackled. She licked at her lips.

This did nothing to resolve the electric charge in the air. "When should I start accepting applications?" he asked, moving closer.

She barked a low laugh. She actually *laughed*.

This, whatever this was between them, felt so normal. Not forced. No arguing. They were talking, laughing, and she had a strange fascination with the way his lips moved.

"Okay," he said, shifting, so he was in front of her, his mouth inches from hers.

"Okay," she said, moving forward to fill the small bit of space remaining.

She drew a heavy breath. She could do this. This was not a huge deal. This was just a kiss.

Rachel stared at his lips. He stared at her lips. Neither of them closed the gap.

There was a lot of staring going on. Not an iota of moving.

Mostly, she *couldn't* move because her muscles seemed to have turned to liquid, she was heating all through, and there were nerve endings firing. She couldn't say why *he* wasn't moving.

Finally, he traced the apple of her cheek with his thumb and started to close the last of the space between them. Her breaths came quicker, the flannel shirt rising and falling swiftly with each inhale and exhale.

God, she wanted him to unbutton the top button. All the buttons.

He didn't, keeping his focus on her mouth. Which was

also nice. He was going to kiss her, and given the way her body was reacting, it was going to be really, really nice. Except—

"Wait," she said, pressing her hand against his chest just as his mouth was less than a breath away from hers.

He paused.

She pulled away a fraction of an inch.

"This has to be totally mutual," she said, gesturing between them. "We need to do it at the same time so it's not like I kissed you or you kissed me. We just do it at the exact same time so it's even."

He rubbed the tip of his nose against hers and, oh, she should stop trying to dictate how this was going to go. "This is getting very complicated," he drawled.

Red flag. Huge red flag. The wielding of the accent was something that should've made her pause.

Yet, in that moment? It made her want him only more. "Welcome to my life." She adjusted herself, pushing forward and basically kneeling beside him on the sofa, so it'd be easier to accomplish the task. Uh-huh, she was practically in his lap. He did not seem to mind.

She definitely didn't.

Her palm met his cheek, tracing the light stubble there. Everything in her turned on like she'd been in a holding pattern her entire life and had just been given clearance to land.

He moved to her, and she moved to him, and then their lips melded. Neither of them closed their eyes as their mouths met.

He moaned and deepened the kiss. She, uh, may have also moaned.

Also, good news, Travis was not a bad kisser. He was a *great* kisser. He knew exactly what to do with his tongue, using it like a professional to coax her lips open and get her tongue into the game.

He could open a kissing booth if he wanted to make his fortune. He was that good.

There were more sounds coming from them both, but she wasn't really paying attention to anything but the feel of them together. She wanted more of him. Wanted more of this—the heat, the sizzle, and the ache between her legs.

She moved to straddle him in order to get better purchase on his mouth.

It was a bold move, sure, but it also seemed extremely necessary because the core of her need was begging for contact.

The softness that was her rocked against the hardness of him, and she nearly came on the spot as they appreciated the hell out of each other.

Mouths and hands and bodies. Travis's hard length pressed against his fly.

"Rach," he said against her mouth. "God."

Gah. She was going to come.

He was gripping the back of her head with one hand and he had a handful of her ass with the other. When the kiss had begun, it was mutual. When she straddled him, she'd been the one in charge. But there was no doubt now that it was Travis calling the shots. He trailed his hand to her thigh, shifting, so he was laying her on the sofa, and he was on top.

She spread her legs. He wasted no time nestling into the cradle of her thighs. His erection pressed against her wet center and this was, quite possibly, the best first kiss she'd ever had in her life.

"So you both know these doors have locks on them, right?" Dane asked from somewhere across the room.

Rachel jerked away from Travis, pressing her sleeve to her mouth. Travis, for what it was worth, didn't look embarrassed.

No, the way he was pinching his lips and working his jaw…he was pissed.

Pissed and still turned on, judging by the twitch of his erection against her flannel pajamas.

"They're nifty, you just push the button. Then no one can come in." Dane was giving an illustration on how to lock and unlock the door, seemingly nonplussed by the way the bottom had just dropped out of Rachel's world. Though the drop was not because of Dane's interruption.

Rachel stared into Travis's eyes, questioning what had come over her. Over them.

No, it was thanks to Travis and his ability to kiss the responsibility right out of her.

CHAPTER 14

TRAVIS

Despite her enchanting qualities, Rachel was not a witch. Of this, Travis was pretty certain. But the speed with which she removed her mouth from his was truly stunning.

Rachel had tasted like the sunshine promise he'd been sure she'd just made. Mouths opened, tongues met, his arms went to her back, wrapping around her so they were a tight unit.

His erection had really been hoping to get in the game, especially when she shifted so she really was sitting in his lap with her legs straddling him.

Dane fucked it all up.

Travis counted to four in his head. Then, careful not to shift all his weight onto Rachel, he moved from her.

She immediately sat up and crossed her arms over her chest.

"Dane." Travis shoved his hands through his hair. "We're a little busy."

"I see that," Dane said, standing inside the threshold, and

moving his gaze between Travis and Rachel. "You two are really going to do this, huh?"

Rachel opened her mouth to speak. "I—"

"Because you know Mom and Dad are going to disown you if you fuck with her." Dane addressed Travis as he spread his stance wider.

Travis glared daggers at his brother. Dane had been his favorite right until that moment. "I'm not going to fuck with her."

"He's not," Rachel said. "We were just doing a little experiment. Turns out, it worked." She laughed, but it came out as an awkwardly stifled giggle.

Travis struggled to process anything further because most of the blood in his body was residing below the waistband of his pajama bottoms.

"Can you at least start locking the door?" Dane asked, resigned. "It'll prevent an unsuspecting someone—mostly me—from finding something I shouldn't."

"What are you even doing here?" Travis asked, eyes narrowed.

Dane's eyebrows rose at the tone. "Lights were on. I was checking in on Rach."

"Please don't tell your mom," Rachel said quickly, standing to pace between the sofa and one of the armchairs. Travis adjusted himself so he wouldn't be pitching a trouser tent, and stood, moving toward Rachel. He wrapped an arm around her shoulders and, thankfully, she let him take her weight.

Pressing a kiss against the crown of her head came naturally.

Flying solo had nothing on what he'd just had with Rachel. What she was giving him even now.

"Please don't tell them," Rachel said, softer this time. The soft seemed to get Dane's attention.

He took in the scene—Travis and Rachel, the puppies

sleeping on the rug, the work Rachel had strewn all over the coffee table by the sofa, the half-eaten bag of milk chocolate Dove candies Travis hadn't noticed before.

"Fucking hell," was all Dane said as he, once again, pressed the lock on the door. Then he turned and addressed Travis. "You need to be more careful." Dane pulled the door shut behind him.

"He didn't agree," Rachel said, panicked.

"He's worried." Travis squeezed her shoulders before turning her to face him. "I've always done this thing when someone tells me I can't have somethin', I want it. So he's worried. Rightfully so."

"Your parents just told you that you can't have me, so you want me?" The vulnerability in her gaze hit him hard, like an overhead punch to the cranium. "That's what I thought."

Of course that's what she'd thought. That's what everyone thought.

He hadn't exactly given them a reason not to.

"No," he assured, keeping his tone gentle like he would if he were talking to the pups or the boys. "This is different. I'm not sure what it is exactly, but the chemistry at the lake and on the sofa…I want to explore that. See where it takes us."

"So it's the other thing," she said under her breath. What the hell was the other thing?

"I'm not usually a see-where-it-takes-us kind of person." Rachel started to extract herself from his arms. "This is all new to me."

He let her move away, because deep inside he understood she needed the space to think.

"But you considered trying it," he said, again, keeping his tone low and soft. "And you did try it."

She brushed a strand of hair from her face. "I can't take that kind of risk long-term. Kissing you on the sofa is one thing…what happened after is something totally different."

"It's me, Rach—I won't let this hurt you."

But he was Travis, so she was certain that's why it *would* hurt her.

"That's not how it works, Travis." She hugged herself. "We both know that's not how it works."

He shoved his hands in his hair. "Fine, agreed, we can't prevent each other from falling."

She nodded.

"But we can promise to soften the landing," he said, hoping she'd agree.

"I would love to do the things I want to do just to see what happens. Within reason, you know? Not skydiving or anything like that, but other things." She didn't have to point at him for him to know what she meant.

"Then take the risk, Rach."

"Who's going to make sure Gavin doesn't re-home the puppies if my parachute doesn't inflate?" she asked. "I can't jump, because there are too many things I need to ensure are taken care of."

"You're not responsible for the entire world." He started toward her, but she stepped back, so he paused.

"There's no plan B for me," she said as though she truly thought it were true. "If something happens to me, everything in my boys' world collapses."

"But what do you want to do?" he asked.

The answer to that was, apparently, simple. "You," she said.

"Okay."

"Okay?" she asked.

"Yes, okay." He stepped toward her. "You need to try somethin' new without risk. I'm willing to give that to you."

"How?" She didn't seem convinced at all that this was possible, but people underestimated him all the time.

Usually, he didn't give them a reason not to, but with Rachel he wouldn't fuck it up.

"I'm going to make you some promises," he said.

She didn't move back when he stepped toward her this time.

"I'm going to promise you that no one needs to know about us. I'm going to promise you that I'll respect whatever you decide when it comes to us. I'm going to promise to have your back, even if we decide things aren't working out."

"And if you decide you don't want me? After we move forward?"

"Then I'll promise that I'll still be there to help you out with whatever you need."

"What if I really piss you off?"

The lump in his throat seemed thicker. "Then I won't do it for you, I'll do it for your boys."

"What do you want in return?" she asked, cautiously.

"A shot at seeing what happens." He trailed the edge of his index finger along her cheekbone. "That's all I'm asking."

Rachel opened her mouth and closed it, open and close—like a trout that wanted to jump back into the water but also wanted to see what else the world had to offer on land.

"Okay," she said, finally.

He pressed a kiss to her forehead.

The door handle rattled. "Mom?" Brady called from the other side of the oak. "It's locked."

Rachel pulled away from Travis. "Hang on, sweetie."

"Can you lie down with me?" Brady called. "I can't sleep."

"Be right there." Rachel seemed to be doing an inventory of her clothing—which was, unfortunately, in order, given he hadn't had a chance to remove any of it.

The door handle rattled again. Travis made a mental note to thank Dane for his intrusion earlier. Better Dane than Brady.

After adjusting her shirt, Rachel leaned forward and gently, so very gently, pressed a light kiss to Travis's lips. "We can continue this conversation tomorrow."

"Tomorrow," he said against her mouth.

She smiled, bit at her bottom lip, and nodded, their noses brushing with the small movement.

"One second." She turned to head toward the door. Travis watched her walk away.

He didn't move for a long while after she'd left the room, distracting Brady and heading down the hallway toward his bedroom.

Travis swallowed and glanced at the dogs, then to the new linens he needed to swap onto his bed, and then to the blank space where Rachel had been earlier on the sofa.

The memory of her mouth against his had his insides pooling into melted sunshine.

Pure Rachel.

He closed his eyes, and he smiled.

CHAPTER 15

RACHEL

"**M**ooom," Kellan said, milking the *O* in her name. "They come two in a bag for a reason."

"One tart, and then you have to eat real food." Rachel was careful to keep her voice low so that if Evelyn or Bob happened to be nearby, they wouldn't hear her.

Evelyn took special offense to Rachel's assertion that the toaster tarts did not, in fact, merit consideration as a solid breakfast option. Mostly, though, sugar wound her kids up tighter than red dye in gummy bears, so she tried to keep it to a minimum.

After popping a couple of the cinnamon-sugar-cream-cheese tarts into the toaster—one for each kid—she started cracking eggs. A scramble would contain enough protein, she hoped, that it would counter the sugar filling, pastry dough, and frosting.

"Good morning, all." Travis sauntered into the kitchen, looking rather dashing with his hair totally messed up. Still in his black pajamas from the night before, now they were rumpled from sleep. He looked great rumpled. Unshaved, he sported impressive stubble, too.

Rachel liked men fresh from the razor. She did. Stubble, however, was her favorite.

She glanced up mid-crack, and the eggshell collapsed in her hand with the pressure she inadvertently used.

Shoot.

Pete and Re-Pete followed Travis into the kitchen, ignoring everyone and going immediately to the kibble in their bowls.

"Good morning," she replied, cheery, despite egg goo dripping down her wrist.

The warm smile Travis gave her made this all feel so domestic. And right. And her stomach did the flippy thing. "Did you boys sleep well?" Travis asked, sitting down at the table.

They nodded as Rachel plated and set a toaster tart in front of each kid.

"Can I get you breakfast?" Rachel asked, turning her focus to Travis.

He glanced up at her, so close and still far away. "I'll get it."

"We're having toaster tarts and eggs." She went back to cracking eggs, careful not to squeeze too hard.

Travis stood and moved closer to her. Not so close that he was in her personal space, but close enough that she could smell his cedarwood shampoo.

"Yum," he said, cracking open a foil packet holding a raspberry tart. The foil was the special kind with a paper outer layer and a foil interior.

He slipped the breakfast pastry into one of the pop-up toasters lining the edge of the counter. The kitchen may have had only a couple of spatulas, but it had four oversized toasters to make up for it. Gently, Travis ran his hand along the waistband at her back on his way to snag a plate from the cupboard to the left of the sink. The movement was barely noticeable, but she still felt every tender spot he touched.

He glanced at the boys. She followed his gaze. They were totally absorbed in watching cartoons on a tablet and, therefore, oblivious to the snap in the air surrounding their mother.

Travis deftly pressed a light kiss onto her neck. "Morning, sunshine."

The low timbre of his voice and his breath against her skin had goose bumps rising all over.

He trailed his hand to her arm and gave a gentle squeeze.

Oh. Oh dear. The bottom of her stomach seemed to fall to her toes.

She cleared her throat. "Morning," she said, though her version was not nearly as smooth as his.

"Sleep well?" he asked, grabbing the plate and moving back to the toaster.

His body brushed past hers that time, too, igniting more nerve endings.

She shook her head. "Not really."

Between Brady, clients, and a brain that wound and rewound around her encounter with Travis, she'd slept like crap.

"Brady didn't settle?" he asked, voice low and only for her.

"Took a bit, but he finally crashed." She pushed the eggs around the pan with her spatula. "I went back to the den after he was out, but…uh…you weren't there."

She hadn't meant for that to sound like an accusation. Really, it'd been good to finish her work without distraction, but she'd been more than a little disappointed that he wasn't waiting when she returned.

Yes, they'd agreed that they'd reconnect the next day. That didn't mean she hadn't stopped thinking about him. Hoping that he'd wait.

A long pause stretched between them. When Travis didn't say anything, she glanced at him.

He was studying her intently. She gulped.

"Next time"—he leaned forward into her space—"I'll be sure to stick around."

Good. That was… "Okay," she said.

Evelyn took that moment to bustle into the kitchen, an orange box of toaster tarts in her hands, chattering to Bob about the varieties of pumpkin and which were most effective when baked into a pastry.

Her eyes narrowed as she took in the scene with her son and the woman he wasn't supposed to be around without a chaperone.

"It's Rachel," Evelyn said. "Good morning." Rachel started to open her mouth to say—

"Good morning," Bob said before she could form the words.

"Good morning," she said at the same time but, since it came a little after his greeting, hers sounded like more of an afterthought.

Bob headed straight toward the coffeepot.

Rachel was mid-swipe with the spatula in her egg scramble when Evelyn stepped beside her.

"What's this?" she asked.

Rachel's pulse paused with the tone of Evelyn's words. "Eggs," Rachel replied.

"Rachel, dear, we are a breakfast pastry family." Evelyn dropped the box she'd been carrying on the table.

"Mama," Travis said low and with what sounded like a great deal of restraint. "Rachel can fix whatever she'd like for breakfast."

"I guess we are a breakfast pastry *and* egg family, while I'm here." Rachel laughed, but no one joined in.

One of the boys pushed pause on their show. The entire kitchen descended into awkward silence.

"Mom, where's the milk?" Brady asked.

Rachel set the spatula beside the stove to go in search of the milk in the refrigerator. Then Kellan needed a refill, Evelyn asked for a glass, and, in the midst of it all, Rachel decided coffee was a very good idea—so she poured herself a cup.

"Are those burning?" Evelyn tilted her head toward Rachel's smoking eggs.

Crap.

She hurried back to the stove.

"Not burned, just really well done." Rachel tried to flip the eggs onto a plate, but they stuck to the nonstick coating that was, it turned out, not so nonstick after all.

Rachel stood, unable to form a sentence, spatula still in hand, staring at the smoke rising from the pan.

The eggs she'd been making for her kids to offset their sugar intake were totally wrecked.

She tossed them into the dog bowls, but even they gave her stink-eye about her breakfast offering.

"I guess it's tarts for breakfast!" Evelyn bustled through the kitchen, grabbing the now-unnecessary spatula and dropping it in the sink. "We've got a new flavor we want everyone to try. It's our first go at pumpkin spice."

"How does she do that?" Rachel whispered to Travis.

"What?" he asked.

"Always get her way?"

"It's her gift." He shrugged.

"Did you know that most pumpkin products aren't pumpkin at all?" Brady asked, reaching for the box and studying the label. "They're really squash that's dyed orange to look like pumpkin." He lifted a shoulder. "It's just easier."

"Pumpkin is gross," Kellan said immediately. "I like eggs, though."

Evelyn brushed him aside. "Eggs are fine for lunch. No one needs that kind of heavy for breakfast." She pressed a kiss to Kellan's temple, leaving a bright red lipstick print. "And don't you worry, we added extra sweetener, so they'll taste delicious."

"More sugar?" Rachel asked, ready to grab the spatula and whack the box from her son's hands.

"I'll try the new flavor," Brady announced, handing the box to Bob who handed it to Travis. "I like pumpkin pie."

"Brady…" Rachel raised her eyebrows in his direction.

She'd been clear about her one-tart rule.

Brady whispered in response, "You said it's rude not to try something when it's offered to me."

Yes, but that was before the dogs ate his burned breakfast.

Rachel made an attempt at the box breathing that April had showed her shortly before she hopped on the plane to Twin Lakes. In for four counts, hold for four counts, out for four counts, hold for four counts. Repeat.

She was on her third round before her blood pressure began to drop back to within a normal range.

"Evelyn and I are heading down to Confluence for the day," Bob said. "We were thinking you and the boys might enjoy taking the scenic route with us."

Um…Rachel had a call starting in thirty minutes and she expected it'd take a while. "That's not possible."

"We'll bring the dogs, too," Evelyn assured, as though that were the problem. She was filling the line of toasters on the countertop with pumpkin pie tarts.

"I've got meetings today," Rachel said. "I was hoping the boys could go swim at the lake or something with the rest of the family."

"They can come with us," Bob said. "We'll have a good time."

"Travis and Dane can come along, too, and you can have the whole place to yourself." Evelyn gave Travis a don't-you-dare look; not subtle at all.

"Nope." Travis chomped his raspberry tart. "I've got an

R&D committee meeting at ten. Then a Distribution meeting at two. I've got to hop on the conference calls."

Bob and Evelyn went still.

"You're meeting with Distribution?" Bob asked.

Evelyn looked like someone had smacked her in the face. "And R&D?"

Does he even know what that means?

Travis finished chewing, looking between his parents and Rachel. "Don't look so shocked, I'm technically the vice-president of distribution. I get the email reminders."

Evelyn's eyes stayed wide. "But you never go to the meetings."

From what Rachel had heard, he never did anything when it came to work.

"Yeah, well, had some ideas I drew up to run past the team." He lifted his remaining tart. "Can we not make a big deal about this?"

"What's an R&D meeting?" Brady asked, looking at Rachel.

"Research and development," Travis answered, ruffling her son's hair. "Where they decide what flavors are coming up next."

"Maybe tell them not to do the pumpkin," Brady said quietly, the words solemn. "It's not good."

"Where's Dane?" Bob asked, changing the subject but obviously having a silent conversation with Evelyn.

"Probably sleeping." Travis said around another bite of tart. "He had a late night."

Evelyn tsked. "Bob, you should go wake your son."

"I wouldn't," Travis said. "When I say he had a late night, he showed up around three this morning. I caught him sneaking in when I took the dogs out."

Bob didn't budge. "After I drink my coffee."

"I guess Dane can stay here, too," Evelyn said, resigned. "We'll take the boys with us."

Bob looked up at Rachel. "That okay with you?"

After Evelyn got them good and sugared up?

Yes, it was totally fine. After an hour in the car with that amount of blood sugar, Evelyn might rethink her stance on the abundance of breakfast pastry the boys consumed.

"Sounds like they'll have fun." Rachel did her very best to smirk only on the inside. "Thank you, that would be great."

"And the dogs," Travis added. "You'll want to take the dogs. Don't leave them out."

Bob glared at Travis over the top of his mug. "How'd I wind up on mutt duty?"

"You married me," Evelyn said, cheery.

Travis's eyes met Rachel's and the heat beneath the surface was enough to…well…toast a breakfast pastry all by itself.

Without any other options apparently available, Rachel grabbed a pumpkin pie tart for herself.

Of all the pies, pumpkin pie was her least favorite. And Brady was correct, this version was *very* not good.

CHAPTER 16

RACHEL

"Where's he going?" Rachel asked as she peeked out the side of the curtain by the front door.

Dane was climbing into one of the black SUVs in the driveway.

She'd finally wrapped up her call and went in search of some lunch. And Travis. Lunch and Travis. Possibly lunch with Travis.

What she'd found was Travis finishing up his first conference call and Dane heading out to whereabouts unknown.

"Don't know." Travis came behind her, his chest brushing against her back as he pulled the curtain a little farther. "But he's Dane, so wherever he's going, it'll probably be fun."

The light way he said that held a tone of wistful. "Meetings weren't so fun?" she asked.

"They were work." He shifted behind her, his chest still right there.

Rachel let her body lean in to his, just a little. "And Dane is now the fun sibling?"

The sibling in question pulled around the half circle drive

in front of the house and onto the road. He headed in the direction of the town.

"Gavin is the serious one. I guess Dane gets to be the fun one." Travis's warm breath brushed against her neck. "And I'm the other one."

"Oh, come on, you'll get a new designation," she said. "Just because you decided to go to a couple of meetings doesn't mean you can't still be fun."

He seemed to lose himself in thought.

Oh. Huh. That idea gave her a stomachache. "Did you go to the meetings because of me?"

"No." He placed his hands on her shoulders. "It's been a while coming. I need to step up."

"Then what are you doing with me?" Because she genuinely wanted to know. *They* as a *them* didn't make much sense, so this was an answer she was searching to uncover.

"I'm taking"—he turned her, so they were face-to-face—"what I want."

The woman he shouldn't want.

That was fine. It wasn't like she should want him, either.

They could just be rebels together.

The air between them crackled. She lifted on her toes but didn't have to move far because his mouth met hers in a gentle sweep of lips and tongue.

The other kisses had been frantic, exploring, and fire.

This one was simpler, but even without the frenzy of the night before, her blood heated all the same.

Her phone rang in her pocket, totally ruining the moment. She extracted it, praying that it wasn't a client who needed her.

Kaiya.

"Do you want to get that?" Travis asked, pressing a light kiss against the side of her mouth.

She shook her head. "I don't want to talk about skin cream right now."

"I have no idea what that means." His eyebrows furrowed, just a little.

"You probably don't want to." She lifted on her toes to kiss him again. Then they were moving, mouths still melding. Somehow, they were moving without having to break the seal of the kissing.

And they were kissing. So, so much kissing.

The gentle quality moved to a hectic need that discombobulated her and made the place between her thighs ache for more.

Travis was an excellent kisser and apparently, he knew what he was doing, because suddenly they were at her bedroom door.

Specifically, her back was against the door as they both breathed heavily into the shared air. He held her hands over her head and took her mouth like he owned it. Oh boy, did he own it.

Her whole body was wired, every inch of her, sensitive and pulsing. Wet heat pooled between her legs as Travis's erection pressed against her stomach.

He tore his mouth from hers, still holding her hands above her head, which was good, because without his grasp there she probably would've dissolved into a puddle on the carpet and later she'd have to clean it up and that would be a whole thing.

"Can I come inside?" he asked, his gaze never leaving hers.

"Inside?" Somewhere in the recesses of her brain she understood his question.

Sex. He wanted to have sex with her. Or do sexy things with her.

Oh, yes, yes, please, her body practically begged. *Let's do this.*

Her mind, however, was starting to come back online after the brief lust-induced logic hiatus.

She pulled her arms free from his, crossing them at her belly.

He could come in. They could make out a little and talk. During this talk she could explain all the reasons he didn't want to have sex with her, starting with stretch marks and ending with poor choices in the bedroom that could wreck her relationship with the only family her boys had left.

Then he could make an informed decision about his future choice when it came to her.

"What just happened?" he asked. "Where are you right now, Rach?"

Still in her space, he was full charm and full frontal and full...everything.

"I'm right here," she said, because she was.

That's not what he meant, though, and she knew it. She rubbed her eyes, probably smearing her eye makeup to hell and back.

"No, you're not. What's going on in your head?" He moved his hands to her shoulders, sliding them to the base of her neck and tilting her head back so their gazes met again. His thumbs against her jaw rubbed small, light circles there, igniting sparks she was pretty sure they should stomp out.

What was going on in her head? That maybe in a different time, in a different life, they could've fallen into bed together and had amazing sex without any consequences at all. But this was now, and this was her life, and she had responsibilities, and no number of Travis's kisses was going to change that.

"Inside is good," she said.

That got her a magical Travis smile. "Okay, then."

"Okay," she said, the word coming from her mouth sounding much more uncertain than his version.

With the hand behind her back, she turned the knob and pushed open the door. She took three steps in. Paused. Looked over her shoulder. Took three deep breaths.

Travis studied her the whole time, like she was one of the puppies and he thought she might bolt. Finally, he pressed the solid wood of the door closed, holding the handle so it wouldn't make a sound as it latched, which was silly, since they were the only two people in the house.

Except maybe the housekeeper or the chef. Evelyn had a chef come in and fix dinner every night. Rachel hadn't made it to the kitchen recently, so she couldn't really say if the chef had arrived yet or not. Then Travis locked the door.

He locked it because she had children who might come home early and search for her.

Children who could not find her in a clinch with their uncle because then she'd have so much explaining to do. And she was definitely going to be making out with their uncle.

The thick curtains were closed in the bedroom, with only a sliver of sunlight peeking through the middle where they came together.

Darker was better when it came to stretch marks. Maybe they could just keep the lights off, and she could keep her shirt on. That was the best idea.

Sex post-children was such a complicated maze.

She toed off her shoes, her toes sinking into the warm carpet, and closed her eyes.

When she opened them again, Travis was right there. His blue eyes soft, his perfectly symmetrical face held a totally gentle smile. Yes, this man was captivating, and sex in pressed slacks.

He moved his hands to her shoulders. "You're tense."

Well, wasn't that just the understatement of the century?

"I don't think we can do this the way you want," she said, her words as soft as the look in his eyes.

She meant the feelings and the bedroom activities and the kisses...those amazing kisses.

"We're already doing this the way I want," he replied, stilling only a moment before he started working a knot where her shoulders met her arm. That knot that always seemed to be there, but that she forgot about most days.

"How do you want to do this?"

He moved away, just a little. Just enough for her to feel the emptiness he'd filled before by being so close.

"We don't *have* to do this, Rach." His eyes were pure heat. His words sincere.

"I know." She swallowed. She wanted to do it. But there were reasons, a lot of reasons she'd carefully laid out in her mind, as to why they needed to press the brakes on whatever this was between them.

"Can we talk?" she asked.

"We can always talk." He pressed a kiss to her forehead, his hands still working their wonderful, delicious magic.

"Let's start with my kids." She crossed her arms under her breasts.

"Rach." With an abundance of care, he unwound her arms, wrapping his own around her waist, holding her up so she didn't have to do it all alone.

"I love your boys," he whispered. "But I don't want to talk about *them* right now."

She gripped the soft cotton of his button-up shirt.

Apparently, he owned two. This one was blue. "If we do this, we'll wreck everything for them."

"What we're doing right now has absolutely nothing to do with them." He tilted her chin up, running his hands over the curve of her hips. "Just us. It's just us here."

He was so wrong. Oh, so very wrong.

"Everything I *do* has to do with them. I have to take them into consideration. Always. What happened in the hallway?" She swallowed the thick cotton in her throat. "I can't lose control like that. They could have *seen*."

What if Brady or Kellan had come home early? How would she have explained what she was doing?

"You're serious?" Travis asked, looking like she'd struck him with a smack of her palm.

For the first time that afternoon, his expression went distant. He dropped his hands from her.

Maybe they could just go back to bickering. That was so much easier than this.

"I've never been more serious." She crossed her arms around herself again because…she had to.

"Rach…" He shoved his thumbs into the waistband of his slacks. "I…"

"Trav…" She needed him to understand.

He glanced up quickly, so many emotions flickering over his face.

"Fuck…" he said.

"Fuck what?" she asked, totally unsure of what was happening with him.

"You have never, not ever"—he lifted a palm to her jaw, stroking the pad of his thumb over the apple of her cheek—"called me"—he leaned in closer—"Trav."

The fire in his eyes seemed to melt everything in her body.

"Really?" That couldn't be true.

"I would've noticed." He turned from her, paced to the wall in the dim room, and took a visibly deep breath.

Was that true? It must be. He'd always been Travis. "Do you even know how long I've wanted you?" he asked.

"Travis." She took a step closer to him, her body seemingly on a mission of its own to get closer to this man even as she resolved internally to stop the forward momentum between them so they could get back to where they were earlier. The comfortable in-between with no guarantees and just…friendship.

Abruptly, he turned back to her. "Don't do that."

She stopped, suddenly unsure how to get back to that comfortable spot she wanted, even as her body craved the opposite. "Don't?"

He moved to her and shook his head.

"You give me Trav, then take it away. That's who I am to you." He grazed his lips against hers in a nearly there kiss that literally made her toes curl. "I'm comfortable. I'm a place you can relax. And you're a place I can be serious. Don't take that away."

This man drove her batty. This man made her wet.

Made her want. Made her need.

Her body hadn't craved a man like this for years. The question was, what was she going to do about it?

CHAPTER 17

RACHEL

"Trav." She pressed the length of her body to his, gripping the button-down cotton shirt.

To be honest, the kissing, and the chemistry, and the desire had already complicated everything. Even if she hadn't wanted that to happen. She'd jumped off the diving board, and now was the time to swim.

She couldn't get her mouth to form the words, because she wanted this. Wanted him. Wanted today.

"What do you say we take a conversation break and use our bodies to communicate?" he suggested.

"Because, Rach, your body has so much to say. Let today be what it's going to be."

Right. Yes. She could do that. That sounded nice. She nodded.

He took that as his cue to unbutton his shirt and pull it off in a swift motion that left his abs bare.

Of course, at the pool (and on the lake) she'd noted his fairly spectacular abdominal muscles, but now she got to touch them and play and…

She reached for his jaw with her palms, lifted on her toes, and pressed her mouth to his. Kissed, sucked, and pushed her fingers into his blond hair. She owned the kiss. Owned the moment. Owned the hope of what came next.

He let her. Let it be.

Until he didn't.

As he took over the kiss, her mind released its hold on logic and let the pure feeling of the day pull her under.

Picking her up like she weighed nothing, he strode to the bed, their mouths barely separating through the movement. With gentleness like she couldn't have dreamed, he laid her head on the pillows and straddled her knees—still clothed from the waist down.

Which was a real bummer.

"Too many clothes," she said softly.

His pupils seemed to liquify, and he reached over to the nightstand, flicking on the lamp.

The lamp had warm white bulbs that cast a nice—dare she say, romantic—glow about the room.

But.

She hadn't had sex with the lights on since the boys were born, so even though she was A-OK with getting the nice warm glow over his abs, hers were…well… "Shit," she said—not in a whisper.

"What?" He stilled the kisses he pressed to her neck, his heated breath against the tender skin just under her earlobe.

Sonofabitch, she was wearing a spandex shaper that was not of the sexy variety. Not like the ones she'd seen at one of the shops downtown with the corset and the lace.

No, she was wearing the full coverage granny panty variety that were decidedly not sexy—unless covered by a kick-ass dress.

"I'm—" She pressed a hand to her forehead. "This is so embarrassing."

Unfortunately, but also fortunately, he dismounted, lying on the mattress beside her, propping his head in his hand.

She should probably just give him a blow job or something for his trouble.

"Say again?" he asked, eyebrows totally furrowed.

"Say what?" She slid her gaze to him.

He didn't look very happy, at all. "The blow thing." Fuck a duck, had she said that out loud? Like *out loud*? Her cheeks immediately heated.

"Oh my God." She pulled her hands down over her eyes.

"Rach." He settled against her, his front to her side. His abs right freaking there, ready to touch. His...holy crap, he had a total hard-on happening, tenting his slacks and...

"I'm wearing a shaper thing. It's not sexy. I'm totally unprepared. I don't even have condoms in here and...I should just do the blow job thing. Then we can both go back to work."

Now, that? That he didn't seem to like. What with the way his eyes turned stormy, and he abruptly sat up.

"What do you think we're doing here?" he asked, louder than she'd expected. "I think we're in two entirely different mindsets. Because it felt like I wanted your body and you wanted my body, and we were going with that."

"I don't know," she said, the truth tipping right out of her lips. "I don't know what I'm doing. The lights are on and you're"—she gestured to the tent pitched at his fly—"and I'm"—she gestured to herself.

"This is because you have a shaper? What the hell even is a shaper?" His forehead creased with clear confusion.

"It's underwear that keeps me all..." She considered the best word for the situation. "Contained."

He stared at her one, two, three, and then four beats, the creases growing deeper.

"I need to ask you a question. I need you to be honest with

me." He moved his palm to her neck, turning her head so their eyes met. "Can you be honest with me?"

"I just told you I'm wearing super unsexy underwear right now, so I'm being more honest than I'd like to be." She sat up, her hair falling over her shoulder in a total wreck that was an echo of what the afternoon had become.

"Do you want to do this? With me?" he asked.

Yes, of course she did. She wanted to do this. Her body wanted it and even her mind was on board.

"I mean sex where we both…pop our toaster tarts," he said seriously.

Well, yes, that would be ideal.

"We don't have to plan the rest of it. Don't give it too much weight. If you want, later, we can spend time together. When you're ready, I'll help you when you need help. Right now, though? It doesn't have to be all of that." He pointed to his bare chest. "It can be just this."

She gulped, because she'd never known Travis to be sincere like that.

What did she want?

Did she want the whole package? Yes.

No question.

No questions with him.

She'd never even considered it until literally yesterday.

Still, she nodded. Not because she told her head to move. It seemed to do it all on its own. "I want that. This. I think I want to try for the whole thing." Maybe this really, really was what she wanted. "I think…"

"You're doin' a lot of that."

"Maybe I'm just off-limits. That's why we're here." She gestured to the bed.

The storm in his eyes raged harder. "Did you ever think that maybe we're here because I just needed the right reason?"

"What's that?" And did she want to know?

"You, Rach." The storm had passed, and his blue eyes settled on her and she knew whatever battle she'd wanted to wage, thought she had to wage, she'd lost. *And* she'd won. And nothing made sense. "The right reason is you."

He extracted his wallet from his back pocket, pulled out three condoms—apparently, he had high hopes—and tossed the wallet to the nightstand.

"Lie down." He watched, a new fire in his eyes this time.

One like she'd never seen before.

"How do you take off the shaper thing?" he asked, settling the condoms on the pillow within arm's reach but not intrusively in the way.

Travis was good at being prepared. Who knew?

"It's just…like…" She wanted to hide her face behind her palm. She didn't, because she had a feeling that would only ignite more of whatever was going on in his eyes. While that look excited her, it also scared the bejeezus out of her.

"Like?" he asked.

"Like underwear."

Just like that—lickety-split—his face hovered over hers. "And you're wearing this underwear?"

"Yes?" She sort of asked and sort of answered.

"It's covering you?" he asked. "Between your legs?"

"Yes?" The sort of asked, sort of answered thing was becoming habit with not-bickering Travis.

"Then, ma'am," he said, leaning heavily on the accent. "I guarantee this shaper thing is desirable, and sexy, and somethin' I want to see. Nothing you say will make it not." He said the words, and he moved to pin her with his hips against her own, the impressive evidence of his arousal against her stomach, and then his mouth descended to meet hers.

Urgent, sweet, and a balm that made her not care what kind of underwear she wore, because pretty soon she'd be wearing none and that was perfectly awesome. Preferable, even.

"Lift for me." His words against her mouth were gravel and crushed marble as he straddled her again, guiding her hips so she raised them, her heels pressing into the white duvet cover.

With her hips lifted, he pushed her dress up to her waist.

His hands touching everything along the way, skimming the skin of her thighs, brushing against spandex, until he got to the waistband nestled high above her belly button.

Then, Travis Frank surprised her, because he removed the shaper without any assistance. Like he was a spandex-shaper-remover professional.

This was impressive because it took her a solid three minutes to get the thing on and off, yet he rolled the material down, down, down, and tossed it off the bed like it wasn't a big deal and she was still desirable and...yes, she was so going to put her mouth on that tent in his trousers. A lot.

A whole lot.

Later, though, because he needed to finish undressing her. And she was damp between her thighs and she had barely moved but was breathing heavily and it would probably take only two strokes from him and she'd come.

With tongue and lips and hands, he pressed butterfly kisses to the scar just above her pubic bone, around the side of her belly where silver stretch marks marred the skin.

He continued touching and kissing all the spots she'd never shown anyone except her doctor.

"Travis, you don't have to..." she started to say but ended on an *ahhhh*, because his kisses had moved to between her thighs and this time they were of the French variety.

Using his thumbs to stroke her sensitive opening, he tongued her core, rolling his mouth over the center of her desire until she was clutching the bedspread. Panting, she was pretty much seeing all the stars that were ever in the night sky.

"I want to." He raised his gaze. His eyes held hers, which

was amazing but also not, because his mouth left the space between her thighs.

What did he want to do?

He should continue doing whatever it was he wanted to do.

She must've somehow broadcast this either telepathically or, more likely, with words she didn't realize she was speaking, because he chuckled. Deep and low and she clenched the bedspread harder.

Seriously? Could a woman come when a man wasn't even touching her?

"Let me see you." He massaged the spot where her thighs met her torso with the pads of his thumbs.

She pinched her eyes shut. They'd come this far. He was into *this*. She was into *this*. He'd already seen most of it.

If they were going to do *this*, she could hold off him seeing her totally exposed for only a little while.

Eventually, he'd catch glimpses.

Hopefully, later, in a shower where they could experiment with aquatic sex and she could do the whole going down on him thing she really, really wanted to do.

"Okay," she whispered.

"Open your eyes, sunshine." The words were commanding and gentle and how he managed them to be both, she had no idea.

She did, however, do as he asked.

He sat back on his heels, looking over her body like he was cataloging all the things that needed changing.

But maybe he wasn't.

Because the heat was back in his eyes. He looked wrecked. In a good way.

"God, Rach." His gaze skimmed her once more, from her face to her core. "You have no idea, do you?"

Okay, or maybe not. Maybe it was exactly as she'd expected.

Mortifying. This was mortifying. She started to pull the dress back down. "I know. I know. It's not—"

He pressed his hand over hers, stilling their descent with the fabric. "You have no idea how beautiful you are."

Um. What?

"No idea at all." He said this, but not to her. He seemed to be speaking to himself. "Fucking stunning and no idea."

"Trav?" She rose to her elbows, which wasn't super comfortable given the way he straddled her at the knees.

Her use of his name seemed to jerk him back to the present.

"No idea what?" she asked softly. "What don't I know?"

He ruffled a hand through the thick blond waves of his hair. "That nearly every man in every room—even some of the women—are looking at you. Wanting you just like I've got you. Wishing they could taste you. Make you moan like that."

Her throat clogged. Well, she hadn't expected that.

There was only a beat before he made some kind of decision, and he nodded along with it.

He unbuckled his pants and quickly removed them. "Dress comes off," he said as he removed his boxer shorts next. "Bra, too."

Not that she noticed, but, okay, she totally noticed the little dabble of pre-cum on the front of them. Given the way the length of him stood straight, he was as worked up as she was.

She pulled the dress over her head—not near as smoothly as he'd done with the spandex, but she didn't fall off the bed while she did it. She was totally claiming that as a win.

There.

They were both out of breath, turned on, and naked. She wasn't even freaking out because…holy crap on a croissant, Travis was a sight to behold.

He. Worked. *Out.*

His gaze melded with hers and he climbed on the bed, pressed up over her, and kissed the hell out of her mouth.

Travis could seriously earn a gold medal in the kissing Olympics.

The hard length of his erection weighed heavy against her thigh as his mouth did amazingly fantastic things to her lips. His hands lightly gripping both sides of her head, she moaned as he swept his tongue along her own.

Her skin tingled with the fire of his touch, her legs parting to make room for him, the ache between her thighs growing with each stroke of his tongue. She was ready to climb him like a tree.

What had come over her? She wasn't really sure, but she nipped at his bottom lip. That seemed to push him further onto the ledge they climbed together, the length of his erection pulsing hot against the inside of her thigh.

They were skin to skin, her nipples pressing against the light smattering of hair on his chest, the friction building *everywhere.*

She moaned and arched. Needing more.

Barely putting any space between them, he grabbed one of the condoms, ripping open the package and rolling it over the length of his erection.

She spread her thighs intuitively in invitation, pressing her fingers against the bundle of nerves at the apex of her opening, pushing there in an attempt to relieve the pressure.

Travis's gaze settled on the way her fingers worked for a beat, the length of him stiffening further, before he took the invitation, lying over her, one hand on his erection, the other bracing himself against the mattress as his mouth met hers again.

She gave up all control as he guided himself inside her body, his mouth never leaving hers.

Okay. So. Clearly, he was an exceptional multitasker when he put his mind to it.

Their bodies melded as she wrapped her legs around his thighs, the hair along his legs giving friction as she groaned.

She continued making all kinds of noises she was pretty sure she'd never made before.

He took the noises as an invitation—as he should, because she couldn't speak at the moment to issue a formal one.

He started thrusting, taking her there in only four movements. They'd barely begun when her body clenched around his, moans escaping her throat that he caught with more kisses, his own groans more subdued than hers but no less urgent.

The next wave began before the first had fully receded. This time he followed her as she clenched around him once more. He seated himself fully inside her, and his expression was one of concentration. Desire. Lust.

"Beautiful." The word coming from his final grunt was so many things—a plea and a promise and...everything.

The word was everything.

"Thank you," she whispered against his earlobe.

"Thank you, Trav."

They were sweaty and spent as he rolled off her, pausing to press a kiss against her temple before he said, "Condom," and left the bed.

The bathroom light flickered on and she closed her eyes. Reality began seeping in centimeter by centimeter.

She'd just had amazing sex. With Travis.

Travis.

The faucet turned on and off and...no, they couldn't stay like this.

The kids were coming home. They'd need her. Then Evelyn might come looking and figure out what they'd done.

Rachel usually kept her phone with her for clients in case they had an emergency.

She should get dressed and go back to work.

That's what she should have done, but instead she climbed between the sheets, and that small movement took everything she had, because her bones had turned to mush. Sleep pulled at her.

Gah, sleep called. Maybe she could take just a little nap.

Nothing big.

Her eyes fluttered closed. She was pretty sure she was three-quarters of the way to REM when the bed moved, and Travis was there.

"Open your legs," he said, the words gruff but filled with peace.

She did as he asked because…what else was she supposed to do?

She opened her eyes as his warm-washcloth-covered hand stroked between her legs.

Travis cleaned up his own messes? She stilled but didn't say anything. Unsure of what to say.

Finally, she settled on, "Thank you."

He tossed the washcloth off the bed and settled in behind her, holding the spot of the big spoon.

Not taking the time to dress, they were both naked, and she was so tired, and he was so warm, and this was so intimate.

What they'd done was intense and fun and…yeah. But this? This was beyond that.

"What are you thinking?" he asked.

"How do you know I'm not asleep?" she responded.

"You think really loud." He snuggled in deeper.

"I'm just wondering why you get to be the big spoon," she said as the sleep that she'd nearly had before started to pull at her again.

"You're such a goof," he murmured against her hair.

"Hey, Trav?" She yawned.

"Umm-hmm?" he murmured against her hair.

"That wasn't like doing the laundry at all."

He chuckled, then he kissed the crown of her skull. As she

drifted to sleep, he took her hand in his, tethering her to a reality she was pretty sure she didn't get to keep.

CHAPTER 18

RACHEL

*S*hit.

She was naked. Travis was there.

Sex. There had been sex. Really good sex. Then she took a nap.

She never took a nap.

Naps were for those who had time to take them. She was not that person.

Travis's warm breath came in small puffs against her neck as his body cradled hers.

Apparently, he'd fallen asleep, too. He'd gotten dressed first, though.

A sliver of light still shone through the curtains, but barely.

"Trav." She rolled so they were face-to-face, and shook his shoulder. "Travis."

He pinched open an eyelid. Then, even half awake, he turned on the magnetism and gave her a grin that would've had her dropping her panties—if she'd been wearing any.

"We fell asleep," she said, already peeling herself from his arms and searching the bedding for her clothes.

"You were really tired." He smiled. "Seemed like you needed to catch some sleep." The just-awake timbre of his voice was so inviting, she nearly found herself jumping him again.

Her stomach soured. The kids could be home any minute.

"You had a conference call." She rubbed her hands over her face, pinching at her cheeks to wake herself up. "I have clients."

"I rescheduled." He moved his hand to hold hers. "Your clients can survive a couple of hours without you." He squeezed her hand.

"You have no idea what my clients can survive." She started to get out of bed, but Travis's arm snaked around her waist.

He spoke against her bare neck. "Even you get to take a nap sometimes."

"We don't *all* get to pick and choose what work we do." Okay, so that came out way harsher than she meant.

He clenched his jaw, tight.

"What I mean is we need a plan," Rachel said because, first of all, they needed a plan. Second of all, they couldn't continue without some kind of direction.

"Rach—"

"I have kids," she continued.

"I know you have kids. We've talked about your kids. I love your kids."

"I can't confuse them." Blurgh. She hoped her tone transmitted the sincerity of those words and how desperate she was to ensure that she didn't mess up her boys. Finding Mom in bed with Uncle Travis was not something she wanted to try to explain.

"No one needs to know anything yet." Travis rolled and

sat, the sheet bunching at his waist. She'd grown really fond that afternoon of what lay under his clothes.

And him. And his dimples. And his humor. And his voice.

"Everyone's going to find out." She fidgeted with the bedspread. "I am horrible at keeping secrets."

"Who is going to find out?" he asked. "Mama? Dad? Gavin?"

"Brady, Kellan," she continued listing in the same tone he had.

"Then don't make it a secret." He moved his palms to her face, stroking her neck. "In your head, while we figure things out, don't make it a secret. It's just somethin' we're not ready to share. There's a difference."

"Your mom is going to be so mad," she said against his lips because, dammit, his lips were right there.

"My mother has no say in this."

"Your mom has a say in everything," Rachel whispered. "She's the Puffle Yum Momster."

"No." Travis shifted, not even bothering to realize that she was still totally naked. Apparently, he was cool with naked. Good to know.

"Mama *thinks* she has a say in everything. The only two people this involves are you and me." He paused, looking lost in a moment of thought. "Eventually, it'll involve your kids, because they're a huge part of who you are."

His fingers met her chin, holding her face up to his. He pressed a kiss to her lips, gentle, with a soft quality that wrapped around her and reassured that everything was going to be fine.

She let out a long breath.

"Are you with me on this?" he asked.

Not like she really had a choice. If they went around announcing what they were doing, she'd get tossed out, and the boys would be confused. "Next time I fall asleep like that, wake me up."

"No." He seemed firm on this, which meant she'd never get to fall asleep in the afternoon again.

"While you were asleep, Dad checked in with me. They're staying in Confluence for dinner, and they'll be back late. He worried when they couldn't reach you. I told them you were taking a nap, and I'd let you know when you woke up." He moved closer to her like a predator and she was his prey. "This is me, letting you know."

Since his lips were right there and her lips were right there, she kissed him. Hard, long, and with some tongue action.

He pulled away from her mouth, adjusting the bedding so it didn't cover any of her.

She resisted the urge to cover her stretch marks with her hand.

"For the record, I haven't worried what my mother thinks about any woman in my bed since I was sixteen," Travis said, nibbling along her neck.

Rachel stilled. "Sixteen?"

"You're thinking again, sunshine." He kissed her, the same way that she'd kissed him. "Don't dig too deep. That's where we keep the skeletons."

She looked up at him and saw the heat of his gaze, felt reassurance in his touch. "What if we mess everything up?"

"You're giving us too much power." He rolled her onto her back, settling between her thighs.

This felt…this felt natural. Like it was always supposed to be this way. Rachel and Travis.

It made no sense, and in that nonsensical way, it made all the sense in the world.

"I really like you," she said as he pressed kisses along the column of her throat.

He didn't stop kissing her, continuing along her collarbone to her shoulder until he said, "Good to know."

Then it was hands and mouths and so much groping.

He was hard, she was ready, and he took everything she gave.

There wasn't a lot of preamble this time, the foreplay made up only of his touches and her groans. He got undressed, donned a condom lickety-split, spread her thighs, and drove home.

She gasped, wrapping her legs around his waist and letting him ride her. She panted, he moaned, the world blurred.

This was new.

This time he didn't make eye contact. He shoved his face into her neck and made feral sounds rivaling her own.

This was…this was something different than before. The feelings coiling inside her were just as arousing, but this time they weren't foggy. It seemed like she'd put her glasses on and the world had refocused.

He gripped her hips, pressing into her with the hard length of him and, suddenly, she realized what this was.

This was his claiming of her body. Making it his. Owning her.

She'd never given her body over like this before.

"Trav," she said on a gasp.

He didn't stop. His name on her lips seemed to spur him further, push him more. With each thrust, she unraveled a little until she became genuinely worried there wouldn't be anything left when it ended.

Except, as he thrust harder, he lifted his gaze so it held hers, and in that moment he was someone she'd never known. This man she was with was making a point that she was pretty sure neither of them understood.

Everything inside her tightened to the point that it was ready to unleash. She pressed her lips together to cover the sounds she was pretty sure were coming from her.

The release took over. She bit into his shoulder to stop herself from crying out. As soon as her muscles clenched around the solid length pressed inside her, he followed. The thrusting slowed. His breaths came jagged, but more evenly spaced.

"To be totally clear. If you want a plan? You are now," he said with a final thrust. "My plan."

She rode the aftershocks of their lovemaking. He didn't withdraw.

Still joined, he kissed her.

"I mean it," he continued. "You're my plan. Your smile is my goal. Whatever I need to do to make it happen, I'm going to do it."

Well...huh. On that note, she couldn't smile, because she pressed her lips against his instead.

CHAPTER 19

RACHEL

The past week, her mind had been a muddle of lust-filled moments with Travis and spending time swimming at the lake—with and without her kids.

Travis made her feel everything, the water brought peace, and the slow pace of summer at Twin Lakes lulled her into a false sense of serenity.

Because then…Rachel missed another deadline.

Well, sort of. She'd missed *a* deadline that the client had last-minute emailed her about. The deadline had been of the tight variety and, generally, this was not an issue due to the attentiveness Rachel prided herself in providing with her service.

The first deadline she missed happened because she'd taken a Travis nap. That one hadn't been a huge deal.

This one she'd missed because she was doing…other things with Travis. It was a massive deal.

"I'm so sorry," Rachel gushed into the phone, really glad this wasn't a video call because she felt like a total wreck, and she was pretty sure her cheeks were flushing. That weird red rash thing was probably going on around her neck—the one that seemed to show up only when she was really and truly flustered.

"I'm not sure what happened," she said, deflated.

"This is really unlike you," Cassie said on the other end of the line. She seemed more than a little distracted, given the way she covered and uncovered her mouthpiece. Other conversations were happening simultaneously, Rachel could tell. Everyone on that end of the line was rushing, trying to figure out how to fix the error of the orders arriving with the wrong coupon code.

"Are you sure everything's okay?" Cassie asked. "I'm worried about you."

Ugh. That was even worse than making the mistake in the first place. Now the rash around her neck itched. "I'm fine. Really, this is just a onetime thing."

Call-waiting chimed and Rachel glanced at the screen to ensure she hadn't messed anything else up for another client that morning.

It was Kaiya.

She'd call her back later.

Rachel declined the call and turned her entire focus back to Cassie. "It absolutely will not happen again."

It wouldn't, because Rachel responded to all client emails within hours and handled everything that came up immediately. She wouldn't slip again. This was the kind of service her clients had become accustomed to receiving. The kind of service she'd become accustomed to giving. She considered herself something of a concierge when it came to her company, that's why she had three *select* clients instead of filling her schedule with multiple smaller clients like she'd done when she first started out.

Cassie's change request for the coupon code had a time stamp of three a.m. that morning, and Rachel had been getting handled by Travis at that time. Then she'd had breakfast with her kids. Thus the advertisement didn't get switched out before seven, as Cassie had requested.

Which meant, the previous version of the ad ran with the old coupon code.

Rachel's lungs had gotten a little heavier and the air in the room denser when she'd checked her email and realized that, while she was eating a strawberry toaster tart with her kids and her ex-in-laws, the timeline had come and gone.

The old ad ran, Cassie's request had fallen by the wayside, and the strawberry toaster tart turned sour against Rachel's tongue.

To be fair, this *was* the first screwup of this magnitude. Rachel kept lists of her lists to ensure that nothing fell into cracks. There were no cracks when it came to her company.

Travis emerged from the shower wearing only a towel.

She pressed her finger to her lips and mouthed, *Client.*

He nodded and went to pull on boxers and a pair of jeans, which was a shame.

They'd become a little bolder in their time together—still ensuring that the kids were out of the house when they were together during the day. And the locks were always firmly engaged. But they'd started seeing each other intimately throughout the day instead of only at night when everyone else was asleep.

"Rachel?" Cassie asked.

"Yes, sorry…again." Rachel turned her focus to the notepad in front of her, pointedly not looking at Travis and his abdominal definition.

Cassie sighed. "You're very distracted."

"I am." Rachel frowned, but it was the truth, so she might as well fess up. "The family summer trip has definitely diverted my attention a little, but that ends now."

Travis scowled at her at that declaration. His scowl added to the heaviness she was already feeling in her shoulder blades.

She stood to pace as she wrapped things up.

Cassie seemed to take Rachel at her word, and the rest of the conversation turned to reconfirming future deadlines, which wasn't necessary given that this was a one-time situation. Rachel tolerated the inquisition because Cassie was clearly perplexed about the situation.

She and Rachel had been working together for three years, and this was the first time Rachel hadn't addressed an issue within the given time frame.

Although, if Rachel really thought about it—as she was right then—Cassie had consistently started asking for more and more on tighter timelines. Rachel had always delivered, so she hadn't thought much of it.

Once she hung up the phone, Rachel fell back on the bed, dropping her cell to press the heels of her hands against her eyelids.

"Didn't go well?" Travis asked, pulling on his tee.

Rachel nodded, hands still against her face. "I really screwed up."

"How bad?" he asked.

"The old ad ran, but Cassie changed the coupon code. So now, she says, customers want both deals, and she's really worried she's going to lose money over the whole thing."

"How much money are we talking?" Travis's baritone was not soothing like usual.

This was a testament to how tense Rachel was, if the sound of his voice wasn't doing the general calming thing like usual.

"I don't know." Rachel slumped farther into the mattress, letting the thick comforter, well, comfort. "Cassie wasn't happy about it, though."

Rachel was going to have to give her a discount on her monthly bill. That meant she was going to have to pull into her savings for the mortgage payment this month. And that meant that she'd have to replenish her savings.

"Do you want to talk about it?" Travis asked, sitting at the edge of her bed, running his hand along her leg.

"No." She rolled over and tried the box breathing thing again.

"Rach." Travis moved his palm from her leg to her back. "Even you get to mess up sometimes."

She looked at him then. Really looked at him. Not his abs, not his body, not the way he made her insides flippity-flop with his mind-boggling sex appeal. No, she really drank him in.

He cared about her.

That thought made her throat go dry.

"I don't get to mess up," she said.

Then she told him. All of it.

"She's in the States?" he asked. Rachel nodded.

"And she was up at three in the morning sending you emails with changes for an ad that was supposed to run within hours?" he asked.

Rachel nodded again. "While we were—"

She gestured to the wall, where they'd had a truly inspired middle-of-the-night romp. It involved inventive use of the curtains. She wouldn't have thought the position was possible.

Travis's inventiveness when it came to bedroom antics was one of the many pieces to that smoldering sex-appeal thing he had going on.

"Rach, you shouldn't have to take calls at all hours of the night." He sprawled out on the bed beside her, rolling to his side. "No one can possibly expect that from you."

Except him, of course. He didn't say it, but she was pretty sure he wanted to.

To be honest, she'd jump when he called because of that thing she'd discovered he could do when they went skinny-dipping at the lake. Let's just say, she was mighty impressed by his flexibility.

"It's just part of the service I provide to clients." A headache was forming just behind her eyes. "I mean, I'd like it not to be." She rolled, so they were face-to-face. "But it's what they expect. I'm definitely not the cheapest option on the virtual-executive-assistant market. My clients have come to know that I will get it done and do it right."

He brushed a strand of hair behind her ear. "Do you charge them extra when they call with last-minute demands?"

She shook her head.

"Have you considered laying out the exact times you'll be available and when they can expect responses?" he continued.

Given that he was starting to show up at work only some-times, he really didn't get to have thoughts on this.

"I've considered it," she admitted. In fact, she'd consid-ered it more than once. She'd even drafted it up in a docu-ment. She hadn't seen it through because she absolutely didn't want to ruin the relationships already established or—more to the point—admit that she was unable to complete the job as asked.

"I think I just need to do better." She waved her hand between them. "At managing my time with you, with the kids, and the work."

"I'd like to spend more time with you, Rach." He shifted so they were touching, front to front. "I've been thinking... we should consider taking this thing between us public."

She kept her gaze steady with his, even as she arched away. Seriously? She was mid-crisis, and he wanted to discuss this now?

"No," she said.

"No, as in *never*?" he asked. "Or no, as in *not right now*?"

What had she meant? She'd meant that she didn't want to deal with Evelyn's passive-aggressiveness, explaining rela-tionships to the boys, or having to have a talk with Gavin, since it affected the kids and they'd agreed—and both had always communicated—whenever they'd had a change in their lives that merited that type of a talk.

"I'm really stressed-out at the moment." The headache was starting to become more than just an annoyance. If she wasn't careful, her morning would brew a full-blown migraine. She had no time for a migraine. "Now is not the right moment for this."

"I think it's a fantastic moment, myself," Travis said, his dimple making an appearance, which caused heat to pool between her thighs. The headache receded a little, too.

They had been taking it slow. Well, slow everywhere but in the bedroom.

And that one time in the study. Also, the lake.

But that had just been once because they really could've gotten caught.

Although, maybe they weren't taking it as slow as she'd thought.

"Can we keep it at just us right now? Until things calm down for me?" she asked, touching his chest because she could, and it was just so touchable. "Then talk about a plan to ease everyone in to you and me being a public us?"

"That depends." He pressed a light kiss to her lips.

"On what?"

"Let me take you out tonight. Dancing. There's a local place Dane says is great."

Dancing. She hadn't been dancing since Molly's birthday two years ago. They'd all decided to try clubbing. They'd ended up spending twenty minutes at the actual club before evacuating to an Olive Garden because it was soup, salad, and breadsticks night.

"We have a problem with going out." She sifted her fingertips through the still-damp hair on his scalp. "Someone *here* will notice we're gone." Or, to be precise, multiple someones.

"Already handled."

He couldn't just have it handled. That would be a lot of handling.

"What do you mean?" she asked.

"Mom and Dad don't know it yet, but they're taking the kids to a magic show at the Twin Lakes resort. Dane is going to cover for us here. I already asked him—bribed him—and he agreed."

"Dane is good with us?" she asked. Ever since the night in the den, she hadn't said a peep to him about it. He, likewise, had pretended it hadn't happened.

"Dane is, officially, staying out of it," Travis said carefully. "But I had somethin' he wanted, so we negotiated."

"What exactly did you have that he wanted?" she asked, cautiously.

Travis shrugged. "Some things are better kept between brothers and air traffic control."

She shook her head with a bit too much force for trying to stave off a headache. "I'm not neglecting my clients again so you and I can go dancing."

He did a push-up over the top of her. "Bring your phone and check it between songs. If we have to head back here, we can. I won't say a word about it."

"You've thought of everything, haven't you?" He grinned a shit-eating grin. "Just wait."

CHAPTER 20

The dirt parking lot wasn't well lit at all—just the full moon above, the stars, and the light coming from a dilapidated old barn that could seriously use a coat of paint and new lumber, but did have a big, professional sign announcing the barn name as Come As You Are.

Under that was a piece of canvas hung along a thick rope with wide hand-painted letters announcing the evening as open mic night.

"This is it?" Rachel didn't seem impressed.

He wasn't impressed, either. He'd have to have a talk with Dane later. "Apparently so."

"Give me a second." Rachel had brought her laptop along and was returning emails from a hot spot she'd created with her laptop and her cell phone. "Almost done."

She needed to set some pretty substantial boundaries with her clients, because they were walking all over her. He'd asked her what they paid for the kind of service she provided —as in, always available to drop everything and do whatever they needed at literally any time of the night. She'd dodged the question.

The only thing she was more committed to than her work was her kids.

Travis was hopeful that soon she'd find room in there for him, too.

He stretched across the interior of the SUV and kissed her on the temple. "Whatever they're paying you, it's not enough."

She gave a soft shake of her head. "You know what I'd like to do?"

"What's that?"

"I'd like to have staff." She was fidgeting with the dangly bracelets on her arm.

He got the feeling this conversation was of the important variety. So he turned in his seat to face her. "Yeah?"

"So it's not just me." She went back to typing away at the keyboard. "I guess that's my dream. So whenever anyone needs anything—at any hour—someone is monitoring the inbox. And they could be from all different time zones so it's not a big deal if a three in the morning request comes through. Where they are, it won't be bedtime."

She was definitely on to something.

"Take some of my money. I'll hire you a staff."

Given the look she gave him, that was not the answer she wanted.

"Or do it your way," he said. "That works, too."

"I need to have enough clients to pay for help, but to do that I need to have more time to build up my client list. I already know I prefer fewer high-paying clientele than lots of smaller ones."

He knew, without a doubt that any of the Franks would invest in her company if she asked. If she didn't want him involved because of their extracurricular activities, the others would toss in for it.

She finished up the email, closed the laptop, and slipped it into the padded case before stuffing it under the seat.

"Okay, let's go." She pushed her door open before he could get around the front of the vehicle to open it for her.

He linked his hand with hers as they headed toward the building. The barn.

Light spilled from the open double barn doors and as they got closer, a loud stream of country music coming from inside filtered out into the mountain air.

Dane had said this was the place in town to hit up on a Friday night. He knew, from his chats with Molly, that Rachel and her friends tended to hit up trend-setting martini bars. Not old barns in the middle of nowhere.

He'd have a talk with Dane later about his suggestions on date locations.

Although he was pretty sure there was not a martini bar anywhere in the Twin Lakes region.

"You've never been here before?" she asked as, tethered together, they weaved through the parked trucks, various off-road vehicles, and a few luxury SUVs that seemed oddly out of place.

"Nope. Dane's the social guy. I usually hang out at the house, hike, hit the lake, that type of thing." They emerged from the parked cars and…the barn had a bouncer.

That was as unexpected as a pair of overalls at The Cruise Room.

A big, muscled guy manned the door. The size of this guy rivaled the bouncers at Brek's Bar in Denver when Dimefront stopped by.

"Name?" he asked, swiping across the screen of an electronic tablet that seemed fancier than the ones Gavin had bought the boys for Christmas.

"Frank, Travis."

A slow smile spread over the bouncer guy's face. "Dane's brother."

Travis nodded, pulling out his wallet to handle the cover charge.

"No charge for Dane's brother." Bouncer Guy held out two gold, plastic wristbands with VIP etched in black letters.

Rachel caught Travis's gaze, her eyebrows raised.

He was certain they were thinking the same thing—*a barn has VIP wristbands?*

Travis took the bands, helping Rachel with hers before attaching his own. The bouncer guy unhooked the thick rope blocking the entrance and jerked his chin, indicating they should pass through.

Rachel gripped his arm and rolled up on her toes to whisper in his ear, "I've never been a VIP in a barn before."

Her breath against his earlobe made his whole body heat.

"That makes two of us." He turned his head so his face was right next to hers, and he kissed her. Quick. The kind of kiss two people shared when they were comfortable with each other. The kind that wasn't any kind of promise because it didn't need to be; it was simply who they were.

That realization had him tripping over his feet a little. Rachel held on to his arm as though if she released him, he'd disappear into the crowd.

There was quite the crowd inside, a wall-to-wall melding of the locals and those who owned seasonal homes. Cowboy hats abounded, paired with worn jeans, right alongside not-worn-in designer jeans and one-hundred-dollar haircuts.

Travis liked it.

What the place lacked on the weathered outside, it made up for on the inside. First, because the inside had new lumber for walls. That squelched his previous concern the place might cave. Even the sawdust on the floor seemed to be more for show than for utility, because the sawdust was way too clean to have been there before that evening.

Rachel was pulling him toward a table set up along the wall filled with a buffet of food, but that's not where she stopped. Behind that table was another with mason jars filled with what appeared to be moonshine and a keg of Pabst Blue Ribbon.

At the end of the table was a tabletop sign announcing the beverages were for the VIPs.

"I've never had moonshine before," she said with a sly grin.

He squeezed her arm. "Be careful with that stuff—it'll light you up."

"That sounds fun."

"Depends on who's holding your hair tomorrow."

"You'd hold my hair?"

"Did I bring you to a fancy barn or what?"

"I guess you'd hold my hair, then. But good news"—she chucked him on the shoulder—"you don't have to, because I have an iron stomach."

This he did not know about her.

She nodded along with her assertion.

"Then I suppose you should try the moonshine," he said.

The attendant offered a tiny, shot-size mason jar filled with clear liquid to Travis.

He took it and passed it along to Rachel. "Enjoy."

"You're not having any?" she asked, doing a little sniff test that made the corners of her eyes water.

He shrugged. Given that he'd driven her there, he was definitely not having any. Plus: "My stomach is not of the iron variety, and I'd prefer not to be throwing up tomorrow."

"I would also prefer you not throw up tomorrow." She lifted a shoulder, and her sweater slipped down a notch, exposing a lace bra strap. "The Frank stomach is notoriously weak. Which is a wonder, given your excellent breakfast choices." She layered on the sarcasm nice and thick.

"Did you just call me weak?" He nudged her.

"It's the only part of you that's weak." She smiled and glanced down to his fly. "Everything else seems top-notch."

That top-notch part of him she stared at stirred under her scrutiny.

"Glad you approve." He stepped aside so another woman with a VIP bracelet could get to the table.

Rachel tossed back the shot like it was apple juice, but then the fire of the moonshine must've punched her in the gut, because her eyes bugged and she gripped his shoulder.

He didn't like that she learned the burn of moonshine the hard way—she should've given it a little sip first—but he liked that she leaned against him for support and held on when she needed it. He practically felt the warmth of the distilled liquor in his own veins. Except his hit wasn't near as bad as hers must've been.

"Smooth," she managed to finally say on a cough.

"Maybe I should try some," he said.

She shook her head. "Take it from me—don't do it."

That wasn't what he'd meant, though. Instead, he leaned forward and pressed his mouth to her lips. She sighed and parted her lips, and he went for a taste. Rachel, and fire, and spirit.

He broke the kiss. "Tastes fine to me."

"Dance with me?" she asked, not moving.

"Always." He touched the indent of her mouth with the pad of his index finger.

It was either that or take her to the car, put down the seats in the back, and find a secluded spot to devour each other.

"That's not entirely true," she said. Suddenly, it was as though everything but his face held her interest. She didn't meet his gaze. "The always thing."

"Then what's the truth?" he asked. That moonshine sounded like it had been a good idea, given the tone of her words.

"There's what I thought was the truth and what I realize now is the truth," she said.

He could relate to that.

They weren't dancing, yet. They weren't even touching. But there was only a wink of space separating their bodies.

The space seemed to stretch for miles in the silence as Rachel started and stopped, started and stopped.

"Forget about it." She gave a halfhearted wave of her hand.

Her hand brushed against his chest. He reached for it and held it there.

"I would've danced with you before this trip, Rach." He lifted her hand and kissed the end of each and every one of her fingertips.

"I wouldn't have danced with you." Her words were quick. "But I will now. And I'm not really making much sense, so we should just get to it." She paused for half a beat. "The dancing thing."

"What you're trying to say is you didn't always like me?"

She nodded. Gulped. "I shouldn't have said that."

"Well, the feeling was mutual." He pulled her to the dance floor. A slow country ballad came through the speakers. He wrapped her in his arms, keeping enough space so he could study her face as she responded. "I know what my problem was. Why didn't you like me, though?"

"I know better than to listen to what other people say. But Gavin had always talked about you like you were shallow."

That sounded about right.

"I took his word for it." She looked up at him from under her lashes. "I shouldn't have."

He pulled her closer, because he could. "Tell me about what he said."

"Which do you want to hear?" she asked, finally meeting his stare.

He wanted to hear anything Rachel was willing to tell him, so he could go about fixing it. Showing her who he really was.

She cleared her throat, swaying with the music. With him.

"You and Gavin don't get along," she stated as though it were fact.

They didn't get along well, this was true. "That's right. Most of the time."

She was tracing little ovals along his arms—the bare skin at the edges of his short sleeves. "Why?"

"Different philosophies, I suspect." Although, in recent years, things had been better between them. They'd kept their relationship to business, and the business was doing well, so there wasn't much to argue about. Travis didn't like Gavin's complete commitment to the company. He wished Gavin would throw that commitment toward his kids. But he'd stayed out of it.

"Why don't you think we get along?" he asked.

"Gavin always said little things about you in passing." Rachel lifted her shoulder, just the tiniest of inches.

He stilled for half a second. "What kind of things?"

"Like that you were always with a different woman."

She studied the floor, then the wall.

"That's not entirely untrue," he admitted with a chuckle.

"And you didn't treat them well," she continued.

Now, that? That was entirely a lie.

"I never treated any of the women I was with poorly. We each got what we wanted from those…"

What was the best word for what those definitely-not relationships had been?

"Sexual liaisons?" she offered.

His cheeks burned. She was right; that's what they'd been. All they'd been.

He nodded. A lump suddenly stuck in his throat.

"I've been a little worried that this thing between us might be you somehow sticking it to Gavin," she said, as though the thought had weighed heavy.

"Gavin has nothing to do with what we're doing." He

pulled her closer. "Gavin doesn't get to be in this thing with us, no matter where it goes."

She nodded.

"He also said you weren't dedicated at work," she continued.

That was also true. "I supposed I've spent a good deal of time figuring out my shit."

"What kind of shit?" They weren't so much dancing as they were clinging to each other in a sea of people.

"What I want to do. I want to fly. Wasn't sure about the family business, but you can imagine how Mama reacts when I bring that up. Gavin takes her side. Things get complicated real fast."

"The thing is…" She paused, nibbling her bottom lip. "I'm not sure Gavin's opinion is the real reason why I didn't care for you. I don't think I ever really believed him about any of it, if I'm being honest."

"Then what was the real reason?"

"I knew if I opened myself up to liking you, I'd go all in on it." She didn't seem to be able to meet his gaze. "That scared me. Gavin and I were trying at that point. Trying to make it work so Kellan and Brady would have stability. We were trying, and you were…distracting."

"So it was easier to stay away." The music changed to another slow ballad. "You were distracting, too," he said against her hair. "And I guess I didn't really do much to prove to you I wasn't a total dick."

"Just a tad bit of a dick?" she asked with a little nose scrunch.

"I *am* a Frank." He pressed a brief kiss to her forehead. "Some of it is genetic."

"I don't believe that." She shook her head vehemently.

"Why?"

"Because my boys are Franks, and I don't believe they need to be jerks."

"Ahh…"

They didn't speak for the rest of the song, but their bodies moved like they were made for each other. Made to move together.

"What are we doing, Travis?" she asked quietly, almost like she didn't mean for him to hear the question.

"Dancing," he murmured against her hair.

"I mean…"

He knew what she meant. They were new; this was precarious. Which was why he said, "Sometimes you can just go with it and not worry about every little thing. Makes life more fun."

CHAPTER 21

RACHEL

Rachel pressed herself against Travis's body. She adored the feeling of his strength as she nestled against him. The way her curves seemed to fit. How her body didn't feel like something she should change or improve upon when they were together. Instead, her curves were something he enjoyed. Therefore, she enjoyed them, too.

Neither of them was even pretending to sway to the music at this point. Standing together, bodies molded to each other, was perfect.

She shuddered a breath. This brand of perfect had the power to ruin everything.

"I'm not ready to tell everyone about us," she said, letting the words out before she had time to think and then overthink them.

"Okay." He pressed his lips to her forehead. "We don't have to do that right now."

"I don't…I don't know if I'll ever be ready." She worried at the lipstick on her bottom lip. "What would we even say?"

"That things are good between us." He traced her neck

with his thumb, the path warming. He had a way of touching her that made her muscles release years of tension. The man's hands were magic.

The tension building in this conversation was starting to make her whole body tighten up. He caught it. He remedied it.

This was life with Travis.

"We'd say that this is going wherever we want to take it," he continued with that mesmerizing quality of his voice. "We don't want it to end."

"That makes it sound so simple," she said, whispering into the cocoon they'd built around each other.

The muscles in her back continued to release with his touch.

"We can take the next step," he said. "Just for us. The rest will fall into place when the time is right."

"We're doing this." She couldn't help it, she pulled herself up on her toes, so her nose brushed against his.

He smiled. "We're doing this."

"Are we going to give each other keys and stuff?" she asked.

She vaguely knew where his apartment was downtown, but she'd never been there. The boys had been, though. Their comments about the space all revolved around his video game setup. It was, apparently, amazing.

"My apartment has a doorman. You're already on the list of people with clearance to be let in whenever you want," he said against her hair.

Her eyes went wide. She was on the doorman list?

Wait…he had a freaking doorman?

"Since when," she asked, "am I on the list?"

"Since you became part of the family."

"Oh." She glanced at his palm, still practicing magic in the muscles at her shoulder.

"It's not a big deal," he said, but it sounded like it was actually a pretty big deal to him.

"Even after the divorce?" she asked carefully, unsure if she wanted to know the answer.

"You're still part of the family." His sincerity pierced through the sadness that came whenever she thought about those times. "Divorce doesn't change that."

The divorce wasn't contentious, but it was still a divorce. She still mourned what her boys had lost when their parents split. Knowing they'd never remember a time when Mom and Dad were together as a couple, not just a parental unit.

"Seriously?" she asked, not fully believing him.

He nodded.

"A doorman is so fancy. I have only a keypad," she said, making the silly face that usually worked to make the boys laugh.

Travis didn't laugh. But his lips twitched, so she'd call it a win.

"I usually just use the garage opener," she said, as they dance-moved closer to the edge of the dance floor. "But the keypad works on the front and back doors. It's, uh, four-zero-six-nine."

"Four, zero, six, nine," he repeated.

She'd given him the code before—the night he brought her margaritas and she'd crashed on the sofa. This time, though, when she gave him the numbers, it felt like more.

They were, somehow, a promise she was making.

"I can write it down for you," she said. "Or the boys know. They're sworn to secrecy, though, so they probably won't say anything, even if you ask."

He grinned.

Knowing Travis, he'd test them on that later.

"And...uh...just to be clear," she chattered on. "We're not seeing other people while we're seeing each other, right?"

"Do you want to see other people?" he volleyed back.

He looked as though he absolutely did not want that.

"No," she said, remarkably fast. "I was hoping this was exclusive."

"Me too." He spoke against her forehead.

"Good. Exclusive is good." She did the whacky face thing again.

Gah, she had to stop doing that when they were talking about serious stuff.

"Exclusive is the best." He gave her a squeeze.

"I'm clean, too," she said. "And I have the birth control thing covered. I mean, uh, I *really* do this time. Not like when I was in college. And I had a physical right before we left Denver. All good on that front."

She might as well have given him two perky thumbs up to top off that morbidly embarrassing data dump.

The song stopped, but they stayed together, holding each other until the next song started. The band played a new rendition of a Bellamy Brothers song she recognized about a man holding a woman against him.

"I'm clean, too, Rach," he said. "If this is your way of asking."

Well, it was. A very uncomfortable way of asking.

He hummed along to the song, apparently waiting to see if she had anything else she wanted to add.

She did, more embarrassing data she needed to dump.

Get it all over with in one night.

"If you want to, uh, not use a condom," she whispered so only he could hear. "Then we…we can just not do that." She met his gaze. "If you want to," she added as a quick addendum to her declaration.

"Is that what you want?" he asked, and his words were remarkably neutral given that she'd just embarrassed the hell out of herself.

For a moment, she stood still, not moving to the music.

"Sorry?" she asked, seeming to not understand his question.

"What do you want, Rach?" he asked. "Whatever you want, we'll do that. I believe you when you say you've got it covered. If you want me to cover it, just let me know."

"You don't have an opinion on this?" She pulled back from him, earnest. *Do you just not care?*

"Rach." His lips brushed hers. "I care about everything when it comes to you. You know I don't like it when you let people walk all over you, so I'll speak up about it. I want you to make time for us, so I'll make sure that happens—even if it means your schedule gets a little fucked in the process. And I want dinner invitations with you and the boys, so I hope we can figure out a way to make that happen for me." He drew a long breath. "That's the shit that matters. It's what I have an opinion about. When it comes to the rest, I'm willing to take your lead."

"Oh." She pressed her temple against his chest as he led, but they mostly stayed in a two-foot square holding on to each other.

"Anything else you want to get off your chest tonight?" he asked. "Or should we start heading back?"

They had a little more time before the boys were due back at the house. But she needed to check her email and follow up with any late-night Cassie crises.

She didn't stir. Didn't move.

There was more. More she needed to say.

"I didn't call Gavin back." This came out as a confession, a choked confession that she whispered into the air at his chest.

"Gavin's not here." He traced his fingers up and down her spine and held her tighter, her cheek against his chest. "It's just you and me."

"After we hooked up, I wasn't going to call him back," she confessed—the confession she'd never told anyone.

Travis stilled. Blood started to thrum in her ears.

"I don't need to hear this." He started to step away, but she held firm. "You know how before I said that I'd have some things that mattered to me? This is one of those times where I don't need to know the details."

"I need you to hear them, though," she said, because she really, really did.

The earnestness in her voice apparently made him pause.

"Please," she continued.

She did her best to relax, ready to give only the abbreviated version of events.

"I wasn't going to call him back, even though he called me, like, four times afterward. I ignored the calls until I found out about the pregnancy. *Then* I called him," she said. "By that point, he'd moved on. As he should have, since I wasn't interested."

Travis hardly moved, but she sallied forth.

"I explained everything, and he said he wanted to get married. I didn't want to. I mean, I wasn't even going to call him back, so why would we get married?" She had pulled away a little and was talking with her hands.

"Why did you get married?" Travis asked, that mask of neutrality covering his expression.

"Gavin and I are friendly. Friends, even. Sometimes. Mostly, before Dakota. She didn't really like that we were friends." She waved away the thought. "This isn't about her, though. All of this is in the past. I don't want to ruin where Gavin and I are as co-parents. But you need to know what happened because it...it affects what we are together."

"Why did you get married?" Travis asked again.

"He made it clear who your family is. Explained to me that you would all support us as a family."

"If you got married." Travis filled in the blank for her.

She nodded. When the divorce had finalized, she swore this was the first and last time she'd ever accept help like that.

Owing Gavin cost her more than she was even willing to admit to herself—a whole heap of pride.

"My parents were angry I was pregnant. They were even less thrilled that I decided not to end the pregnancy," she pressed on. "I convinced myself I could be a good mom on my own. But then there were two babies. How was I supposed to raise *two* babies? Even if Gavin shared custody." She swallowed against what felt like a rising tide ready to sweep her away. "Gavin was my nuclear option so my world wouldn't implode. He stepped in. He offered an alternative. He made it so I didn't have to make a decision that I really, really didn't want to make."

And it cost her only her dignity.

"It's not his fault we didn't work out." Rachel gripped Travis's arms to hold him in place. "He just...he didn't forgive me. For not calling him back. For not wanting him. Eventually, I thought we forgave each other for everything. We were both doing the best we could. The divorce wasn't angry or anything. He took care of the boys, wanted to ensure we stayed comfortable—but I didn't want alimony."

"You should've taken the money," he said through gritted teeth, because there was more than enough of the stuff to help her out. She didn't have to work so hard all the time.

She gulped. No, she wouldn't do that. She'd spent the last years rebuilding her self-esteem. Proving she could make it herself.

"The thing is...I would've called *you* back," she said, pressed against his chest. "I had to tell you about what happened, so you'd know what a big deal that is to me."

His hand pressed against her hair. His breaths jagged pieces of glass slicing through any hardening of her heart she'd used as armor.

"I would've called you first," she whispered again. "I think Gavin will know that. I think he'll know it if we tell everyone. And I think it's going to hurt him." She drew a deep breath. "If it hurts him and he lashes out, it could hurt the boys. I can't let that happen."

He pulled away from her, ran a hand through his hair, and paused as he saw the expression on her face. "We should go."

Her lower lip trembled the smallest amount, a small bit of wet appearing at the edge of her eyelids, but no tears fell. She crossed her arms under her breasts, doing that thing she did to hold herself up.

"You wouldn't have had to call me, because there's no way I would've been able to walk out the door the next morning. I would've ordered pancakes—scratch that, I'd have *made* you pancakes myself. From scratch. We would've spent the whole day together. That's what we would've done."

She smiled a watery smile. "Are you really that good of a guy, Travis Frank?"

"Don't let the word get out. I have a reputation to uphold."

The tear that she'd been holding back finally fell, but it didn't make it past her cheekbone because he wiped it away with his thumb.

Another fell. He repeated. Another.

Another.

"Don't cry, sunshine," he said, still swiping as she hiccupped. She pressed the back of her hand against her mouth.

She smiled then.

The fact that she was smiling—really smiling, not one of those fake ones she'd gotten so used to using—the smiling was a good thing, but that didn't change that there was a whole bucket of water falling out of her face.

"What's going on right now?" he asked.

"I don't know," she said, wiping at the tears herself.

"First guess, then?"

"I think because I'm happy," she said on a throaty laugh.

"I'm happy, and I don't know what to do with that when it could ruin everything for my kids."

"We're going to figure this out." He sounded like he really believed that.

For now, for that moment, she decided to focus on the happy instead of the laundry. The dirty, messy, daily chore kind.

CHAPTER 22

TRAVIS

Nearly a full three days since their date night and Rachel had been scarce. She wasn't avoiding him; he understood this because they were still connecting for...entanglements... every night. But the amount of time she spent working was becoming cumbersome for even the boys.

They wanted their mom around, and even when she was present, the laptop or her phone was her constant companion.

He got it. Understood that she was worried she'd miss another request or make a mistake.

Her attention to detail was one of the things he liked most about her, because when it was just the two of them?

Oh yeah, her attention to detail was meticulous, which led to other things that were exceptionally...thorough.

He was pretty sure he was becoming addicted to Rachel's particular brand of precise.

"Hey." Travis pushed the door closed softly behind him, pressing the lock with his thumb.

He held her toothbrush in his other hand. She'd left it on his sink that morning.

Rachel, sitting crisscross-applesauce on the bed with her laptop open in front of her, lifted her gaze to him and raised her eyebrows. "Hey."

"Hey," he said again. He held up the toothbrush. Set it on the table by the door. "Thought you might want this."

She hadn't messed with her makeup that day, so her face was bare, her hair piled on her head like she wore it only when she didn't expect anyone else to see her. At least, that's what he'd noted. She never kept it up like that when anyone else was in the room. He gave her thirty seconds before she remembered that it was in the pile before she removed the band and let it hang loose.

He liked it both ways. He didn't particularly have a preference.

"Are you busy?" he asked, hand still on the doorknob, ready to leave if she couldn't take time away for him.

She nodded, the almost-there smile edging at her lips. "Always."

"I'll leave you to it, then." He turned the door handle to leave.

"Trav?" she called before he pulled the door open more than an inch. "Did you need something?"

Yeah, he needed something. Someone.

"You," he said simply, turning back toward her.

She smiled, her cheeks turning pink, her teeth nibbling her bottom lip. "Good thing I'm here, then."

"Good thing." He shoved his hands into the pockets of his jeans, glancing at his bare feet.

She closed the laptop, carefully, and moved it to the nightstand before patting the bedspread in invitation.

He pushed the door closed and made it two steps into the room before she reached for the rubber band and pulled her hair free.

"You don't have to do that," he said, moving to the bed and stretching out beside where she sat.

"Do what?" She tossed the band on top of her laptop and snuggled in to his chest.

He relaxed immediately. Breathing around Rachel just came easier. Having her against him like this made him feel like he hadn't been breathing and never even realized it. Then suddenly she was there, and the world was full of oxygen.

"The hair thing. I like it up." He shuffled his hands through the strands, piling it on the crown of her skull like she'd had it with the band.

The kiss he pressed to her mouth didn't go as planned when she frowned against his lips.

He didn't like it when she frowned in bed. Didn't particularly care for it when he frowned in bed, either.

"Okay." She turned from him and reached mechanically across the mattress toward the nightstand until her fingertips grazed the hair tie. "I can put it back in."

He caught her, pulling her back in to him so the front of her meshed with the front of him. "I like it down, too."

That got him a smile and a press of her lips against his. "Oh."

"I like it both ways. You don't have to change it when I'm around." His lips were barely away from hers, sharing the same air, firing all his senses, making him want to sink himself in all that she was and escape.

Unfortunately, it was the middle of the day and she had work, and he had a call with distribution, and if they weren't careful, someone would come knocking at the door.

"Wanna make out?" he asked instead of what he really wanted to do.

"The kids with Dane?" she asked but didn't wait for his response before running her hands up the edge of the bottom of his tee. Her palms against his abs lit a trail of fire along his skin that was all Rachel.

"Yeah." He brushed the tip of his nose against hers. "We're alone."

"Then by all means, yes. Making out is good. Add some groping too, if you want." The last word barely passed her lips before he rolled her to her back and reached up her top, under her bra, to toy with her nipples as his mouth melded with hers.

He broke the kiss only long enough to pull his shirt over his head and toss it to the chair beside the bed.

"Good call, fewer clothes." Rachel laughed against his mouth as she rolled him to his back, straddling him.

There was no doubt about it, he was falling tart over toaster for Rachel.

"Rach." Travis held her face as she continued to kiss the hell out of him.

The things this girl did with her mouth couldn't possibly be legal. Her T-shirt stretched across her breasts, her nipples pebbled into tight buds, he was hard, and she was riding him over his jeans. This was so much more than a make-out session.

"We aren't good at the just-kissing thing, are we?" she asked.

He chuckled. "It's probably a good thing to know."

"Tonight, I expect you to follow through with the promises your body is making to me right now." She laughed as their mouths melded and the center of her heat rubbed against his length. She groaned as he pressed his hips up and into the warmth between her thighs.

The barrier of their clothing barely registered, and the moan that filled the space between them could've been either of theirs. He had no idea if it was him who was making the noises. It didn't really matter. What did matter was that he was going to end up finishing in his pants, and wouldn't that just be embarrassing?

"Mom," Kellan called from the hallway, the pounding of

his footsteps getting closer to her door. "Brady took Mr. Pretzel and won't give him back."

Once, Travis had taken the twins to the water park and there was this huge bucket of cold water that would drench anyone standing in the wrong spot. That's exactly how his body reacted right then. Like fifty gallons of cold water had been tossed over them on the bed.

Travis was a little worried that Rachel might pass out, because suddenly she was holding her breath, not moving, and her eyes had gone wide.

Rachel scrambled off the top of him, her eyes still huge, round orbs. She threw his shirt at him.

"You locked it, right?" Even as she asked, she headed toward the thick wood as he dealt with his own thick wood. He rearranged his pants and grappled with his T-shirt.

"I locked it," he assured.

Yes, he had. He distinctly remembered pressing the lock.

Rachel's mouth had the appearance of a thoroughly kissed woman, her lipstick smeared over her lips and up onto her cheek. "You run to the bathroom, wait there. I'll open the door once you're—"

The door swung open. Sonofa—

Kellan barreled through the entry, skidding to a stop nearly comically. "Uncle Trav, what're you doing in here? Why's your shirt off?"

Travis gripped his T-shirt against his naked torso, wishing he could become one with the mattress.

"And what happened to your face?" Kellan asked, moving his gaze from his uncle to his mother, then back again.

Kellan settled his gaze on his uncle sitting on his mom's bed with a T-shirt gripped to his chest, a set of blue balls, and apparently his mother's lipstick smeared all over his mug.

His heart tripped over itself as he grasped for ideas on how to play this. There could be no collateral damage for Rachel. Unfortunately, the commands from his brain weren't working, because though he opened his mouth, no sound came out.

"Uncle Travis was helping me look for my toothbrush," Rachel said quickly. She raised her arms and then dropped them to her sides. "But we found it. Yay."

"Brady stole Mr. Pretzel. He won't tell me where he hid him." Kellan was on a rant and clearly wasn't too concerned about the current state of his mother, his uncle, and their... toothbrush situation. "I know it was him because I left Mr. Pretzel under my pillow and only Brady knows where I keep him."

Rachel turned her rabid gaze to Travis, mouthing, *Help.*

Travis pointed to her lips.

She must've understood what he meant because she was swiping around her mouth with her fingertips. "Tell you what? I'll go put my toothbrush away. Then Uncle Trav and I will come help with the Mr. Pretzel search."

"Hurry." Kellan's shoulders slumped. Travis could relate to that feeling.

Rachel shooed her son out of the room with the ease and practice of someone who had done it a thousand times before.

As soon as he was gone, she clicked the lock on the door.

"You said you locked it." She turned a fiery gaze on Travis. This time it had nothing to do with the fire from their chemistry experiments.

No, she looked like a dragon about to breathe fire. To be honest, she scared the piss out of him with the way her skin flushed.

"I did." He scrambled to his feet and pulled on his shirt. "I guess I accidentally unlocked it, too."

"Accidentally?" she said with a hiss. "Do you know what happens when there are accidents?"

Um...the kid walks in on his mom in an awkward position with his uncle?

"There cannot be accidents." As quickly as it started, the

fire banked, and she fell against the wall, her back to the plaster.

"Rach?" Dane knocked. "Have you seen Mr. Pretzel?"

"No," she called back. "Give me a minute to finish changing. I'll be right there."

"Okay," Dane replied before his footfalls disappeared down the hallway.

Travis moved toward Rachel, hands up like he was prepared to be arrested. "Scale of one to ten, how pissed are you right now?"

She rubbed her forehead. "That depends," she said, and suddenly she was smiling. "Are you going to help me find my toothbrush again later?"

"Tonight." He let out a holy-fuck-thank-God-that's-over breath. Then he ran his hands up and over her shoulders. "After everyone is in bed and I've installed a second lock on your door, I will help you find *all* the toothbrushes."

That got him a smile.

"Then I'm not mad." She wiped around the edges of his mouth with her thumbs. "There's makeup remover in my bathroom. You should probably use that—it's in the pink bottle."

"Will do."

"And…uh…wait five minutes after I leave…so…"

She didn't finish the thought—*so we don't get caught together*. She didn't have to.

He understood why they needed to be secretive, for now. He didn't like it. Didn't like the way it made his back teeth set on edge or his limbs itch, but he understood.

Standing on her tiptoes, she pressed a breath of a kiss against his lips. "When you're done here, we'll probably need your help to find Mr. Pretzel."

"It won't be as fun as the toothbrush hunt, but you'll be there, so I'll deal," he murmured against her mouth.

She smiled, but the effect of it didn't quite meet her eyes.

Yeah, they'd need to figure out how to handle this thing between them before they had a real accident. The kind of accident they couldn't cover with a toothbrush and Mr. Pretzel.

The problem was, he wasn't sure how they could approach the situation reveal without facing the damage of a fallout.

Deep down in his gut, he worried it would affect everyone.

But it'd be Rachel who suffered most.

CHAPTER 23

"Brady." Rachel was only yay-far from losing her shit. "Where did you put Mr. Pretzel?"

"He ate my gummy bears." Brady shoved his index finger toward his brother.

This was the response Brady was giving to everything.

"We don't point like that." Rachel glanced to Dane and Travis, who were tearing apart the closet in search of the missing stuffed pretzel toy. "It's rude."

Apparently, if Rachel was following the train of activities correctly, Kellan had eaten into Brady's special stash of gummy bears. The ones Rachel didn't know existed that someone had bought in Confluence.

In retaliation, Brady had held Mr. Pretzel hostage in an unknown location until Kellan replaced the candy or came up with a suitable alternative.

So far, none of Kellan's suggested resolutions had been acceptable to Brady and his demands.

"Fine. How about you can have all my underwear, you

jerk," Kellan said this with not an ounce of concern that his mother was standing right there.

Rachel did not have time for this. Or patience.

She opened her mouth to explain to Kellan the consequences for name-calling—no electronics for the rest of the day—when there was a throat clearing from the doorway.

"There are my boys," a deep male voice said.

Gavin?

Rachel turned and, sure enough, Gavin was standing, arms wide, waiting for one of his boys to run in for a hug.

Neither of them did as he expected, seeing as they were currently in a standoff.

No, they did what *Rachel* expected. They took their argument to the new authority figure in the room.

"He stole Mr. Pretzel." Kellan ran to Gavin, but not like he clearly had hoped. There was no hug, no welcome, just more finger pointing.

"He. Ate. My. Gummy. Bears." Brady clenched and unclenched his fists.

On any other kid, it would've been cute because it wouldn't have been Rachel's issue to deal with. As it was, the clenching and unclenching was not cute. Not at all.

"They. Were. Left. Out." Kellan went into a showdown with his brother.

Shit. Shit. Shit.

"Boys." Rachel strode to them. "Separate."

Kellan had a look in his eye. She knew that look. It came right before he got physical with his brother.

"What's going on?" another voice asked from behind Gavin. Female. Damn.

Yes, that would be Dakota and her impeccable timing.

"I'm not sure," Gavin said with a misplaced chuckle. "Sounds like there's a problem with gummy bears."

Kellan took that moment to shove Brady right into the wall.

Brady shoved him back, harder. Rachel gave a heavy sigh. "Stop it!" she said. "Both of you."

They did not stop it. Instead, they continued back and forth three or four times before Rachel finally dove between the two of them. Gavin stood at the door with his mouth open like he was trying to catch flies.

"Give me my gummy bears back, and I'll give you your pretzel." Brady's little body heaved with self-righteous indignation while Rachel played bouncer, keeping them apart.

Gavin finally broke free of his trance and scooped Brady back. Dane took Kellan.

This, this right here? This was why twins were hard on a single mom. Sometimes you needed two full adults—or more—to deal with the conflict.

Kellan got a look in his eye. Some might call it a gleam, but whatever it was, Rachel didn't like it.

Yes, she clocked the exact moment that Kellan had the idea.

The idea that he could throw up the gummy bears to instigate the return of the pretzel. She couldn't say exactly how she knew this was his intention, just that every hair on her body was standing on end with the way Kellan looked at his brother. And the only thing that could make the night worse?

Vomit.

"Don't you do it," she said, big breaths heaving from her chest now. "Do not throw up those gummy bears." She was pointing, even though she'd just told her other son not to do it.

Meanwhile, Kellan was already lifting his index finger to his mouth in what felt like a slow-motion drama.

"If you throw them up on purpose, there will be no more swimming for the rest of the summer." Rachel managed to grab hold of Kellan's wrist before he made it to his mouth.

Gavin apparently took issue with her punishment. "Rach, we just got here; that's not really fair to Dakota and me—"

"Rach?" Travis cleared his throat.

She ignored him because she had two boys who needed a reminder that she was in charge. And, apparently, their father needed a not-so-subtle reminder that he needed to back her up. Even when it "wasn't fair to him."

"No electronics for the rest of the week." She started counting out their punishment on her fingers.

None of them decried the unfairness of the punishment. Probably because her tone was the one that she used only when she was really serious.

"Early bedtime tonight. And if Mr. Pretzel is not returned in the next thirty seconds, I'm going to follow through on the no-swimming rule. You can watch your dad and Dakota swim, but none of your body parts will touch the lake again for the entirety of the summer. You can sit here at the house and…color…or something."

Dammit. She'd been on a great roll until it fizzled out at the end.

Travis slipped Mr. Pretzel into her counting hand. "I found him."

Well, that put a damper on the mad she'd been nursing.

"Where?" She gripped the stuffed pretzel in her fist.

"In the bathroom. Under the towels," Travis said, tilting his head toward the room in question.

He also held out an oversize bag of gummy bears that was still decently full and two boxes of s'mores-flavored toaster tarts. "These were with the pretzel."

Dane loosened his grip on Kellan, his expression one of pure compassion. "Sorry, Rach. I think the gummy bears came from our last trip to town. I didn't realize that's what he bought, or I'd have given you a heads-up."

"Okay, well." She blew out a breath. "Crisis averted, I guess."

She handed the pretzel to Kellan.

"I'm keeping these." This she said to Brady.

"That's not fair." Brady seethed.

"We'll discuss their return after we've all had time to cool off."

"Rach." Gavin stepped toward her. "Why don't I take the boys for a bit? You really look like you need a break."

"Really, Gavin?" She did. But she did not need Gavin pointing out that she needed a break. "Do I?"

He took a step back.

She turned her full attention to him. "*You* didn't mention you were coming."

They'd spoken, oh, only twelve hours ago, and he'd said nothing, nada.

"Gavin has news," Dakota said, her eyes sparkling with excitement. "We both do."

"What kind of news?" Travis asked.

"News I need to discuss with Rachel." Gavin didn't even look at his brother.

"What kind of news?" Rachel asked, since Gavin wasn't talking to Travis, apparently.

"Things…there are some things I need to talk to you about." Gavin had the look that he'd had when he told her that he was proposing to Dakota. The same one that Kellan had had when he'd gotten the idea to throw up gummy bears. The one that made the little hairs on the back of her neck tingle.

Rachel's cell buzzed in her pocket. She pulled it out and checked the caller ID, then she immediately slid her thumb across the screen to turn it on. "Cassie, hi, what's up?"

She hurried through the call as best she could, leaving the boys with Gavin and their uncles while she returned to her bedroom to grab her laptop and send out an emergency newsletter for Cassie.

When she pulled open the door to her bedroom, it wasn't Travis pacing the hallway; it was Gavin.

"Hi." She shoved her hands into her back pockets, then

realized that it might make her breasts stick out, so she dropped her arms. "Have you been waiting for me this whole time?"

He shook his head. "Got here a minute ago. Was just rehearsing a little before I knocked."

Rehearsing was not reassuring. She forced herself not to assume anything about what he wanted to say. They'd always been sensible when it came to the boys. There was no reason to think that would change now.

"What's up?"

"Can I come in?" He nodded to her bedroom.

Now it was her turn to shake her head. "Let's go to the study. That's where I usually work anyway."

He gave a subtle nod. "Works for me."

She followed him to the study, tracking the lope of his stride. Something was bothering him. Her mind started cataloging the things he could be upset about. From Dakota being pregnant to him asking her to head back to Denver, since they were here now, none of them was that big of a deal. It'd stink if she had to go back to Denver without Travis, but it wasn't the end of the world. She'd see him when he got back.

"You might as well just spill whatever it is you need to say." She scrubbed at her cheeks with her palms once they were inside.

He took a deep breath. She raised her eyebrows.

He gulped and finally said, "I'm moving to Boston."

CHAPTER 24

RACHEL

Gavin was moving? *Gavin was* moving?

Whatever she thought could've happened after his appearance didn't hold half a candle to this.

Boston was much, much worse than anything she could've cooked up with her imagination.

So much worse. The worst.

Moving across the country meant rehashing custody agreements, child support, explanations to the boys.

Rachel couldn't seem to get her limbs to move.

"What?" Rachel finally asked. "What's in Boston?"

"Dakota."

"Dakota?" Now she was just repeating him, and that was ridiculous. "Dakota lives in Denver."

"She's opening a gallery in Boston."

Why Boston? Couldn't she get animal inspiration anywhere? And Rachel happened to know for certain that there were plenty of bathtubs to use for inspiration in Colorado. Animals, too. Loads of animals *and* bathtubs. Dakota didn't need Boston when she could have the Rockies.

"But your family is in Denver. The boys are in Denver," Rachel said, instead of the other stuff that she was thinking but was best left unsaid.

Thank goodness she hadn't dropped her filter in the midst of this ridiculousness.

Yes, his family was the obvious reason he should stay, but it also seemed that in this case, the obvious was the most pertinent.

"How do you feel about bringing them to Boston?" Gavin asked, glancing up at her with Brady's same piercing eyes full of hope.

"For a visit?" It would totally wreck her schedule, honestly. Even if Travis agreed to fly them out in the company plane.

Wait.

That look on Gavin's face. Shit.

He didn't mean a visit.

"You don't mean for a visit," she clarified, sitting on the leather sofa because her legs didn't seem to be able to hold her up anymore.

Her face had turned numb.

Damn. Dammit. No, he didn't mean for a visit.

She gripped the edges of the cushion. "I feel like you've lost your mind to even ask me that."

"Okay." He ran his hands through his hair. "This is okay. We'll just have to adjust our schedule with them. They can fly out to Boston a few times a year." His voice got pitchy.

She got splotchy when she got upset. His voice got pitchy.

"Your job is in Denver." Rachel could not believe this was happening. He couldn't be serious, asking her to uproot their kids to move across the country.

He paced. Again. "I can work virtually, like you do."

Working virtually was not a walk to the lake. It was a full-time, all-the-time exhaustion fest that drained a person. It would be extra hard for him, given he was in charge of the actual staff in the Denver office. Of course, it was possible.

Still…

"Don't do this to the boys," Rachel whispered. *Don't take away their dad, too.*

She could be a lot of things for her kids, but she was beginning to think she couldn't be everything.

"Rach…" He studied his feet. "We'll figure this out. We always figure this stuff out. This time, it's no different."

"Is this really what you want?" Rachel asked. "You want to upend our boys? Even if it's just you who moves to Boston, their whole lives change."

"No." He shook his head. "It's not what I want."

"Then why are you even considering it?"

"Because if I don't go with Dakota"—he stood, paced to the window, then back again—"she's going without me."

That didn't sound like an excellent start to their soon-to-be marriage. Not that Rachel was the expert on that kind of thing.

Rachel's cell rang. She checked the caller ID. Cassie. Gah.

She clicked it off and shoved it in her pocket.

"Do you need to get that?" Gavin gave a pointed glance at the pocket where she'd shoved the phone.

She *did* need to get it, but for once she didn't have to question her priorities. "This is more important."

"Rach." Gavin sat next to her on the sofa. "I have to figure this out because it's my issue to sort. But we've always worked together when it comes to the kids. I don't want that to end."

"Do you love Dakota? Do you love her enough to see your kids only a few times a year?" she asked.

"Honestly?"

"I think we're being honest here, aren't we?"

"No." He dropped his face to his palms. "I don't love her like that. But it's what I've got."

The silence that descended wasn't awkward, but it was heavy. She had the intense urge to reach out and hold his hand, but it wasn't her place.

The deep inhale that came from the other side of the room clearly shocked both of them, given the way both of their heads twisted in that direction.

"I guess it's a good thing we discover this now, before the exchange of vows," Dakota said.

Rachel rolled her lips between her teeth and stared at Dakota standing at the entrance to the room.

Huh. Dakota's neck did the same splotchy thing Rachel's did when she got upset.

Gavin stood, wiped his palms on his slacks, and with a nod to Rachel, he moved to his next future-ex.

And Rachel? Rachel wasn't quite sure what to do with herself.

So she went to search for Travis.

She didn't really know why she needed to find him, but it felt important. Important to her.

* * *

TRAVIS

Dakota was pissed. Really, really pissed.

The family lake house had, apparently, totally wrecked her mellow. What with all the yelling going on behind the door of the study.

Dakota was yelling. Gavin was not. Gavin was, surprisingly, calm and doing his best to utilize reason. Travis never thought he'd live to see the day that *Gavin* was the reasonable one in a relationship. Turned out anything could happen at Twin Lakes.

"You think they're okay?" Rachel asked. She wasn't

talking to anyone in particular. Because they were all standing outside the door.

Well, technically it was the living area right off the study. Even Mom and Dad were there. They kept giving each other looks that communicated a lot more than words. And Mama kept side-eying Rachel like this was just the opportunity she'd been waiting for to nudge Rachel back into Gavin's arms.

Travis did not fucking think so.

Dakota was really on a roll, and this was the kind of thing the boys probably didn't need to hear when it came to their dad.

"I don't think they're okay," Dane said, shooing the boys toward the kitchen when they came out after a particularly loud Dakota f-bomb.

Travis didn't think they were okay, either. This was definitely mid-relationship implosion magnitude.

"I think we should mind our own business," he said, turning to follow Dane, the boys, and the dogs, who were always ready and willing to go into the kitchen because that's where the good stuff happened for them.

"Maybe I should go in. See if I can defuse things." Rachel had her arms crossed at her chest again. Travis felt the pull to go to her, help hold her up, so she didn't feel like she had to hold the world up herself.

"I think the one thing that could make this relationship ending worse is the ex-wife stepping in," Travis said. He tilted his head toward the kitchen.

"Then *I* should go in." Evelyn started toward the door.

Right, so Rachel was probably *not* the worst thing to add to the recipe of their relationship destruction.

Bob shook his head. "No, sweets. Let them figure it out."

Instead of going to the kitchen, Rachel headed toward her bedroom.

Travis gave her a few minutes, made an appearance in the kitchen, and then followed her.

He found her sitting on her bed, laptop in front of her, clicking away.

"You're exhausted," he said. She was gorgeous, of course, but the smudges under her eyes were becoming more and more prominent.

Also, she looked like she was ready to cry.

"Do you want to talk about it?" He stepped toward her, carefully, because she looked easily spooked at the moment. She shook her head, a little too quickly, a little too jerky.

"Is this about Gavin? Did he say somethin' to you?" Because if he did, Travis would need to have more than a word.

"No, it's Cassie. She called when Gavin and I were talking. I didn't pick up. So she sent me an email detailing her concerns about my availability." Rachel gulped, pasting on a smile. "I'm so tired of this, Trav. So freaking tired."

Fucking hell. This Cassie was a piece of work. "It's fine, though. I'll fix it. Somehow."

"You get to have a life, too." He continued moving toward her, keeping his voice even. "And you get to spend time with the boys, with me, with whoever you want."

She nodded.

"That's why I wrote this." She turned the laptop toward him.

"I wrote this after we got back from dancing the other night. But I wasn't sure if I should send it," she continued. "I figured if I doubled down on my dedication, I wouldn't have to."

Rachel had drafted an email laying out her office hours, the time required to respond to requests, and guidelines on the best ways to communicate.

It included scheduling links, bullet points, and an abundance of organization. Not that he'd expect anything less from her.

"I couldn't bring myself to send it." She turned the laptop back to herself and scrunched her forehead while she reread the message.

The message, for the record, was perfect. Firm, but not terse.

"Limits don't mean you're weak." He traced his fingertip down her forehead, tucking a lock of hair behind her ear. She hadn't bothered taking out the knot she'd put it in when he came into the room. "They actually mean you're strong enough to recognize the importance of the other things in your life." He nodded to her screen with the blinking cursor. "This lays out the terms of the relationship. There's nothing wrong with that. Isn't this what we did that night? Doesn't make us weak."

"I don't want to tick her off." Rachel squinted at the screen and then scowled at it.

"Isn't *she* ticking *you* off?" Travis asked, because Cassie sure ticked him off on the regular.

Rachel nodded. "I should send this to everyone I work with."

She inhaled. Exhaled. Glanced to him. Worried her top lip with her teeth.

Her finger hovered over the button.

He wanted to make this easier for her, but there was nothing he could do except stand there like a doofus with a stone in his stomach, waiting for her to make the call.

She pressed the button and closed her eyes.

"Do you want to take a minute and send it to everyone. Or do you want to do that later?"

"Now." She clicked through her screen. "I should just do it all now."

He sat on the bed beside her, running his palm up and down her back while she finished clicking send.

"There," she said.

"There," he echoed.

She stared at her screen, unmoving. He continued what he hoped were reassuring brushes over her back. "The world didn't end."

The edges of her lips twitched. "It didn't."

He pressed a light kiss against her temple. "How do you feel?"

"Scared." She adjusted how she sat on the bed, so their mouths were close. "But I had to do it."

He deleted the space between their lips, brushing his lightly against hers.

The commotion of Dakota and Gavin—mostly Dakota, since Gavin wasn't fully participating in the scream fest—passing in front of the open bedroom door in the hallway had Travis pulling away.

Then the front door slammed.

"I think she left." Rachel's wide eyes met Travis's. "Where are the boys?"

"Kitchen with Dane, last I checked. Mama was showing them how to crumble cinnamon sugar toaster tarts over ice cream for a special topping."

"Great." Rachel rubbed her forehead. "Gummy bears *and* cinnamon."

The motion made his stomach cramp. He didn't want this for Rachel. She deserved easy for a while.

"Maybe I can drag them out with me for a run?" Travis asked. "Give them a way to burn off all the sweets?"

Rachel's email chimed, and Travis's gut turned over on itself again. Rachel seemed to feel the same way, because her skin had gone chalky.

"It's from James," she said. "He said he understands the changes and is happy I'm working with him."

"Who's James?" Travis asked.

He'd heard all about the guys in Australia, and Cassie, but she'd never mentioned James.

"James makes these sandal things. They're pretty neat. We started working together recently, and we have a pretty set schedule. He doesn't veer from it very often."

"Does he pay on time?"

"So far. He's got it automated with his bank."

"So he's an A-list client."

She laughed. "I guess so. That's one way to think of it."

"If you had to assign a designation to Cassie and the other guys, what would you give them?"

"The guys get a solid C. But we're still getting used to understanding how we can work together."

"Cassie?" he asked.

Rachel picked at the bedspread. "I don't even think she'd get a letter."

She followed this with a light chuckle, but it was pretty clear she meant it.

Her email dinged again.

"So far you're one for three; let's see who that is," Travis said, squeezing her hand.

Rachel sucked in a breath. "Shit."

He glanced at the screen, and it was an email from Cassie dissolving the contract with Rachel's company.

Yes, that really made Travis's gut turn over. Rachel slumped a little.

"No matter what, you're going to be okay."

She nodded, but didn't really seem to believe it.

Another email chime, and this time he had to stand because the unknown was totally making his stomach cramp.

"The other guys want to have a meeting tomorrow to 'discuss the nature of our future projects.'" She read aloud from their email.

"Rach." Travis shoved his hands in his pockets. "You did the right thing here."

"That leaves me just the one." Her expression seemed to freeze.

"You don't know that." Travis started to step toward her—

"Rachel?" his mother called from down the hall.

Rachel looked at Travis, then at the open door. It wasn't like they were doing anything inappropriate.

Rachel tilted her head toward the bathroom, her expression earnest.

Today was probably not the day to fight that battle. Travis started toward the bathroom to hang out until his mother skedaddled.

"Trav." His name on Rachel's lips stopped him cold.

He turned. His mother stood in the doorway. And the Puffle Yum Momster—as Rachel called her—looked like she was ready to eat her young.

That would be him.

CHAPTER 25

RACHEL

"Travis, what are you doing here?" Evelyn asked innocently, like she didn't know.

Rachel knew her well enough to know that after the momentary shock dissolved, she knew. Yes, the look on her face, that glint in her eye—Evelyn knew. She knew exactly what she'd just walked in on.

"Are you two?" She waved a finger between them.

Travis shook his head. "Don't get involved in things that don't involve you."

Rachel had just witnessed the start of the implosion of her company, Gavin may or may not be moving to Boston, the boys were fighting like they hadn't in forever, and the only thing in her life that felt remotely like a rock was Travis. And that was about to be snatched away.

"What on earth do you think this will lead to?" Evelyn's expression steeled. "Doesn't this just take the tart?"

Rachel refused to feel ashamed over her feelings for Travis. Or setting boundaries with her clients. Or any of the other things she did because, dammit, she got to be happy, too.

"Even my cat can't believe you're considering this," Evelyn said on a huff.

Oh, well, goodness, if it was the cat struggling with Rachel and Travis's relationship, then they should absolutely dissolve it immediately. The difference was that this relationship was real where the cat was…not.

Perhaps the pretend cat might need real executive assistance. *Oh God. Is this what my life has come to? These kinds of thoughts?*

The room seemed to get too hot. Her skin too itchy.

"Mama." Travis strode toward Rachel. "Rachel's having a pretty rough day. Lay off a little?"

"I have no idea what you're talking about," Evelyn said. If Rachel didn't know the Puffle Yum Monster and her innate ability to get whatever she wanted, she probably would've bought that line from her. As it was? She did not.

"I'm just looking for my son and the mother of my grand-children so they can come enjoy ice cream with the rest of us." Evelyn waved a hand between them. "But I find this instead."

"What exactly did you find, Mama?" Travis asked. "Because all I see is Rachel having a rough day, me talking to her, and you barging in and yapping about your cat."

"You two are in a *bedroom*." Evelyn glanced very pointedly toward the bed. "Together. Alone."

"Believe it or not, Mama, I don't just drop my pants every time I enter a bedroom with a beautiful woman," Travis said.

They continued volleying back and forth, but the room was getting too small, and Rachel couldn't catch her breath. She evacuated to get her boys, so she could take them for a long, long walk and try to figure out what came next. How, without Cassie, she was going to make ends meet next month. And the month after.

Catching her breath got harder as she hurried down the

hall and into the kitchen. She found Kellan, Brady, Bob, Dane, and Gavin all indulging in Evelyn's homemade cinnamon toaster tarts and ice cream.

"Meemaw says cinnamon is the next *it* flavor," Brady said with his mouth half full. "I don't know what that means, but it's yummy."

"Boys." She kissed them both on the tops of their heads. "I was thinking we might take a walk. What do you say?"

"My tummy doesn't feel good." Kellan started to push his bowl away. The residual bit of melted sugared cream and mushy toaster tart sloshed in the bottom like a reminder of Rachel's present life circumstances.

Evelyn knew.

Rachel had lost any semblance of control of the situation. What was going on was definitely not perfection.

"Well, sweetie, you know that when you eat gummy bears, and ice cream, and pastry, it's probably not going to feel too good on your tummy." Rachel rubbed his shoulders. "Let's go walk it off."

Kellan apparently changed his mind about the tummy ache because he pulled the bowl toward him again. Then he dove right back in like he was in a food-eating competition. Evelyn's voice slid down through the door to the kitchen.

"I'm just asking why you two couldn't talk in the living room. Why the bedroom? This is not a hard question to answer."

"Mama, stop." Travis's words were curt.

"Do you not understand what is inappropriate and what is not?" Evelyn asked, emerging from the hallway and glancing around the kitchen. "How are we all doing?"

"Dakota left." Gavin had shoved his sleeves up to his elbows and continued to drown his sorrows in sugar.

"She left the ring, too," Dane added, also diving into his ice cream.

"We'll look for it tomorrow." Gavin spoke to the bowl, not looking up.

Dane lifted a shoulder. "She tossed it in the lawn over by the stairs."

Rachel made a mental note not to allow the dogs over there when they took their middle of the night bathroom break. Also, throwing the ring in the lawn was a tad bit cliché. If Dakota was going to throw a drama, Rachel expected a little better. Go all in and get creative.

Not that she'd ever thrown a drama. But she'd thought about it lots of times.

Evelyn was whispering to Bob about what she'd discovered in Rachel's bedroom. Rachel's chest was feeling tighter and tighter by the moment.

"Uncle Trav, did my mom lose her toothbrush again?" Kellan asked.

Rachel's tongue turned to ash, and suddenly toaster tart ice cream seemed like an excellent idea. Maybe she'd even have some cake. And ask Travis to make her a pitcher of margaritas for her and Evelyn's cat to share.

"Her toothbrush?" Dane asked, raising his eyebrows in the general direction of Travis.

"Yeah." Kellan continued through his stomachache to dive back into the remnants of his not-so-much dinner. "I don't know why he had to take his shirt off to find her toothbrush." He lifted his little eight-year-old shoulder in a hell of a shrug.

"He what?" Evelyn practically shrieked.

Okay, so it wasn't really a full shriek. It was more of a sound of surprise with a dash of high anxiety.

"Oh dear lord," Rachel said under her breath. She rubbed at her skull, not looking at anyone.

"Uh," Dane said, clearly unsure how to continue. Which was apt, because she had no idea, either.

"Mama," Travis said, stepping toward his mother, who was taking a play out of Gavin's book and opening her mouth, closing it, then opening it again like she was trying to catch any variety of flying insects.

"In my house," she said finally.

"It is not what you think." Rachel, still not looking up, gripped the back of Kellan's chair until her knuckles turned white.

"I *think* you two have been carrying on right under my nose this entire time." Evelyn shoved her hands on her hips, staring Rachel down.

"Well, then, I guess it's exactly what you think," Travis said.

Now it was Rachel's turn to shove her hands onto her hips. "Trav…"

"What's carrying on?" Brady asked.

"It's like what Uncle Dane did with that lady at the park that one time." Kellan was thinking so hard he was going to break his brain. "Back behind the dugout."

"This is not about me." Dane held up both hands. "I'm just here because Dakota took the car, so I don't have a way to leave."

"Rachel?" Gavin asked, his eyebrows falling. "Since when do you call him Trav?"

Okay, so Gavin got a little leeway, since he'd been involved in his own drama. But Rachel's life was currently imploding, just like his relationship with Dakota. So *she* also deserved a little leeway.

"Since we became a couple," Rachel said to the back of Kellan's chair.

The room went silent. A heavy, wet blanket with weight even Dakota's dramatic departure couldn't touch.

Even both boys were quiet, and that never happened.

"Boys," Rachel said. "Why don't you head outside and play?"

"They are fine. They need to hear this, too." Evelyn stuck her nosey nose right where it didn't belong. "They're old enough to understand that their uncle Travis and their mother are an *item*."

"Like Dad and Dakota?" Brady asked.

Well, without the whole door slamming and the throwing of the ring.

"Both of you, go outside and play." Rachel grabbed the bowls from the table and went to rinse them in the sink.

"C'mon boys, this is a grown-up talk." Gavin gave Rachel a look with a subtle head bob. He had her back on this.

She wasn't quite sure how to feel about that. Mostly good. Unexpected. But good.

Thankfully, both boys seemed to get the vibe in the room and headed outside. The soles of her feet itched to follow them. Instead, she went back to cleaning the dishes.

"I care about her," Travis announced. "A lot."

Rachel stopped rinsing Brady's bowl, seemed to stop functioning altogether. She glanced up at Travis. He was staring at her intently.

He cared about her, and he wasn't afraid to say it in front of everyone.

She gulped. The water poured over her hands, over the now-empty bowl, to swirl down the drain.

"I'm not entirely sure how she feels about me, but I want to make it clear that I care deeply for her." Travis continued his announcement like it wasn't a big deal.

It was, in fact, a big deal. Huge, even.

"No." Evelyn's word was curt, to the point. "This is unacceptable."

"Mama," Gavin said, setting his bowl aside. "Let's hear them out."

Rachel turned to look at Gavin, and his warm brown eyes rested on her. They weren't angry. She wasn't quite sure what they were, but they weren't upset.

"If they want to talk about it," he continued.

Rachel didn't. She didn't want to talk about it with Evelyn, etc.

Not until she talked about it with Travis. They should've formed a plan when he'd suggested it. Then things wouldn't have gone wildly off script.

"What will the boys call you now, Travis?" Evelyn was all piss and vinegar and southern sour. "Unca-Daddy? Unca-Step?"

"Mama." Gavin set his bowl aside and stepped forward. "This is uncalled for."

"What is uncalled for is your brother and your Rachel—"

"She's not my Rachel." Gavin stared down Evelyn in a way that Rachel had never seen before. Stared her down and stood right up to her.

"I'm no one's Rachel," Rachel said. "I'm *my* Rachel. I'm the mother of Brady and Kellan. And Travis and I are a couple, and we're figuring things out, and we were waiting to announce it because we knew this, this right here, is what would happen. You'd lose your mind. It'd drip into the boys' lives, and people would get hurt."

"Mom," Brady squealed from outside. He ran straight to the door of the kitchen that led to the back patio. "Kellan's sick."

Rachel quickly dried her hands and hurried toward the door.

"He threw up all over," Brady went on. "It's like he ate gummy bear ice cream and it exploded everywhere." He made dramatic hand motions to illustrate the point.

Wonderful. Ridiculous Evelyn and her toaster tarts, and ridiculous Gavin and his breakup drama, and her ridiculous clients with their demands—

All of a sudden, Brady's face turned the funky shade of green it always turned right before…

"No, no, no," Rachel said under her breath.

She reached for the trash basket kept under the sink.

Then she lunged toward Brady.

No one else moved, but Dane asked, "Is he going to—"

That's when it happened. Brady followed in Kellan's footsteps and, because he was Brady, his lack of aim was impressive when it came to all bodily fluids.

He did not hit the trash can. He did hit the floor. Also, Gavin's shoes.

Mostly, Rachel caught the mess in her hand. She gritted her teeth.

But she did not break.

CHAPTER 26

RACHEL

Rachel's life was the perfect symphony of defective and she was the conductor. Yes, someone had seriously tossed handfuls of dysfunction glitter all over her, and that shit got in everything. It was, apparently, also impossible to get out.

All the Franks—including Evelyn and Bob—had come down with whatever virus had joined them on their vacation. Rachel had been up all night taking care of them, because of her titanium stomach and an immune system not fueled by toaster tarts.

After Brady's impressive demonstration in the kitchen, they'd all fallen like dominoes.

Click. Click. Click.

One Frank after another.

Rachel had started a log for each of them to document their medication usage, temperature, and any other pertinent information. Given that she hadn't slept all night, she'd seriously started to worry she'd forget who was who. Writing everything down became extra important.

She sent the dogs to stay in her bedroom so they wouldn't get in the way. Because when it all went down, they *seriously* got in the way.

Like, a lot.

"Rach?" Gavin rolled over on the leather sofa where she'd set up his triage station. That's what she called it in her mind, anyway. It sounded more impressive than "his spot on the sofa."

She'd just checked his temperature—it was finally under a hundred. She was pretty sure he'd be holding down some fluids soon.

It'd hit him last, but it'd hit him hard when he finally went under.

"What's up?" She set a cup of ice chips beside him on the coffee table.

Gavin started to sit. "I can take over."

Rachel pushed him back down. "I'm good for a while longer. Rest. Then I'll catch a nap. The worst seems to be over."

Well, for most everyone.

Travis's triage station was still in the bathroom. She'd set him up with a pillow on the floor and a couple of blankets.

Mostly, he wanted to be left alone. She knew this because he requested that exact thing. She still required temperature checks so she could be sure he wasn't going in the wrong direction.

Evelyn and Bob had eventually moved back to their bedroom, but Evelyn had a bell to ring for Rachel.

The bell thing was super lovely. Insert all the sarcasm.

"Ask Mom," Kellan said with a huff to something Rachel hadn't caught and probably didn't want to know. "I gave back the gummy bears. You can go get them out of the trash whenever you want."

"No, you may not," Rachel said, tucking their blankets back around them. She positioned the two of them on the sofa across from Gavin. Brady at one end, Kellan at the other.

The boys, because they were kids, were bouncing back quicker than the rest.

Having everyone in the same room was easier for her to manage. She'd even set up the other couch for Travis, when he decided to get up off the floor and join them.

He wasn't going to his bedroom because she was not giving him a bell. One bell per virus was plenty.

Also, when this was all over, Rachel was not allowing gummy bears ever, ever again. The boys could have them when they were old enough to vote. Not a second before.

Yes, she understood it was not the gummy bears' fault that everyone got sick, but she couldn't ban toaster tarts. She had to draw the line somewhere.

"We should play video games," Gavin said, directing this statement to the boys. "You think we can convince your mom to set us up out here with a console?"

Yes, they could. Because if they were well enough to play video games, they were well enough for her to go crash for a while. At least, until Travis peeled himself off the floor or Evelyn rang her bell.

"*Yesssss*," Brady said, his gaze settling on his dad. "We have this new game that makes everyone happy. Even Mom."

"'Cause she gets five minutes of peace," Kellan parroted in a voice that sounded remarkably like Rachel's, if she did say so herself.

She couldn't help it, even in the midst of the destruction of their vacation, she smiled.

And wasn't that really what motherhood was all about?

"Ha." Rachel set up one of her hey-so-you-threw-up packets on the floor beside Kellan. It included a bowl, a wet washcloth, and nitrile gloves she'd stolen from the first aid kit —because she'd learned her lesson on not wearing *those* in the kitchen with Brady.

"I kind of wanted to talk to you both about Dakota first." Gavin gave Rachel a look that seemed like he was asking for backup.

Actually, she was really interested in this conversation, too. So she was happy to give him that backup.

Gavin stared at his hands, fidgeting with them over the top of the blanket. "We broke up. She's not going to be around to see you boys anymore."

His words held strength, but Rachel heard the hurt beneath them. Gavin was in pain. It wasn't just his stomach. And that sucked.

"She's really upset about that," Gavin continued. "The not seeing you anymore."

Not from what Rachel had heard. She was upset about a lot, but none of it had seemed to revolve around the boys *or* the dogs. But whatever Gavin needed to tell himself, and the boys, to lighten the blow of losing her.

"Okay," Kellan said, nodding.

"Sorry, Dad," Brady followed. "She was nice."

Then they went back to watching whatever animated show they'd found on Netflix. Like Gavin hadn't just given them information that was seriously going to change their lives.

Gavin was blinking hard. And a whole lot.

"Are you okay?" Rachel sat at the end of the sofa where he stretched out. He didn't look okay, but she couldn't think of what else to ask him.

"I'm..."

"It's okay not to be okay," Rachel said, softly, so only Gavin could hear.

Fine. Maybe she said the words for herself a little, too. Even pale, even exhausted, he gave her a sad smile.

"That's a very Rachel thing to say."

"Is it?" She tilted her head to the side, studying him.

He nodded. Then he cleared his throat. "How's Travis holding up?"

Presently he was lying down. On the tile floor of the bathroom. At least, that's where she'd left him when she peeked in on him last.

"Apparently, he prefers silence while he recovers." Rachel slid her gaze toward the hallway leading to the restroom where he'd taken up residence. "I've been checking on him, though."

"He always did prefer to do things his way." Gavin closed his eyes for a minute.

So did Gavin, if he decided to be honest with himself, but now was clearly not the time to point that out.

"Once you're well enough, we can go someplace and talk about what's happening between Travis and me. If you want to," Rachel said, toying with the edge of the blanket. "It sounds like you and I have both had an eventful summer."

"Eventful" being the least appropriate word ever.

Gavin didn't say anything for a bit; he seemed to be intently studying the wall behind Rachel.

"Are you happy with him?" he finally asked.

The way he said it sounded like her answer really mattered.

But that question was an easy one. "Yes. He makes me really happy."

"Then that's what counts." Gavin smiled. It seemed forced, but he was trying, and she appreciated that more than she'd ever be able to show.

The bone-deep satisfaction she experienced at Gavin's willingness to let her be happy made her smile. Maybe they could be real friends, beyond just co-parents.

"I thought you might be more upset about it," she said, not able to meet his gaze.

"I knew you'd meet someone eventually. I'm not *thrilled* it's

Travis." Gavin glanced at her. "I wish it were anyone but one of my brothers. But he makes you happy. You're both important to me. *Your* happiness is important to me. I'll deal with the rest of it, so it doesn't affect what you've built for our family."

"What have I built?" She had an idea of what she felt like they'd constructed as a team, she was just suddenly really curious what *he* thought, too.

"You built a pretty awesome situation for our boys. They know they're loved. They know you'll be there for them. I wish I could say that I had a huge hand in it, but I don't think that's true. Mostly, it's you, Rachel."

Rachel swallowed hard. "You're not giving yourself enough credit."

They both sat in silence, the only sound the television the boys were watching nearby.

This was how it should've been. Well, without the vomit and convalescence part. Two parents, two kids, two dogs, the television on in the background. Nothing falling apart for a change. And yet...

"I think I'm falling in love with your brother," she said, the words surprisingly easy, given the weight they held.

Gavin looked at her like she'd just suggested they all eat toaster tarts for dinner. "That's good, because I'm pretty sure he's already there."

"You think?" He seriously thought so?

Gavin nodded, a sly smile tipping the edges of his mouth. "He's in pretty deep. Deeper than I've ever seen him."

Her heart seemed to expand, even though she was pretty sure nothing had changed at all. And that was...that was...

Her eyes got a little wet. She parted her lips. Then pressed them together.

"Thank you," she said. Meaning every bit of the words.

"For what?"

"For starting me down this path." She would not cry.

Refused to do it.

"You know, Rach, I didn't want to stay away. But I didn't want to make your life harder, either. You always seemed like you preferred it when I stepped back so you could run the show."

She stilled. That's what he thought?

The sticky, bitter taste of regret seemed to coat her tongue. "That's not what I wanted at all."

She wanted her kids to have their dad. To have everything.

When Gavin had stepped back, she'd done all she could to fill that gap. Maybe…did she not need to?

They did the silent thing again until she stood to go check on Travis.

Was she the one making things harder than they needed to be? She was, she knew. And she hadn't even realized it.

Suddenly, she really wanted to check on Travis, to ensure he was okay.

She drew a deep breath. This conversation with Gavin was just really uncomfortable, and she wanted to get away from it. From failing.

So she did the hard thing. She sat back down. "I'm sorry you thought that's what I wanted."

"Besides, it's not me you need to worry about on the Rachel and Travis front." Gavin pursed his lips, then gave a wry smile. "It's Mama. She's got ideas for all her little chicks, and Mother Hen did not have designs on you ending up with her Travis."

Rachel sucked in a breath. "What do you think I should do about her?"

"Well, I think you and Travis have to decide together what's important and what's not. If she's important—and, I kinda think she should be, but it's not my call—then you work it out with her."

That was a problem, then, because, "I have no idea how to work anything out with your mom."

"Show her how much you care for Travis. She'll come around."

Rachel nodded. She could do that. She wasn't sure it would be enough, but it was something she could do.

"It won't hurt the situation that all I want, Rach, is for you to be happy." This time he smiled a genuine smile. "If that means it's with Travis, then it means you're happy with Travis. He's a good guy."

"That's not what you used to say." In fact, that was the opposite of what he used to say.

Gavin shrugged. "He takes things too casually at work. But I assume he's treating you right, and it helps the way he looks at you like you're everything. He's never looked at anyone that way."

That brought a whole dash of wet to her eyes.

"I want the same for you. The happiness," she said.

"I screwed up my chance…twice." He stilled and closed his eyes.

"But did Dakota really make you happy?"

He opened his eyes, seemed to study the vacant air before him. "Dakota gave me hope."

"Then I'm sorry you lost that." Rachel fidgeted with her hands because she wasn't quite sure what to do with them. She should probably reach out to him. But that didn't feel right, either. "Hope is a good thing."

"I'm not sorry it's over." He yawned, closed his eyes again. "Because it shouldn't take someone else to give me that hope. Not when I've got two of the best little miracles puking their hearts out with me."

"You're going to be more actively involved with them?" That would not suck. Not at all. The boys needed this from Gavin.

"Yeah." He nodded, opening his eyes briefly again to stare at the boys with a total look of love. "I don't want to miss any more."

That look he gave them made her heart do flips on their behalf. They had a good dad. He wanted good things for her. And that meant a lot.

He was also wrong. She hadn't built all of this. They'd done it as a team, and now they could both move forward, together as co-parents who wanted each other to be happy.

Even if that happiness was with other people.

"You need to get some sleep." She moved to him, tucked him in like she'd done with the boys, and patted his arm.

"Video games later," he said before he did as she asked.

She glanced at the boys. They were drifting off, closing their eyes even though they were clearly fighting to watch Netflix, to avoid sleep. Just like their dad.

Gavin snuggled under the blanket she'd put over him earlier in the night.

"I promise I'll do better with them," he added.

"Good." She said it to him, but mostly to herself. And, with that, she went to find Travis.

CHAPTER 27

RACHEL

This was not how Rachel thought the trip would end. Granted, she wasn't sure what she'd expected, but this felt… this felt…defeated.

"Evelyn." Rachel jogged toward her ex-mother-in-law at the lounge where they waited in the small airport just outside Twin Lakes. There were no commercial flights here; this place was just for the corporate jets to come and go.

They were at the airport because Evelyn had canceled the rest of the trip.

Just like that.

No big announcement, just, "We're going home."

Everyone, even Bob, agreed this was the best idea.

"Yes?" Evelyn said, crossing her ankles where she sat.

"I…I just want to thank you for letting the boys and me come up this summer. They really had a good time. Despite… the ending."

Rachel still half expected Evelyn to pull a creative drama the likes of which would've made even Dakota jealous. So far, that hadn't happened. Evelyn had not even mentioned her cat.

"Why don't you sit?" Evelyn patted the chair next to her.

It did, early on, occur to Rachel that Evelyn didn't want to continue to have her and Travis staying in the same house— even if Evelyn didn't come right out and say it. And, as everyone recovered over the following days, Rachel had wondered how Evelyn would conspire to keep them apart.

She'd expected something creative. So the cancellation of the rest of the summer did make sense. It was also very non-Evelyn.

A little too on-the-nose.

Rachel trailed her gaze to where Travis stood by the coffee and tea cart. Even though he swore his stomach was feeling 100 percent, he was still gulping peppermint tea like he owned stock in it.

Which, he might. Rachel really didn't know much about his investments.

He pinched his lips in a thin line when she sat next to his mother.

And that made Rachel's stomach hurt.

The guy was more than a touch grumpy that he wasn't flying them home. Evelyn had called in a pilot—since it'd been only a few days and Travis, while recovered, was not in any condition to fly.

Rachel was pondering the realization that she would've preferred he fly them home. Not some unnamed pilot she didn't know.

"I'm worried that you're angry," Rachel said finally.

"Did you ever hear the story of my meemaw?" Evelyn asked.

"The one who made the first toaster tart?" Rachel shook her head.

"She loved to bake because it brought her family together.

The kitchen was the heart of the family when I was growing up."

Rachel could relate to that.

"Meemaw was the heart of the family." Evelyn adjusted so she leaned closer to Rachel. "She never got to meet my boys, but she would've loved them. She would've loved my grand-babies, too. She would've wanted them to have a stable home with a mom and dad who put them first."

"Evelyn…"

"Hear me out." Evelyn looked between Gavin and Travis.

Travis was scowling in their direction. Gavin was talking to Dane about something that animated his expression.

"Evelyn, I'd like you to hear *me* out for a minute." Rachel set aside her cup of coffee and faced Evelyn head on. "You love Bob. I'm certain that your meemaw loved her husband. Gavin and I never had that."

Evelyn pursed her lips.

"We didn't. We made a mistake one night, and he was stuck with me. We did our best, but it wasn't the right thing. So we adjusted. That's what you do in a family. You adjust. My family wouldn't adjust to the idea that I had kids the way I did. They still haven't. And you know what? It makes me sad, because they're missing out on two of the best humans on the planet." Her voice trembled a little, dammit. She stood, then she turned to Evelyn. "I'm not making threats, because that's not how I work. But I have watched my boys lose one set of grandparents to what they thought was right, even when it was really, really wrong. I don't want them to lose you and Bob, too, because I'm with the wrong son."

Evelyn didn't say anything. She didn't have to.

"Just don't do the wrong thing for the right reasons," Rachel said as a parting shot.

Then she went to Travis.

"What did she say?" he asked as soon as she was in front of him.

"I…" Rachel turned back to Evelyn, who was staring intently at the interaction between her son and Rachel. "I told her she needs to knock it off before my boys lose both sets of grandparents."

Travis drew her in for a hug. "Are you okay?"

He smelled of spice and the mountains and…the man she loved.

"I'm okay," she said.

How often over the years had she said those words, and they'd been half-truths said to make the other person feel better?

She smiled against Travis's shoulder because this time, she meant it. "I was hoping you might take Brady up in the single-engine? I mentioned it, and he really wants to."

Travis's look of shock was nearly comical.

"Will you come along?" he asked, recovering quickly.

"No way in hell." She shook her head.

He draped his arm around her. "Small steps, sunshine."

* * *

TRAVIS

Travis couldn't kiss Rachel like he wanted to, not with the boys loaded in the SUV with the dogs. He stood outside the driver's-side door with Rachel as the sun set over the Rockies. It cast a beautiful glow behind her.

He wished he had a camera.

They'd touched down at Centennial Airport in Englewood. The flight had been remarkably uneventful. He hadn't been able to fly, but he got to sit with Rach. Even held her hand most of the flight.

He had no idea what the hell had gone on between the two women. But whatever it was, his mama was straight-up confused. She now looked at the two of them like she didn't want to wring both their necks and make chicken soup out of their souls.

If he had to guess, Mama was softening toward the two of them like butter left out in the Tennessee sun.

This, he figured, was a welcome improvement.

Even the walk across the tarmac holding Rachel's hand was not given one iota of side-eye.

"I'm starving and there's no food at home," Rachel said, glancing inside the car to give Brady direction on the proper usage of a seat belt before turning her attention back to Travis. "I guess we'll hit a drive-through on the way."

Molly and April had dropped April's SUV off at the airport for her. They'd been ecstatic about the coming home early.

He couldn't blame them. He'd also grown fond of her company. More than fond. He couldn't quite put a name on it, but he needed this woman.

"Here." He handed her a plastic container with his mama's homemade tarts. "Don't tell her I sent them with you."

"Thanks." She took the container and stuffed it into her bag.

"Do you want me to come by and help you find a tooth-brush later?" he asked, because asking if he could stick his tongue down her pants was probably inappropriate.

"Let me get the boys settled first." Rachel glanced to the back seat of her car.

"I can do that."

"Two boys, two dogs, suitcases, my purse, and keys." She went through her checklist, then held the keys up. "Mr. Pretzel."

She didn't know how cute she was when she did that. He hoped she never figured it out.

The boys couldn't have cared less that this was a huge

step in their relationship—the going-public-in-front-of-everyone thing.

Rachel said she and Gavin explained to the boys that she and Travis were in a relationship, and they could ask any questions they wanted.

So far, their only question had been if Uncle Travis would bring them gummy bears to replenish the stash that Rachel tossed out before they left for the airport.

Travis hadn't been able to answer, because Rachel answered for him.

He was fine with this, because he had a feeling no matter what he answered, somebody was going to be pissed off at him.

"You promise you'll call?" He gave her a sly smile.

She rolled onto her toes and kissed his cheek. "Of course I promise."

"Bye, Rach." He pressed a kiss to her forehead.

"See you in a bit." She gave him a little wave that he felt deep in his bones.

CHAPTER 28

TRAVIS

Rachel didn't call. Not like she said she would. And that stuck in his teeth like a broken toothpick.

Travis had called her, but she didn't pick up.

She had finally texted him that the boys were having a hard time settling, so they'd need to rain check.

He hadn't wanted to rain check. He wanted time with Rachel.

Gavin propped himself against the doorway of Travis's office.

Yes, Travis was in his office. He'd even gone to a meeting that morning to discuss his idea to sell mini toaster tarts to his CEO buddy at Integrated Airlines.

"Do you want to talk about it?" Gavin asked. No, Travis did not. He shook his head.

"If you'd rather sit in here and stew alone, I can go talk to Dane instead." Gavin started to move away from the door.

Travis glared at his not-ringing cell phone. He and Gavin were going to have to have this conversation at some point. Might as well be now.

"Sure, yeah, let's talk." Travis pushed his chair back from the desk, stood, and strode to the door. He closed it. Then back to the chair.

He needed to get new art for the walls. His mother had picked out the pastel watercolors currently hanging. He'd never cared because he was never there.

That was changing.

He had ideas, and he was going to see them through. Mini-tarts was only the beginning.

"You really care about her?" Gavin asked, like he didn't really know if he believed it.

Travis nodded. "I do."

"That's good. I'm happy for you both." Seriously? Huh.

Who would've thought?

"Hey, have you heard from her since we got back?" Travis asked.

"I talked to the boys this morning. They didn't say anything. Haven't you talked to her?"

"Not since the airport. I've been calling, but she hasn't answered. I figured she needed some space." Space sucked, and he'd keep calling. He hoped like hell his mama hadn't done something to sabotage him, and he planned to stop by at lunch to ensure that had not happened.

He'd meant it when they'd danced—he wouldn't just let her walk out of his life, not until she told him that's what she wanted.

"I care a lot about Rachel," Gavin said, clearly choosing his words carefully. He sat in the chair across from Travis's desk.

Of course, Gavin should care about the mother of his kids, but the words still stuck sideways in Travis's craw.

"I don't love her, though, not like that," Gavin continued. "I...I guess I screwed up her life and have always felt the responsibility for that."

Now, that got Travis's attention. "You didn't screw up her life."

"Trav." Gavin dropped his elbows to his knees. "I can see the remnants of my mistakes with her all the way from California to Colorado. Those boys are the best things that ever happened to me, but I still managed to screw it up."

Gavin had been distant with Travis since the big reveal. Travis was pretty certain this was because the twins dug him, and Gavin felt threatened by it. Which was ridiculous because they adored their Uncle Trav, but they loved their dad. If he'd given them half the time of day that they deserved, then he'd see how much he meant to them.

"They love you."

Gavin nodded. "I'm not going to continue that screw-up. I'm going to be there for them. They're the priority."

"What changed?" Because this was a pretty big change.

"I thought Rachel needed me to be absent. I thought she preferred to do things herself. It's who she is, you know?" Gavin asked, but he didn't wait for an answer. "The only thing I want is for her to be happy, the boys to be happy. I'd like a little bit of that for myself, but Dakota wasn't that for me. I wasn't it for her, either. We both held on to hope a little too long. I guess that's one thing Rachel and I did get right—we stopped trying before we really hurt each other."

"You're really not pissed we're together?"

Gavin gave a light shake of his head. "I'll get pissed if you hurt her. She's had enough of that in her life. She's already lost most of her family. We're her family now. I won't let anyone—not even you—fuck that up for her."

Travis chuckled.

"What's so funny?" Gavin asked.

"I've just been rehearsing to say something similar to you."

"Then I guess we're on the same page." Gavin held his hand out to Travis.

For the first time in a long time, they were on the same page.

Travis shook his brother's hand.

Gavin went back to his office, and Travis tried Rachel again.

Voicemail.

Straight to voicemail. Dammit.

"Rach," he said into the receiver. "I'm starting to get really worried about you. Can you call me back? Even just send another text. Let me know you're okay. Okay?"

He disconnected and stared out the window at the Denver skyline.

The knock at the window beside his door had him turning.

"I called the kids," Gavin said, his words stone. "Brady said Rachel's sick. She's been throwing up all morning."

Sonofabitch. Travis should have known better than to give her time to readjust to Denver. Giving someone space meant they spent a whole day throwing up all by themselves.

This is why a guy didn't give the woman he cared for *space*.

Travis grabbed his wallet and his keys and jogged to the bank of elevators before Gavin could say anything else. He made excellent time and was in his car and out of the parking lot, before Gavin even emerged from the glass revolving door painted like the latest variety of toaster tarts that led to the lobby of the building.

Gavin, however, did catch up to him at the stop sign just outside the industrial park where the Puffle Yum factory was situated. He tailed Travis the entire way to Rachel's house.

Travis kept to the speed limit, but it took everything he had.

Rachel was sick.

That's why Rachel hadn't answered his calls.

If Rachel was so sick she didn't have her cell with her, then she was really ill.

She couldn't be really ill because she was Rachel. That made not a bit of sense, but there it was.

He jogged up the stairs two at a time, then tried the door. Locked. Instead of pounding on the glass panes, he punched the code into the pad, and when the lock clicked, he pushed it open.

"Rach?" he called, leaving the door wide open for his brother. "Brady? Kellan?"

The living room was a wreck. Worse than the birthday party aftermath.

He shoved his fingers through his hair.

Shit. He'd never seen her living room this bad—throw pillows all over the floor. They had pulled the couch cushions off the sofas and lined them along the wall to make some kind of fort. Toys were everywhere. Literally, everywhere. The place was a minefield.

There were even cups filled with unknown liquid on the coffee table.

It looked like an eight-year-old version of a frat party.

They hadn't been back that long. How the hell had the boys managed this? The kitchen was even worse—used plates, bowls, and silverware covered the countertops.

"Kellan? Brady?" Gavin called, heading up the stairs to their bedroom.

"Rach?" Travis called, and goddamn it, his voice cracked a little.

He followed Gavin up the stairs. The boys had strategically placed themselves in their beanbag chairs, playing some game with cars and lots of crashes.

"When you do it like this, the car explodes." Kellan screeched and made explosion sounds, puffing his cheeks and throwing his whole body into the turn.

Brady laughed hysterically at the ensuing explosion. He

laughed so loud, Pete gave a bark from where he and Re-Pete were lounging at their feet.

Everyone seemed fine.

"Where's your mom?" Travis asked, his blood pressure absolutely not fine.

"What're you doing here, Uncle Trav?" Kellan asked, his eyes wide.

"He asked where your mom is." Gavin said, turning off the television so they had to give him all their attention.

"Um…" Brady looked to Kellan.

"In her room sleeping," Kellan said. "I think. That's where she was when we took her lunch."

"We brought her toast," Brady added. "She wanted it plain."

Travis hurried to her room. He didn't bother knocking, just pulled open the door and waited for his eyes to adjust to the darkness.

"Rach?" He said her name low, gentle, and did his best to keep the building feeling of terror from his tone.

She groaned from under the blankets.

He moved to her. "Rach, sunshine, it's me."

The two pieces of toast were on the nightstand, untouched. The boys had also, apparently, brought her an apple juice box. Also untouched, since the straw was still in the wrapper.

"I'm gross, go away." Rachel didn't move, and the words were raspy.

He knelt beside the bed, careful not to move the mattress, and pressed the back of his hand against her forehead. He did it just like she'd done for him at the lake. Her forehead was slick with sweat, and her skin was on fire. "How long have you been like this?"

"Really sick." Her words were a croak. "Just need to get better. Don't look at me."

She wasn't gross. She could never be gross. "I'm going to look at you because you're beautiful, and I'm worried."

He started to lift her in his arms so he could get her into his car. Take her someplace where there was a doctor and medicine and people who could help fix whatever was wrong with her.

"What are you doing?" She pushed away from him.

"Taking you to the hospital."

She batted his hands away, but there was no force behind the movement. "It's just a bug. I don't need to go anywhere. I just need my bed and the dark and sleep."

"Rach, you're burning up." He set her back down on the bed and pressed his hand against her forehead again. Still slick, still hot, and her skin was pale and flushed.

She sighed, pointing to the thermometer on the nightstand. "I've been watching it. It's not bad."

He grabbed the thermometer and ran it over her forehead. "It's at a hundred and one. We need to get you to a doctor."

His thoughts were all jumbled. He needed to do something. Something that would make a difference. Something to make Rachel healthy again.

"Travis says it's a hundred and one." Gavin spoke from the hallway, just outside the door.

He was speaking into his cell, hopefully to a physician who could fix this. Because they needed to find a solution, so Rachel could go back to being Rachel again.

"Brady says she's been like this since right after they got home." Gavin nodded at something whoever was on the other end of the line said. "Yeah, the house is a total train wreck."

Rachel groaned at that announcement.

"We'll help the boys clean it up." Travis kept his tone soft, because he was pretty sure if she felt like he had when he'd had the bug, she probably had a decent headache happening along with the fever.

"What did the doctor say?" he asked when Gavin was off the phone.

"Mama says to get a cool washcloth for her head, ibuprofen for the fever if she can keep it down, and a popsicle for dehydration." Gavin shifted on his feet.

Well, crap. He'd called their mother.

"She also said she's on her way," Gavin continued, and this time he sounded apologetic.

Rachel groaned louder. "Maybe let's do the doctor thing. A hospital visit sounds fabulous. Maybe they'll even poke me with a bunch of needles."

"Mama's really good when someone's sick." Travis reached for Rachel's hand.

She let him hold on to it, not moving or batting him away when he slipped his palm against hers.

"I'm fine. I'm up. I don't need Evelyn's help." She started to lift herself to a sitting position, apparently ready to illustrate how fine she was.

Then she swayed a little and fell back to the bed. "I think I'm just going to lie here. If your mom's coming over, can somebody go get me a bell?"

He was absolutely not going to give her a bell—she'd probably bonk his mother over the noggin with it.

When Travis had been sick, he hadn't wanted anyone to touch him, move him, or talk to him. Rachel had managed all of that while still taking care of him and everyone else.

Perhaps it was time they all took care of her for a change.

"Rach," he said, wanting to touch her so badly, it bordered on painful. "Can I stay here with you?"

It was subtle, but she nodded. "Someone's got to play interference with your mother."

"I think she's feeling bad about how it went up at the lake," he said.

And she should, because she was a total... How would Rachel say it? Puffle Yum Momster.

"Can you bring me my computer? It's on my desk," Rachel said into the pillow, the words muffled.

He touched the crown of her head, gently so he wouldn't make the room spin. "You need to rest, not work."

"I need to email my client." She turned so her mouth wasn't pressed into the pillow.

Travis winced at the way she said, "my client." The one client. The last one. Travis wanted to fix this for her, but she didn't want him to. The truth of the matter was that she didn't need him to. Rachel would fix it. He knew she could.

"To let him know I'm out right now."

Ah. Well, that made sense. If she wasn't answering for Travis, she probably wouldn't answer for her client, either.

"Can I take it back downstairs as soon as you're done?" He moved his hand lightly over the knots in her hair.

She gave him a look that would melt the plastic right off a light switch.

"So you can rest," he added, removing his hand from her hair. "And get better."

The glare continued.

"Rach." He moved so they were face-to-face. "What would you tell me to do if I were the sick one?"

She grunted. "Fine. One email and you can put it away."

"That's my girl," he said softly. "Leaning in to self-care."

"If you start talking about airplanes and me needing to put my own oxygen mask on first, you can stop now. Molly gives me that lecture all the time."

"Ahh..." He pressed a kiss against her forehead. "But Molly is not a licensed pilot."

Rachel smiled then. A barely there lift of the edges of her lips before she closed her eyes again.

"It's nice doing business with you," he whispered.

CHAPTER 29

RACHEL

The first thing Rachel noticed was that her body felt like it'd been through a war, childbirth, and a plane crash simultaneously. Still, remarkably, this was an improvement from the day before.

The second thing Rachel noticed was there was a man in her bed.

Travis.

His eyes were closed, his breaths even. He seemed… peaceful.

She smiled.

He hadn't gotten under the blankets with her. No, he was sleeping on top of the comforter, fully clothed, breathing softly.

The third thing Rachel noticed was that she liked waking up next to him.

They'd had sex, cuddled after, but she'd never seen him sleep. Not deeply. Not like this.

There was the time when he was recovering on the sofa up at the Lakes. But that hardly counted, given his broken sleep, her boys and Gavin slept in the same room, and she cared for them all.

She reached for the thermometer and took her temperature.

Normal. Totally normal.

As though the past day hadn't even happened.

"How are you feeling, sunshine?" Travis asked, his voice rough from sleep.

She turned to him. "Like I need to invest in a bell."

He smiled. "Mama found the container of cinnamon tarts and has convinced herself that she's responsible for poisoning all of us."

"But I didn't eat one." Rachel moved to sit up, and the room didn't even spin. "Not after watching all of you deal with the aftermath. I put them in the fridge, but I didn't eat any."

Travis leaned on an elbow, reaching out with his other hand to push her hair behind her ear. "Let's not tell Mama that part, yeah?"

Rachel laughed. "You're being bad."

"You have no idea how bad I can be."

She wavered a little as she stood to make her way to a shower and then some dry toast. "I think I have a pretty good idea." She rolled her tongue over her bottom lip before saying, "When I don't feel like I just rose from the dead, do you…uh…want to look for a toothbrush with me?"

His expression was one of total sincerity. "I want to look for all the toothbrushes with you."

That declaration made her warm all over. And for a moment, she forgot how crappy she felt otherwise.

Then her cell rang from her nightstand. He'd placed it on top of her laptop at some point.

She raised her eyes to meet his.

"I brought it up last night after you'd slept for a solid seven hours."

That was…sweet.

She glanced at the screen of her cell.

"Kaiya?" Rachel said.

"Rachel," Kaiya said, excited like always. "Molly said you're back in town."

"I am. Hey, sorry I haven't gotten back to you. Things went a little sideways this summer."

Travis stood, his gaze holding hers as he moved behind her and pressed a kiss to the back of her neck. Then he moved to pull on his shirt.

"I wasn't calling about that," Kaiya said, even as Rachel's gaze tracked Travis's movements. "Molly said you do the personal assistant thing, and I'm drowning over here. I was hoping we might be able to talk? I just hit international sales director level. Now there are all these meetings I'm trying to keep track of, and orders to put through, and I could just really use some help."

Oh, well… Rachel helped. That's what Rachel did. She rolled her tongue over her bottom lip, widening her eyes in Travis's direction. This was good. Great, even. Fantastic. "I'd love to talk to you about what I do," Rachel said, hoping to keep an air of professionalism even as her heart beat faster. She grabbed a pen and made a new list so the sieve of her mind wouldn't forget this later. "I'm getting over this stomach bug thing, but can we get together later this week?"

"Yes." Kaiya's voice filled with her smile. "Absolutely. That would be amazing. Also…"

"What's up?"

"This is weird…" Kaiya let out a sigh. "I told myself I wouldn't make this weird."

"It's okay, you can tell me whatever you need."

"I know some of your other clients had been difficult in the past." The smile in Kaiya's voice dimmed, just a little. Barely noticeable, really. But Rachel did notice.

"I just wanted to assure you that I'm not a dick with work stuff," Kaiya finished.

Rachel grinned. She glanced at Travis and smiled bigger because he was standing there in her bedroom. He looked as happy as she felt inside. "I appreciate that."

She wrapped up the call with a promise to meet later, and then she met Travis's gaze once more.

"That sounded promising," he said, not moving, just standing there like he belonged.

Which, for the record, he did.

"Maybe things will work out, after all," Rachel mused.

"For now Mama's also being extra nice," he said.

"She was worried about you yesterday and made it a point not to leave until your fever broke. I think she's coming around to you and me being an us."

Rachel turned back. "Seriously?"

"She spent a lot of time yesterday cleaning up downstairs. Man, your boys were like an unsupervised tornado while you were out."

Gah. This was exactly why she couldn't get sick. Ever.

Ever again.

Speaking of... "Where are the kids?"

"Gavin took them to his house with the dogs. They wanted to make you lunch today. Brady suggested they grab you some soup from that place you like over on Champa."

The thought of food was not a welcome one. For the first time since she could remember, "I'm not ready to think about eating just yet."

"When you are, they're waiting for the go-ahead."

She grabbed new clothes from her dresser—nothing special, just a clean set of yoga pants and a sleeveless T-shirt with a shelf bra built in. "Thank you for staying."

Travis swallowed, the Adam's apple in his throat bobbing up and down. "I think we need to discuss that."

"The staying?" She wasn't following.

"The fact that I don't want to leave."

Oh. That.

"Do you think we're at the stage of the relationship where we should be having sleepovers?" she asked. "I don't want to confuse the boys. Maybe we're more at the almost-sleepover stage of things."

"Were they confused when Dakota and Gavin had sleepovers?"

She shook her head. "It's totally different."

"Because I'm their uncle?" he asked.

"Because I'm their mom."

He sauntered toward her. Well, he stalked, really. Then he wielded the southern. "Rach. I'm not goin' to push you on this. But I want you to know that I want *this*, when you're ready to give it. I want it all, and I'm ready to wait."

She couldn't bring herself to meet his eyes.

"Rach," he said, his voice serious.

She met his gaze, and he didn't quite look like himself. "You just let me know, okay?"

Oh. Oh, no.

"I'm not…" She was so not ready for that. Not at all. "I don't know if I'll ever be…"

He didn't seem disappointed. Not at all. And that was weird. It was weird, right? Yes, odd. Except, this just felt like a conversation, not a grand declaration of love.

"You just let me know," he said, pinning her in place with his gaze. "I won't ask again."

Oh.

A lump formed in her throat.

He moved his palm against her jaw. She couldn't help it, she turned her cheek in to his touch.

"Okay," she murmured against his hand.

"Okay." The conversation apparently done, Travis headed for the hallway. "Just toast?"

She nodded, even though he couldn't see her. "Yes. Nothing heavy. Just…toast. Maybe some tea?"

"All right then. Toast and tea." He gave her a flash of a grin that made her seriously wish she wasn't on a dry toast diet because she sorta wanted to jump him right then.

And given her previous day's activities, *that* was a horrible idea.

So she went to shower instead. This time, she didn't step on the scale first, because there was nothing it could tell her she didn't already know.

She was probably always going to have her curves, and it didn't matter, because she was finding she also had a whole heaping of happy. So she was going to hold on tight to it for as long as it let her.

The thing about perfection, she realized, staring at that damn scale, was that it didn't really exist. It's a phantom that drove her to try to do better when she was doing her very best to begin with.

Turned out, sometimes making a mess of things actually made her happier.

CHAPTER 30

RACHEL

"The Puffle Yum Momster poisoned you?" Molly said… well…really, she shrieked the statement. She punctuated this shriek by smacking two hands on the table in front of her.

Rachel shushed her. "The boys will hear you. And, no, she didn't *actually* poison me, but she thinks she did. Thus, she's now being super awesome."

So far, Evelyn had not brought up Gavin plus Rachel equals true love since they'd been back. She also offered to take the boys for an evening so Travis and Rachel could have some time alone. More than that, she'd added Rachel to the family text chain.

This last one was both a blessing and a curse. Turned out, Evelyn texted her kids a *lot*.

"I'm confused," Kaiya said.

Turned out she sold the hell out of skin care products. Who knew?

And she needed a whole lot of Rachel's help. During working hours.

Kaiya had no problems with boundaries and set her own firm office hours. It made for an excellent working relationship.

She also paid on time and provided all the free lavender skin cream Rachel could ever need.

This get-together was taking place in Rachel's backyard. All the kids were bouncing on the trampoline, April poured margaritas, and Sadie served cookies she'd brought along from Heather's Cookie Co.—the good kind with extra icing she got because she was friendly with the owner.

"What are you confused about?" April asked, topping off Kaiya's glass.

"So Evelyn is just okay with everything because she thinks she accidentally gave you guys food poisoning?" Kaiya confirmed. "That seems unlike her, from what you've said."

She was right, it did seem unlike her. But it wasn't about food poisoning. It was about Evelyn realizing things might just be okay anyway, even if she didn't get her way.

"That's her excuse," Rachel said with a sly smile. "But I think she came around because she realized her sons aren't going to beat the crap out of each other over the situation between Travis and me."

"How do you feel about it all?" Sadie asked.

"I have Travis. So things are pretty great." Rachel settled back against her chair, gripping the cocktail with two hands. On the scale of great, things were magnificent. He'd found her toothbrush three times just that morning before she kicked him out before the boys woke up.

He ate dinner with them every night in the week they'd been back—except two nights he had corporate dinners. On those nights, he stopped by afterward to say goodnight and give Rachel what he referred to as "a proper goodnight."

To be clear, there wasn't much proper about the way he said goodnight. Hence the, *ahem*, magnificent.

Even the thought made her cheeks heat and her heart

flutter like it always had when a relationship was brand-new. The thing was, this relationship still had the flutter, but it was definitely not new.

In truth, they'd been working toward it for years. She just hadn't realized. For the record, the bedroom activities weren't the only thing she adored about Travis. They were a definite perk, for sure, but more than that, he fit seamlessly into her life.

Like he was always meant to be there. Like the splintered pieces of the life she'd planned all pointed straight to this place. To him, and to her boys, and to her family.

"Well, I don't know about the rest of you, but I for one am really ticked off that you didn't even try the produce thing," Molly said with a huff.

"What's the produce thing?" Kaiya asked.

"Don't ask." April held up her hand. "Trust me, it is not something any of us should entertain."

"Okay, what about this?" Molly shifted and faced April. "Car seat fittings."

"What?" April asked.

Rachel pressed her tongue against her teeth so she wouldn't ask questions. Asking questions when Molly had ideas was not a good choice.

"We all love firefighters, right?" Molly asked. "I mean, did you see the calendar they did this year to raise money?" She fanned herself. "Do you know where a girl would go to meet a firefighter?"

"I have no idea," Kaiya said. "Where do you go?"

Total mistake with all the questions.

"To the firehouse. But you can't just walk on in there unless something is on fire. Unless"—Molly held up her finger like she'd just had a brilliant idea—"there is a car seat fitting."

"You know what?" Kaiya said. "I went to one of those once and the guy who installed the seat was really cute and sweet. He even asked about special hand soap to get the gunk off his hands after he went on a call."

"What else did he ask about?" Molly zeroed in on Kaiya. "Did he ask for your number?"

"Uh." Kaiya looked from Rachel to April to Sadie. "Just so he could buy soap. He liked the idea of all-natural hand soap."

"Hon," Molly sat forward, elbows on her knees. She set her margarita on the table. "When a man asks about hand soap, he probably wants your number."

"Here we go again," Rachel said dramatically.

"Just stop, Molly!" April laughed. "Next you'll be telling her to go skydiving with Kent."

"Is he still doing that?" Molly asked.

"All the freaking time." April let out a long breath. "It's just a midlife-crisis thing. He'll get over it soon enough."

Rachel shivered. Jumping out of a perfectly good aircraft was not her idea of a "midlife-phase" anything.

No one needed to jump out of any moving transportation, as far as she was concerned. Not with the kids laughing in the background, fresh margaritas in the pitcher, and good friends to spend time with.

Rachel felt an expansion in her chest. She closed her eyes, soaking it all in.

"You know what?" Kaiya said finally. "I think Evelyn did get her way."

If there was one thing that could ruin the goodness soak, it was the mention of Evelyn.

Rachel peeled one eye open.

"I'm not quite sure how you got from A to B on this one," Sadie said, popping a bit of cookie into her mouth. "But I want to hear it because it doesn't involve skydiving, produce, or car seat fittings."

"Okay, hear me out. When you have a person who consistently acts in a certain way—always—and then all of a sudden they seem out of character, there's something up. In this case, if we drill down Evelyn's main plan, it wasn't to keep Rachel and Travis apart, was it? It was to ensure that Travis and Gavin were happy, right?"

This made sense. Rachel nodded.

"I'm following you so far," Sadie said.

"Despite everything that happened, that end result *has* happened. So Evelyn did get what she wanted, just not in the way that we expected."

Huh. Rachel stared at Kaiya. She was totally right. And that was whacked.

"What did you do before you sold skin cream?" Sadie asked.

"I was head of pharmaceutical sales for a large medical supply company." Kaiya licked at the margarita salt along the rim of her cup. "My ex always said I was a drug dealer. But that's not really accurate, because I didn't have access to the medications myself. I think he just thought it was funny. He was an ass, though, so his sense of humor was iffy."

The things you learned about a girl over margaritas and sugar cookies.

"Hello, ladies." Travis strode out the door, stopping to kiss Rachel on her temple. "Can I crash your party?"

"You can always crash my parties." Rachel glanced up at him.

"Isn't that good to know?" He nodded to the margaritas. "Are those for anyone?"

"No," Molly said. "They're only for people we like. *Therefore*, you are welcome to one."

"Rach." Gavin stepped out onto the patio. "Thought I'd pick up the boys a little early so this lug could take you to dinner. I didn't realize they had friends over."

"For example," Molly said to Travis. "They aren't for your brother."

Travis shook his head. "He'll grow on you, Ms. Molly."

"Not likely." She shook her head, brown curls bouncing against her shoulders.

"Mom," Brady screeched. "Kellan spilled slime all over the trampoline."

"It's in my hair," Ollie squealed. He didn't sound too torn up about that fact.

Molly rolled her eyes and stood to go investigate. "They've been alone for like only sixty seconds."

Gavin followed her, as did April and Kaiya.

Sadie said her goodbyes and headed toward the front door.

"You two have a good night," she hollered behind as she pulled the door closed.

Rachel took in Travis. He was grinning a goofy smile. "Where'd they get slime?"

"They kept it from their birthday party." She shrugged. The stuff was water-based. A good dose of the hose, and the slime would come right off.

Only a month ago, she would've lost her utter shit over the slime situation. But it didn't seem to matter as much these days. Not with the lightness she felt all the time.

The happy.

Oh, for sure, things were still a bit of a mess, but she was making do.

She'd dipped into her emergency fund to make the mortgage payment, but James was looking to increase her hours— during regular business hours, of course—and things seemed promising with Kaiya. Even Sadie and April had asked if she could do some side jobs for them.

Most of all, though, she'd been getting an appropriate amount of sleep at night. Therefore, the weight of her world didn't feel quite so heavy.

She stared at Travis. He wasn't looking at her, though—he was watching the chaos happening at the trampoline.

There was literally slime everywhere.

Where the hell had they gotten so much of it?

"I love you, Rach," he said, out of the blue, but like he'd been trying to figure out how to say that for forever.

Rachel's heart seemed to stop beating for a moment, encapsulated in the feeling that she'd been alone, and now she wasn't. Everything seemed to be all right in her extremely imperfect world.

"Took you long enough," she replied, finally catching his gaze and holding it. She savored the moment, because it was definitely a moment worth savoring.

All the moments with Travis were. Then she stood, and kissed him.

"I love you, too," she said against his lips.

She hoped, really hoped, this would be enough to get them through whatever the future tossed their way, because she had no doubt their story was only beginning. The last chapter ended for her, but it wasn't the end. It simply led to the next part.

There would be fractures, and splinters, and she'd probably want to invest in poisoned toaster tarts at some point.

But, then again, that was the funny thing about perfection being measured by degrees. The imperfection—the ugly and dirty and messy parts—those are the bits and pieces that brought meaning to her life.

She understood that now.

The ugly parts were the ones that made the goodness shine extra bright.

EPILOGUE
FOUR MONTHS LATER

TRAVIS

He was late, and that was unacceptable.

Rachel was expecting him for dinner, but he'd gotten caught up with a supplier at the office.

Finally off the phone, he grabbed his wallet and his keys and headed out the door.

"Travis," his mother called.

He tried the box-breathing thing Rachel had showed him. It never really seemed to work.

"Try this for me, sweetie." She lifted a toaster tart to his mouth.

He shook his head. "I'm late. Gotta get to Rachel."

"One bite. Tell me what you think." Evelyn tried again, holding the pastry only millimeters from his mouth. "It's for the airline."

"Seriously, I'll try it later."

"When is the last time you ate?" she asked, following him as he moved to the elevator, still holding the tart to his mouth.

"Lunch, Mama." He pressed the button to call the elevator.

"You go too long between meals." She did not move the pastry from in front of his mouth. "There's a correlation between sugary treats and the pleasure center of the brain. One bite produces oxytocin, dopamine, and raises your serotonin levels. I think if you ate the product we produce more often, you'd be a much happier man."

He was a very happy man, thank you.

She didn't move the pastry from his mouth. Fine.

He took a bite. Then he gagged.

Her newest Puffle Yum creation was not good. At all.

Pastry dough with some kind of cream filling that held a ridiculously unappealing mouthfeel. The mini chocolate chips in the filling were not helping matters at all.

"What is in that?" he asked, barely able to swallow the concoction.

"Cinnamon toast *with* chocolate cannoli filling," she said with pride, as though this were a good thing. "The perfect pie for the sky."

Travis did not believe in putting cannoli in a pop-up toaster. He had some standards. He also had dinner plans with Rachel.

"Let's rethink this one." He gave the remaining tart a glare before stepping into the elevator.

He beat foot out of the office. Then he hit every construction zone in downtown Denver while wishing he had grabbed a bottle of water to delete the taste of the toaster tart from his tongue.

He had texted Rachel before he left the office, but she didn't respond.

Not that he expected her to, given that she'd made a new habit of keeping her phone away from the dinner table.

Rachel now preferred to give her full focus to whatever it was she was doing.

This new philosophy of hers worked out well for him,

quite often. Especially when they were together in her bedroom.

"Rachel?" he called from the front door of her house, toeing off his shoes.

Usually, her house was filled to the brim with noise, and kids, and dogs when he arrived. Tonight it was quiet. Lately, Brady had been the first to barrel into him because they'd been going flying on the weekends.

Brady was a natural.

Rachel had warmed to the flying. She said something about how Brady had found his "thing" and she would embrace it.

The look on the kid's face was all smiles when he talked about his favorite airplanes—to anyone who would listen.

Embracing her son's adoration of aviation did not, however, mean going up *in* the single engines herself.

Yet. Travis still held hope. Probably misplaced hope, given Rachel's unwavering thoughts on the subject.

Gavin even tagged along at the airport sometimes to see what all the fuss was about with Brady's new extracurricular activity. Now, *he* would actually get in the planes. He got a kick out of it when Brady showed him the ropes.

And he hadn't missed any of Kellan's games that season, at all.

Dare Travis say that for the first time his family was… normal? Totally, obnoxiously normal.

"Over here," Rachel called from the dining room.

"Sorry I'm late, I got caught up and lost track of…"

He came around the corner to the dining room and paused. Rachel had set the table with her good dishes—and only for two. With candles. And they were lit. The boys must not have been on the premises, because there was no way she would've put fire right in front of them.

"Hey." She fidgeted with the fork beside one of the plates.

She was all decked out in a little back slip of a dress that made him want to immediately peel it off so he could get a glimpse of what lay underneath. She'd tucked her hair up into a mess of curls that he guessed took her forever to create, because her hair was definitely not of the curled variety. Most of all, she seemed…nervous.

"What's going on?" He moved to her and kissed her firmly on the mouth.

She melted against him like she always did when he kissed her.

"I…" She heaved a deep breath. "Okay, so I have a little gift for you. I don't want it to be a huge deal. You don't even have to accept it. But the boys and I talked, and we all decided that it made sense. They spent all morning helping me clean out the garage." The words spilled from her lips and made no sense at all.

"Rach." He placed his hands against her shoulders. "What are you talking about?"

She handed him a small wrapped box from the middle of the table. "This is for you. It's not just from me, though. It's from all of us, but they're not here because Gavin took the boys to your parents' house so you and I could have the night alone. He said something about your mom and cannoli. I stopped listening at that point."

A night alone with Rachel was a rare treat. A night alone with Rachel made him plot what they'd do next.

Spoiler, it probably wouldn't involve food.

Then again, maybe it might…

"Does that mean we get to have a sleepover?" he asked, hoping his eyes held the glimmer of excitement he felt in his bones.

Rachel nodded toward the box. "Open the box."

He ripped off the paper and held up a garage door opener. He raised his eyebrows.

"There's now room in the garage for your car. And there's

this—" She handed him a large framed sign that matched the others she'd made for the house.

Turning it over, he studied the craftmanship. The vinyl words she'd added to the cream background read, The Perfect Blend: Travis, Rachel, Kellan, Brady.

"It's for the entryway. So everyone knows you live here, too." She was wringing her hands again.

His pulse started pounding in his ears. Did she mean…?

"If you want to live here, too," she added quickly.

He stood in stunned quiet. She wanted this?

Yes, *of course*, he wanted this, but he hadn't been certain that *she* wanted this.

"Ask me again," she whispered, knocking him out of his funk.

Travis's heart did a ka-thump that he was pretty sure wasn't healthy.

"Rachel." Her name on his lips came with a heavy dose of southern that he wasn't able to filter out, even if he'd wanted to. He stared at the sign she'd made like she'd crafted it from gold and diamonds instead of reclaimed wood and vinyl.

"I'm ready now," she continued.

She didn't look ready. She looked nervous as all hell, what with the way she worried her bottom lip and continued to wring her hands.

Then she crossed her arms at her middle, and that was unacceptable.

She didn't have to hold herself up alone anymore. They held each other up now.

Until that moment it'd been an unspoken agreement, but it seemed like it was time to make it more formal.

He stepped into her personal space, slowly, because it felt like she might run. And if she ran, it wasn't because she wanted to, it was because she put herself out there to him and Rachel was not used to making herself vulnerable like this.

Tilting her face up with a fingertip under her chin, he asked, "Marry me, Rach?"

A heavy teardrop fell from her eye. "Yes."

So that's what it felt like to hear a yes. His heart squeezed tight and gravity felt lighter. Pretty damn amazing.

He pulled her close for a hug, holding her while she held him.

"What else do you need from me?" Travis asked, holding her tight against his chest.

"Just you," she said against his shirt, without hesitation.

"Okay." He closed his eyes a little.

She smiled and looped her arms around his neck, bringing her lips right to his. "What do *you* need from me?"

"Just you," he said, just as quickly as she'd said it.

"Okay." She gave a small laugh and snuggled closer.

"I think I love you a little, Trav," she said against his collarbone.

He moved his hand to the back of her head, holding her close. "I think I love you a whole lot, Rach."

Then he kissed her, to illustrate exactly how much. And it was perfection.

***Get ready for a Rachel and Travis
Bonus Epilogue!***

Visit christinahovland.com/twtbonus
to read a special bonus epilogue
just for newsletter subscribers!

ACKNOWLEDGMENTS

Writing a book about a heroine struggling with perfectionism hit very close to home for me. I am still working to learn the lessons that Rachel uncovered on her own journey. But perfection is in the imperfections. Learning is in the mistakes. I try to embrace that.

Thank you to my fabulous reader Quinn Fforde for naming Dakota when I was stuck on names.

My own mom brigade deserves a shout out here: Karie, Kiele, Sereneti, and Victoria. Life would not be nearly as fun without you in my life.

And my virtual mom brigade: Courtney, Dallas, Leeann, Lindsay, Sarah, and Shasta. Thank you for always being online with a listening ear.

Thank you, as always, to my agent Emily Sylvan Kim.

Thank you to my critique team and beta readers: Serena Bell, A.Y. Chao, Dylann Crush, Patricia Dane, C.R. Grissom, Jody Holford, Diane Holiday, Deb Smolha, Renee Ann Miller, and Becky Wesnidge.

My husband, Steve, and my kids deserve mad props for patiently eating French bread pizza way too many times while I wrote and edited this story.

And, finally, I would be remiss if I didn't mention my own mom, Shirley. I am able to do what I do because you taught me by example. Thank you for being my mom.

ENJOYED THE STORY?

**Turn the page for Chapter One of Gavin Gets It,
Book 2 of the Call Him Daddy Series!**

**A single mom dating guru. A single dad trying to get his
life together. One fake relationship that gets way too real.**

Meet Molly Princeton. She runs a popular dating advice
channel that helps everyone else find love while her own
romantic life has been stuck in neutral for nine years. Between
raising her son, Ollie, juggling bills, and clinging to her
"single mom confidence," she has zero time for real-life
romance or the emotional mess that comes with it.

Then her best friend gets married, Molly's date falls for
someone else before dessert, and her kid accidentally cannon-
balls into the lake. The man who dives in to save him? Gavin
Frank. Single dad. Newly reformed. Former slacker. Also her
best friend's ex-husband. The one she is absolutely supposed
to hate on principle.

Which is inconvenient.

Because he's hot.

And kind.

And entirely off-limits.

So of course he ends up being the perfect person to help when Molly gets roped into a high-stakes matchmaking competition with a cash prize she desperately needs.

The catch? She needs a boyfriend for her videos.

Gavin volunteers. Fake dating. Zero consequences. What could go wrong?

Now their pretend dates are getting too flirty, their on-camera chemistry is impossible to ignore, and one unforgettable conversation nearly breaks the internet. Molly knows falling for her best friend's ex could tank her reputation, her show, and her carefully protected heart, but resisting him is starting to feel impossible.

Molly has to decide if real love is worth breaking her own rules, because the only thing harder than faking a relationship with a single dad like Gavin Frank is admitting you never want it to end.

GAVIN GETS IT
CHAPTER ONE

MOLLY

Of all the things Molly Princeton understood for certain, there was one thing in particular she had no doubts about—a woman was only as confident as her underwear.

For real, she'd ask anyone to hear her out on this point. A girl could always spit shine the outside, but it was what lay underneath that told the true story.

This was the reason she generally wore lace.

Lace, unfortunately, that no one but herself ever saw. She sighed, a disappointed sigh that came from deep within the soul.

Today, however, her life theory was thrown into a bit of a pickle, seeing as she wore no underwear at all.

The no undies thing? Not her fault.

Well, maybe a little her fault. She was the one who had forgotten to pack undies that wouldn't show through the silk sheath dress her bestie Rachel had picked out for her as the maid of honor at her wedding.

A wedding in the total boonies where there was no Nordstrom's or even a Walmart to grab something that wouldn't leave a panty line. Thus…she might as well join the Army because she was commando.

"Let's ask Kaiya. I bet she has a whole new package," Rachel said, looking up to the vaulted ceiling of the bedroom they were using to prepare for her fast-approaching wedding. Her makeup artist applied a touch of jawline shadow before moving on to the powder foundation. "Or you could just take me up on my offer."

Nope. Nuh-uh. Molly had a firm *don't share underwear* rule.

"I'm not asking Kaiya. I'm not asking anyone," Molly said. Her issue was hers alone. Unfortunately.

And, really, it wasn't a big deal. The dress Rachel had picked for her, in a gorgeous blue silk, kissed the carpet, so no one was going to see up her skirt, anyway. Even with a gust of wind.

Molly's bestie and the bride-of-the-day did not need to concern herself with Molly's undergarment situation.

She really shouldn't have said anything.

Except they usually shared everything with each other, and she'd vented to her friend about her ability to forget something so important.

But perhaps this might even be the change she needed to get out of the rut her dating life had been in for the past nine years. Of course, no one knew how deep the rut had become. No one except Rachel, who wouldn't ever say a word about it. Best friend code, and all that.

No one *could* know.

Molly gave dating advice on a popular YouTube channel as her profession. *Good* dating advice, given the number of wedding invitations she'd collected from those who had used her tips in the past. Enough viewers tuned in regularly that she was able to pay her bills with sponsorships, and a few years ago had given up the nine-to-five office gig she had always loathed.

"Kaiya always brings spares of everything." Rachel turned as the makeup artist adjusted her angle. "*Brand new* spares for just this kind of emergency."

This was true. Kaiya brought extra of everything. For everyone.

She was their prepared friend.

Also, their multi-level marketing friend. Kaiya discovered this skin care system when she was traveling through Eastern Asia, visiting her family there, and, honest to God, it was better than lace underwear that didn't show through silk. Kaiya brought the system to the States and sold the heck out of facial creams and serums. Rumor had it, they'd be branching into color cosmetics soon, too.

"I shouldn't have said anything," Molly said. "You've got other things to worry about other than my inability to remember important clothing items."

"I," Rachel said with a huge grin, "am not worried about anything. I have Evelyn for that."

Evelyn was Rachel's soon-to-be, and *also* former, mother-in-law. It was complicated.

"I love Evelyn," Molly said. This was true. What she'd give to have someone with the persistence of Evelyn on Team Molly. They could move mountains together.

Rachel already knew what that felt like. The Evelyn thing.

"You only love her because you've never had her as a mother-in-law." Rachel raised her eyebrows. "I happen to know *all* her quirks. Fake cat included."

"And you don't love her?" Molly asked. The fake cat Evelyn always talked about in lieu of her emotions was brilliant as far as Molly was concerned.

"Oh, I love her," Rachel assured. "She wouldn't have it any other way. But I still can't believe I'm signing up for this again."

And, willingly.

Mmm hmm, Rachel was marrying the brother of her ex. Some might think that was unconventional. Molly held a different opinion. She'd seen the spark from the beginning. Thus, this wedding was not a surprise, not to her.

Besides, Gavin—Rachel's ex—was very…unappealing. Yes, that was a good word for him. The perfect word.

Molly absolutely understood why Rachel had ditched him. Though ditched might be an extreme assessment. There was no ditching. Their relationship had been like a wet sparkler: the fizzle at the end was spot on, but they'd never really had that initial blaze to push them through for any length of time.

Oh, for sure, Gavin was very attractive—in the carnal sense. Broad shoulders, black hair he kept just long enough to touch his ears, and a face that would make even Calvin Klein want to pan up from the boxer briefs, just to glimpse perfection.

But he was a nonstarter. The kind of guy who was perfectly pretty, but that was about it.

"You look like you're thinking about Gavin," Rachel said with a laugh. "Or you accidentally ate a bug."

"Well, I was. The Gavin part, not the bug, ew." Thinking of Gavin always made Molly's mouth pucker like she'd indulged in one of her eight-year-old son Oliver's Sour Patch Kids gummies.

"While I appreciate your commitment to me"—Rachel closed her eyes as the artist applied eyeshadow—"I have to remind you that Gavin's not a bad guy. Be nice to him today. Please."

The bad guy thing? That was debatable as far as Molly was concerned. She dropped her shoulders, shook them out.

"Best behavior." She made a cross over her heart. Rachel rolled her eyes.

Fine, Molly hadn't liked how he relied on Rachel for everything regarding the care of the two kids they had together. Their boys were best friends with Molly's son, Oliver.

Yes, recently, Gavin *had* stepped up. Molly was required as a human being with eyeballs to notice. She was not, however, required to forgive him for the years he had slacked.

Molly didn't appreciate slacker baby-daddies—seeing as she had one of her own and understood first-hand how hard life could be on a single mom. Exhaustingly hard. Frustratingly hard.

A small child-support check every month didn't take that hard away.

"He's been amazing about the wedding," Rachel continued. "And he didn't have to be."

No, he didn't. He could've made the fact that Rachel had fallen in love with his brother a whole thing, and he hadn't. Point in his favor. That made it, what? Like, two points? Out of a billion?

"I'm glad that the wedding thing hasn't caused a rift," Molly said, because she was relieved that Rachel was well on her way to forever future happiness and a wedding that would be worthy of every magazine spread.

She wanted that for herself—forever future happiness, not the princess wedding. Though she wouldn't object, it'd never been part of her happily ever after dream package. Truly, most of her life wasn't part of that dream package. She rolled with it.

Even the fancy maid of honor treatment she'd received from the makeup team and the designer gown had been princess worthy. The hair stylist had gone above and beyond with Molly's unruly black curls. She'd wrangled the beast of a mane into submission, and it actually looked…good. Half pinned up, half falling over her shoulders. She'd really wished she'd made time to go to one of those spray-on tan places so the difference between her dark hair and oh-so-pale skin wouldn't have been so in-your-face.

There hadn't been time. And the good places charged a lot. And Ollie had needed new cleats for baseball.

"I want to hear all about you and Cam the Man." Rachel drew out the name of Molly's wedding date.

Sort of date. They hadn't travelled to the location together —he was good friends with the groom, so he was attending anyway. Given that the wedding was a small affair, and he knew Molly from Little League practice where he was one of the coaches, it made sense that they agreed to attend together. Sit together at dinner. Avoid awkward small talk with other people. All that.

She'd agreed to his suggestion without hesitation, even though her track record with first dates was more than a bit of an issue.

"I haven't even seen him yet." Molly willed a spark to flash when she saw him today. The sparkler kind with lots of fizzy firework attraction.

Up to this point there had been no voltage between them. But he was a handsome guy, and he liked kids, and she was getting a touch desperate. Who trusted a dating advice guru who never went on more than a first date because she always found a better match for her guy than…well…herself?

"I like him." Rachel waggled her blonde, perfectly threaded brows. "I think there's something special about the way he looks at you."

Wouldn't that be nice? Molly scraped away the hope bubbling up and pushed it aside.

"Maybe." Molly could really go for something special in her life.

Perhaps the no panties thing might just be her ticket out of her rut. Change things up underneath and it would shine through to the surface.

She should mention that in her video series next week.

Maybe Cam would give her lots of ideas to work with.

Uh-huh. Today would be different. *Dear God, please let it be different.*

"Do you need anything?" Molly asked.

Rachel's makeup was nearly done. They'd accented all her best features, but they'd made her blue eyes the center of attention. And it worked. Rachel's blonde hair had been teased and then pulled into a loose chignon at her neck. She could be a model for a bridal magazine.

She even had some pretty kick-ass lingerie under it all.

Molly had helped her pick it out.

And Rachel hadn't forgotten it. Because she was the organized friend.

Molly was more the hot mess friend.

But today was about Rachel. Everyone was heading down to the dock in about fifteen minutes to watch her best friend marry the man she was meant to be with.

"Is there a Coke in the fridge?" Rachel asked, stretching her neck to the side. "I'd kill for a soda right now."

Molly moved to the mini-fridge and knelt to open the door. Several bottles of white wine lined the shelves, a few bottles of water, but no soda.

"No." She stood. "I'll go grab one from the catering staff."

"You're my favorite friend right now," Rachel said, standing so the makeup artist could check her work in the light near the window.

"I'm your favorite friend all the time," Molly countered, because it was true. She and Rachel knew more about the other than they did themselves.

She didn't even try to fight the grin smeared across her face as she headed for the kitchen. This was her first time at the infamous lake house where the Frank family summered and concocted new plans for their Puffle Yum Toaster Tart empire. Seriously, that's how the family had made its fortune.

Deep in thought about how they got their blueberry tarts to be the same funky shade of teal as her current dress, she turned the corner to the kitchen and stalled mid-step.

Gavin stood near the sink with his twin boys and Ollie. He leaned in, whispering something that left the boys in stitches.

He glanced up, and his gaze snagged uncomfortably with hers—like she'd run her hand the wrong way on a piece of textured fabric. Then he smiled like he meant it. Which was bananas. He didn't get to smile at her like that.

A curt nod was what he got in reply as she did her best saunter toward the refrigerator.

She glanced back at him with her kiddo, who was intently eating a toaster pastry and laughing with his buddies. Gavin leaned in again, saying something to Ollie that she couldn't catch from across the room.

Ollie pulled a face. Gavin nudged his arm.

Her kiddo pulled his lips to the side and said, "You look pretty, Mom."

Her heart dipped. That was…sweet.

"Bud." Gavin shook his head. "We've got to work on your game. Be specific when you're complimenting someone."

"His compliment is fine. You don't need to micromanage my kid's compliments," Molly said the last part under her breath.

"I do when he needs to up his game," Gavin said, also under his breath.

Reluctant, she glanced over her shoulder to toss some glare daggers his way. Hey, it was sort of their thing.

Ollie stared at her, thoughtful, his tongue flicking to a crumb of toaster pastry at the corner of his lips. Finally, he seemed to settle on something—

"I like what you did to your face," Ollie said cheerfully.

She smirked. "Thanks, kiddo."

"The dress is a pretty color," the oldest twin, Kellan, added.

"Thank you, Kellan. That's *very* specific. Your mom picked it out." She gave him a smile for his effort while ignoring his dad.

"That dress makes your butt look small," Brady—the younger—added.

Say whaaaa?

"Brady." Gavin shook his head. "No. Don't mention her bum."

"For the first time *ever*, I agree with your dad. No one mention my tush." Molly shook her head. "But thanks for the complimentary effort."

"What?" Brady said, apparently ready to defend himself. "It's true. Mom says clothes are best when they make her butt look smaller."

"Okay." Molly closed the door to the fridge for a moment. "You shouldn't compliment anything about a person that has to do with things in their swimsuit area."

"Why are girls so weird, dad?" Brady asked with what seemed to be genuine curiosity.

"That is an excellent question." Gavin shrugged. "We may never know the answer."

That's it, she was going to kick him in the nuts—right in his swimsuit area.

"He's right. You do look pretty." Gavin smiled again.

"Too little, too late," she said, mentally tossing a few more daggers his direction. "You'll need to up your game."

"Be specific." Ollie raised his little eyebrows at Gavin.

"I'm good." Molly smoothed her dress. "I don't need specifics."

She pulled open the door to the refrigerator and scanned the shelves. Every soda lining the shelves was of the Pepsi product variety. Damn. Rachel wanted a Coke. This was her big day. If that's what she wanted, then Molly would figure it out.

"That color blue makes you look like a real-life princess,"

Gavin said from behind her, his deep voice rumbling over her nerve endings and stirring up butterflies she'd expressly reserved for Cam. "It suits you."

What was his game?

She cleared her throat and threw up the wall she was so excellent at erecting.

"You look handsome yourself." Well, he did.

"I had a haircut," he said, like this was a big deal and he deserved a gold star.

Before Ollie could tell her to be specific, she said, "Your ears are looking very symmetrical today, and I like the way the tuxedo helps you keep track of Ollie so I can fulfill my wedding duties."

The wink she tossed at the end was added to mess with him. This was her way.

He chuckled.

"Yes, ma'am. We all clean up nice." She turned back to the fridge. Still no Coke.

She pinched her lips together.

"Everything okay?" Gavin asked, and dammit all, he was right there beside her staring into the Coke-less void with her. Didn't he have a swamp to go lounge in or something?

"Rachel wants a Coke." Molly forced herself not to bite at her bottom lip. The makeup artist who had troweled on Molly's look had done a brilliant job. Now it was Molly's job not to do anything to muck it up—like nibble at her lips.

"I don't think staring at the shelf is going to make one appear." He inched just a tad closer to her. "But I'm willing to try if you are."

"Har." She willed her feet to step away from him and lifted her hand to rub at the space between her eyebrows, but stopped herself. No. Messing. With. The. Makeup.

"Did you check the pantry?" Kellan asked, pointing toward a door near the back of the kitchen. "Maybe they're in that refrigerator."

"Were you going to mention the other fridge?" Molly asked, tossing more eye daggers at Gavin.

He nodded. Pulled his lips to the side. "I was getting to it."

Molly gritted her teeth—another few minutes with Gavin and she'd need some serious dental work. "I'm not wearing enough underwear to deal with you right now."

"I have no idea what that means."

"Yep." Molly popped her lips and said quietly so only Gavin could hear, "Probably best you don't know that I'm not wearing underwear right now."

His lips parted. His cheeks flushed. "I'll check the butler's pantry."

Gavin turned and strode away.

Molly's face heated. Gavin did not need to know about her underwear situation. Ever.

He returned with two familiar red mini-cans with a white swish on them. "Apparently, Mama hides the Coke in the back of that one."

"Oh, thank hell." Molly scooted forward to him as he passed over the soda.

"You're welcome," he said, like he was the one who recommended that refrigerator.

"Thank you, Kellan." She held up the cans to him. "For these."

Kellan kicked his feet against the cabinets. "You're welcome."

Despite what anyone who saw her in that moment might think, she did not bolt away from the kitchen.

No, she didn't saunter like she wished she had.

But she didn't run.

No. She didn't.

That was her story. She was sticking to it.

What she should have done was look up before plowing into her date for the night.

"Oh my gosh." She held up the cans, careful they didn't get shaken up in the head-on collision.

Cam reached out to steady her. "Hey, you," he said.

"Hey…you." Nothing. She felt nothing. The butterflies she had been dreaming of dancing all around her belly were totally, traitorously silent.

Reaching for his arm, she gave it a not-at-all-awkward squeeze, willing a spark to flare.

Nothing.

"I'm—" She held up the sodas. "On a mission to give the bride something to drink."

Cam gave her a lopsided smile and his eyes freaking twinkled. Her nerve endings were dormant. Dead. Not interested in him at all. This was ridiculous.

He eyed the drinks in her palms. "Well, I happen to think there's something special about a woman who is prepared."

Well, then, crap, he was gonna have to keep looking.

Because *that* was not her.

She forced a smile as Kaiya rounded the corner behind Cam. She waved to Molly, hurrying toward her, her glossy black hair swishing as she moved with purpose. The subtle bow shape of her red-glossed lips pursed, and the beige skin of her cheeks pinked, apparently from hustling on her search to solve the undies situation.

Two brand new packages of Fruit of the Loom undies were in her grip. Seeing Cam, she tucked them at her side so it wasn't so obvious what she had. "Rachel said you have an issue. I have a solution."

Cam turned to Kaiya and drank her in like she was one of the Cokes in Molly's grip.

And the Molly first-date-curse struck again.

"Cam, I'd like you to meet my friend Kaiya," Molly said, already preparing herself for their upcoming wedding announcement.

Dammit.

Enjoyed the sample?
Grab your copy of Gavin Gets It
at christinahovland.com/ggi

www.ingramcontent.com/pod-product-compliance
Lightning Source LLC
Chambersburg PA
CBHW020054310726
48970CB00002B/307